THE COVENT GARDEN MURDER

By Mike Hollow

THE COVENT
GARDEN MURDER

Mike Hollow

Allison & Busby Limited
11 Wardour Mews
London W1F 8AN
allisonandbusby.com

First published in Great Britain by Allison & Busby in 2023.
This paperback edition published in by Allison & Busby in 2024.

10 9 8 7 6 5 4 3 2 1

ISBN 978-0-7490-3032-2

Typeset in 10.5/15.5 pt Sabon LT Pro by
Allison & Busby Ltd.

By choosing this product, you help take care of the world's forests.
Learn more: www.fsc.org.

Printed and bound by
CPI Group (UK) Ltd, Croydon, CR0 4YY

For Phoebe,
dawn to my dusk, with a world to inherit

CHAPTER ONE

It was the same thing. Every time. He only had to look at the Prince Albert Theatre in Drury Lane for the memory to come stealing back. It was the same now: vivid in his mind, though a quarter of a century and more had slipped by. Vesta Tilley was up on the stage, singing 'Your King and Country Want You' like the accomplished recruiting sergeant that she was, with the crowd roaring back the chorus through a patriotic haze of beer and cigarette smoke. And he was in there, with them. Before he knew it, he'd signed up, taken the King's shilling, and pledged his life to fight the foe.

By rights, he reckoned, he should be dead now, like most of those who'd volunteered so early in the war. But somehow, by the grace of God he'd never had to fight. In fact, he'd never seen the enemy. As soon as the army found out he could cut hair, they had him for a barber. He'd spent the rest of his war in Catterick camp, in North Yorkshire, inflicting a lightning short back and sides on a never-ending stream of men, at first volunteers and later conscripts.

The Great War hadn't taken his life, but did undoubtedly change it. When he was finally demobbed, sick of clipping Tommy Atkins' hair all day and every day, he resolved to become a high-class gents' and ladies' hairdresser. Early in the war he'd met a wounded Belgian soldier who told him he had the same name as their king's second son, Charles, only the Belgian pronounced it the French way – something like 'Sharl', as far as he could tell – which sounded much grander than his plain old Charlie. He'd taken a fancy to it, and when he started working with the ladies he got into the habit of saying his own name the same way. Somehow a French name sounded more classy for a hairdresser, and classy was what he intended to be.

He'd done well, if he said so himself, and now he owned two shops – or salons, as he preferred to call them – both trading under the name 'Maison Charles'. And here he was, in 1940, back in uniform again. Instead of British Army khaki, however, today he was smartly turned out in the blue serge tunic and matching tin helmet of London's Metropolitan Police Special Constabulary.

No one had ever explained to him why it was called 'special': all it meant was that he was a part-time volunteer, and unlike a soldier or even the War Reserve police recruited to fill the wartime ranks, he worked forty hours a month as a policeman without being paid a penny.

Not everyone's cup of tea, perhaps, but it was what he'd chosen to do. Having staff to run the two salons meant he wasn't obliged to work every day of the week himself, so he could make his own small contribution to the war effort by helping to keep the streets safe. Not that anywhere was safe these days – especially for hairdressers, his wife Betty had said, worried that his professional background might not command much respect on those streets. She was anxious about the risks. Not just the German bombs, but the London drunks too, some of whom weren't past trying it on with a copper, especially if he wasn't a regular.

It didn't worry him, though. He'd met people with preconceived notions about hairdressers before, but he wasn't what they took him for. Over the years a number of smart Alecs had learnt to their cost that snide remarks about his profession, not to mention impertinent comments concerning his character, could lead to sudden and humiliating retribution. Hairdresser he might be, but Charlie Stone had been raised on the streets of Bermondsey, and while he was now on the wrong side of fifty, he was still not averse to a fist fight if the need should arise.

He wondered what the theatre looked like on the inside now. Like just about every other theatre in London it was closed because of the air raids, so he imagined a sad spectacle of dust and cobwebs. There wasn't much fun to be had in the capital these days, and it looked as though the approaching festive season would be a dull affair too. Christmas might still be coming, but the goose was certainly not getting fat, and by all accounts neither were the turkeys. The war had put paid to supplies from the Continent, and imports of turkeys from America had been banned. Home-grown birds were going to be scarce and therefore expensive, and Betty had been playing down his expectations for weeks, playing up instead the merits of getting a nice piece of mutton, but he wasn't persuaded. It wouldn't be the same without a decent Christmas dinner.

Warm recollections of long-gone festive meals began to fill his mind. He'd just begun to recapture the sweet aroma of a roast turkey ready for carving when all such thoughts were dispelled by the scream of an aircraft engine. Not the pulsating drone of Luftwaffe bombers high in the sky, but the relentless, terrifying roar of a fighter plane. He whirled round as it burst into view above the Victorian flats to his left, a flash of grey with a bright yellow nose cone, flying so low that he instinctively ducked. In a flash it was gone, heading south towards the river, but not before he'd glimpsed the cross of the German air force on its side and the swastika on its tail. A split second later he was knocked off his feet by an explosion. Down the street, the Prince Albert Theatre had disappeared behind a cloud of dust and flying debris.

He picked himself up and ran towards the scene, choking on the unbreathable air. The nearest corner of the theatre had been demolished, three storeys of stone, brick and timber collapsed into a jagged heap. He couldn't imagine anyone surviving if they'd been caught in that, but a heavy rescue squad would no doubt be there in moments to start digging. First, he must do what he could on his own. The main entrance was still standing, its doors and windows blown out into the street, and he could see a woman running in, rushing, he assumed, to the aid of any injured survivors. He dashed after her into the foyer just in time to

10

hear her gasp in horror. She had stopped in her tracks, her hands clapped to her face and her eyes staring.

'It's him,' she said, appalled. 'He's dead.'

Stone looked past her to where a man lay motionless on his back against a wall, his clothes dusted white with pulverised plaster.

'Can't you see who it is?' said the woman.

Stone peered more closely, and recognition dawned. First the face, a very famous face, and then the hair: he'd cut it many times. It was Roy Radley, the comedian who'd once strutted the stage here and made it his own, now lying on the floor, lifeless. And there was something else. Something that suggested he was not the victim of a random bomb: what looked like a slim dust-covered handle was sticking out of Radley's abdomen.

'Oh,' the woman gasped again. 'He moved – look!'

Stone had already seen it. An almost imperceptible movement in the handle as the man's abdomen rose by the tiniest fraction of an inch and fell again. There was breath in the body.

He dropped to his knees in the debris beside the victim and touched his shoulder. Radley's eyes half opened and he whispered something. Stone slipped his steel helmet off so he could get his ear closer and spoke gently. 'What did you say?'

Radley struggled to speak. 'God have mercy . . . Forgive . . .' he said faintly, as his eyes closed again.

'Do you want a priest? I'll send for one.'

'No – it's too late . . . I'm dying . . . stay with me.'

Stone reached for Radley's hand and held it. 'All right, I'm here.'

He turned to the woman, who was standing nearby and watching. 'Quick,' he said, 'try to get an ambulance. This man needs one urgently.' She nodded and ran off, but he doubted the man beside him would live long enough for the ambulance to arrive.

Radley gave his hand a feeble squeeze. He spoke again, his whisper growing fainter. 'I . . . I confess . . . thought, word and deed . . . I'm sorry . . . forgive . . .'

Stone couldn't tell whether Radley was speaking to him, to himself, or to the priest who wasn't there, but he kept silent lest he miss any of the dying man's words.

'Stolen . . . lied . . . killed . . .' Radley continued, his words interspersed with the weakest of snatched breaths.

'Who did this to you?' said Stone. 'Who stabbed you?'

Radley gave a feeble cough. 'My fault . . .' he said. 'Forgive me . . . I can't—'

Whatever he intended to say next remained unsaid. His grip on Stone's hand relaxed, his eyes remained closed, and there were no more breaths. He was dead.

CHAPTER TWO

Detective Inspector John Jago brought his car to a halt outside the Prince Albert Theatre. The sky was clear, the sun was glinting on the silver-grey barrage balloons overhead, and the air on the street below had an icy December bite to it. Detective Constable Peter Cradock was beside him in the front passenger seat, and in the back they had Nisbet, the Scotland Yard photographer, with his assorted professional apparatus. Dr Gibson, the pathologist, would be making his way there separately, from St George's Hospital at Hyde Park Corner.

The theatre was a sorry sight, and half a dozen members of a heavy rescue party clad in dust-covered blue dungarees were working as a human chain, passing baskets of debris from hand to hand and tipping it onto the back of their truck. As the three men got out of the car, a uniformed police constable picked his way across the rubble-strewn pavement towards them.

'Good morning, sir,' he said. 'Special Constable Stone. I got a message saying you were on your way.'

'Good morning,' said Jago. 'You're the man who found the body, right?'

'Yes, sir. I've made sure nothing's been touched.'

'Good. Tell me what happened.'

'Well, I was making my way up the road here, everything quiet, a few people around on their way to work or the shops, but then suddenly I saw a plane coming straight at us, very low and very fast. I think it was one of those Messerschmitt fighter-bombers Hitler's been sending over on daylight raids – they've just got the one bomb, so they drop it and scarper.'

'Yes – the papers call them "tip and run" raiders, don't they? Makes it all sound like a game of cricket. Carry on.'

'The bomb hit the corner of the theatre and made a right mess of it, as you can see.'

'Time?'

'Two minutes past nine, sir. The blast knocked me off my feet, but that was the first thing I checked.'

'Well done. And when did you find the body?'

'Well, it wasn't actually me who found it, sir. A woman who was passing by dashed in as soon as the dust cleared and spotted him. But I was there seconds later – four minutes past nine, it was. I sent her to try and get an ambulance and stayed with him, but he died.'

'Time of death?'

'Seven minutes past nine, sir.'

'Very good. Take us to the body, then.'

'Yes, sir – this way.'

14

He led them through the wrecked doors of the theatre's main entrance and into the foyer. 'Over there, sir.' He pointed to a corner where an internal wall had been blown down, revealing what must have been the gents' toilets, with a row of handbasins still intact but the mirrors on the wall behind them shattered. On the floor lay the body of a man in an overcoat threadbare at the cuffs. It was open, revealing a shapeless pullover from which protruded the handle of what appeared to be the instrument of his death.

Nisbet got busy with photographing the body and its surroundings, while Jago captured his own pictures of the scene in his mind. The dead man looked as though he'd been doused with flour from head to foot, like many people Jago had seen after they'd been caught in air raids. Some dead, some alive, but similarly encased in grey-white powder as a building's interior was reduced to dust by a bomb blast.

'Do we know who he is?' he said.

'Oh, yes, sir,' Stone replied. 'His name's Roy Radley.'

'Roy Radley the comedian?'

'That's the one, sir. The woman who got here first recognised him immediately, and so did I. He's well known round these parts – he grew up in Covent Garden and used to live here. He's still got family here. A brother called George, who works in the market – he's a trader, runs his own business – and a sister too. You've heard of Roy, then? He was quite famous on the stage.'

'Yes, I've heard of him. Never seen him close up, though.'

'Top of the bill he was, a few years back. It's tragic to see him come to this sort of end.'

'Do you have any idea why someone would want to do this to him?'

'None at all, sir. Sorry.'

'Where can I find this brother of his? In the market?'

'That's right. If you go down to the Theatre Royal and turn right into Russell Street, that'll take you straight there. Once you get inside the market building, look for a little shop with his name over the top, and if you can't see it, anyone working there should be able to tell you where to find him.'

'Thank you – that's all for now. The pathologist should be here soon, so go outside and look out for him – his name's Dr Gibson. Bring him straight here when he arrives.'

'Yes, sir.' Stone set off towards the wrecked entrance.

'Now, then, Peter,' said Jago, 'let's see what we can find in this man's pockets.' He knelt down and reached carefully into the dead man's coat and trouser pockets. 'Here we are,' he said, handing the contents to Cradock. 'An identity card in the name of Roy Radley, a few coins, a couple of Fox's Glacier Mints and a comb. No surprises there, then. Put these things in a safe place and then see if you can find any useful fingerprints in all this mess.'

'Yes, sir,' Cradock replied. 'Can't say I'm optimistic, though. I mean, I'm supposed to put special fingerprint dust on smooth surfaces, but look at the handle on that knife – it's covered in dirt and plaster dust. By the time I clean all that off there'll be no fingerprints left for me.'

'Don't worry – just do what you can. And by the way, I'm not so sure it's a knife. Look at the shape of that handle – it looks to me more like a chisel or a screwdriver or some sort of tool like that. We'll see what Dr Gibson says when he takes it out and has a good look at it.'

Jago paused, feeling a little queasy and hoping he would not be present when the pathologist extracted the weapon. Cradock, meanwhile, got busy with the task of fingerprinting, with Nisbet photographing his findings. Before long the crunching of boots on broken glass heralded the return of Special Constable Stone, and following him the familiar figure of Dr Gibson with a battered leather medical bag in his right hand.

'Good morning,' said Gibson. 'And what do you have for me today?'

'The late Mr Roy Radley,' said Jago, 'a professional comedian, who appears to have been stabbed in the abdomen.'

'Right, I'll take a look. I suppose you'll want an estimated time of death?'

'Not this time, no. There was a police constable with him when he died, so we know exactly when that was – seven minutes past nine this morning. What I'm interested in is your estimate of when he was stabbed, if and when you can confirm that that's what killed him.'

'Very good. I won't be able to do that until I get him back to the hospital, but it won't take me long to do what I have to here.'

'OK, I'll leave you to it. I need to talk to the constable.'

Jago took Stone to the far corner of the foyer. 'By the way, who's in charge here? Responsible for the theatre, I mean.'

'That'll be Sir Marmaduke Harvey, I suppose – he's the

17

owner. But if you mean day to day, it's the caretaker. He's called Stan Tipton, and I believe he lives on the premises. The theatre's been closed down since the Blitz started in September, of course, like nearly all the others in London.'

'Where can I find Mr Tipton?'

'Not here, I'm afraid. He was injured in the bombing this morning and he's been taken to St Thomas's Hospital. They say he's not badly hurt and should be out soon, but if you want to see him, you'll have to go there.'

'Very well. Now, is there anything else you can add to what you've already told me?'

'There is actually, sir, yes. Just before Mr Radley died, he said something. It was just a few words – disjointed, you might say, on account of him being weak, I suppose – but I thought it might be important.'

'Did he say who'd stabbed him?'

'No, sir, he didn't say anything about that. To be honest, it was more like a confession.'

'Can you remember what he said?'

'Oh, yes, sir – I wrote it all down in my notebook, just after the poor man died.'

'Did anyone else hear what he told you?'

'No, sir – there was only one other person close by, and I'd sent her off to get an ambulance. Sorry, sir.'

'Don't worry. Tell me what he said.'

Stone took his notebook from his pocket and read out what he had written. 'They were his very last words. Is that what they call a dying declaration?'

'Strictly speaking no, it's not. As far as the courts are concerned, that's what the victim says about his injury before he dies – who did it, when and how, that sort of thing. It sounds like Radley didn't tell you any of that, but on the other hand, if it was some kind of confession, and if he talked about lying, stealing and killing . . . well, it could indicate something he'd done that could've given someone cause to murder him. That makes it valuable to me, so I want you to get it typed up properly, as close as possible to a complete record of your conversation – your questions and his answers – and then sign and date it and get it to me. And well done.'

'Thank you, sir.'

Cradock joined them. 'Sorry, guv'nor, I'm getting nowhere with those prints – there's too much dust and soot everywhere. And anyway, in a big old place like this that's been standing empty for months on end there's every chance whoever did it had gloves on to keep warm, wouldn't you say?'

'I'd say not necessarily, but it's possible. But if you can't get any prints off that handle it's just hard luck. Now, while you've been busy our colleague here's been telling me something very interesting, which I'd like you to hear too.'

Stone repeated his account of Radley's last words, and Jago sent him back to keep guard over the body before continuing his conversation with Cradock.

'So what do you make of that, Peter?' he said.

Cradock nodded sagely. 'Like you said, sir, very interesting. So do you reckon he was confessing to doing all those things – even killing?'

'I'm not sure – it wasn't a clear and complete statement, but it's a possibility we need to keep in mind.'

Jago was interrupted by the return of Gibson.

'I'm all finished here,' said the doctor. 'I'll get the hospital to collect the body and I'll do the post-mortem examination, then I should be able to give you a more detailed account of what happened to him.'

'Are we looking at a case of murder?' said Jago.

'At this stage I'd say it's certainly a suspicious death, but come and see me later this morning at the hospital and I'll let you know. I'll be off now.'

Jago watched as Gibson headed for the door. He was about to look away when he noticed the doctor sidestepping abruptly to avoid an older, shorter man who was bustling into the theatre. It was Detective Superintendent Hardacre.

'Ah, Jago, there you are,' he barked. 'Thought I'd better drop by and make sure you're coping here.' He looked round the remains of the foyer like a general surveying his battlefield, and his eye settled on the body lying on the far side. 'Who's the victim?'

Jago noticed that Cradock had edged slightly to one side, behind him, as if keen to put someone between himself and the marauding superintendent. 'He's Roy Radley, sir, a variety performer.'

'Not *the* Roy Radley, the comic?'

'That's him, sir. Found here with a stab wound to the abdomen – a special constable was with him when he died.'

'Good Lord. Roy Radley's famous – who'd want to murder a comedian?'

'I don't know, sir,' Jago replied, 'but I've heard that audiences in Glasgow can be unforgiving, especially to English comics.' His regret was immediate when he saw

Hardacre's face crease into a baffled frown.

'This is Drury Lane, man, not Glasgow,' the superintendent continued. 'In a theatre, for goodness' sake. What kind of lowlife creeps into a theatre to murder a comic? As if we haven't got enough on our plates these days – the whole country's going to pot.'

'Yes, sir.' Jago was learning to concur with his superior officer's observations.

'I blame the blackout – every crook in London's out at night getting up to whatever they like because no one can see them. We're the only men standing between civilisation and anarchy. So who's your killer? Got any leads?'

'Not yet, sir. We're waiting for the pathologist to confirm that it's definitely murder, and we're about to go and see Mr Radley's next of kin, his brother – Special Constable Stone's told us where we can find him.'

'This special – local, is he?'

'Yes, sir.'

'Reliable?'

'He seems to be, from what I've seen so far.'

Hardacre grunted. 'Well, you know what the old song says about specials and old-time coppers. If I've learnt one thing in my time, it's don't trust anyone – not even a man in uniform. Did you hear about that business over in Southwark last week, on M Division?'

'Er, not sure, sir – what happened?'

'There was an empty warehouse – got burnt down in an air raid, and it turned out the bloke who owned it had paid an ARP warden to slip inside when the bombing started and set fire to it.'

'That was a bit risky, wasn't it? For the air-raid warden, I mean.'

'I suppose he must've been desperate for the money – some men'll do the stupidest things if you wave some cash under their nose. But it turns out all that warden had to do was nip in and out with some matches – the owner had got it all set up inside with wood and petrol and probably decided he'd prefer it if some other bloke actually took the risk. But an air-raid warden – you don't expect one of them to be a crook, do you?'

The faces of one or two upright citizens that Jago had had cause to arrest over the years flitted through his mind, and he might have begged to differ had he not been reluctant to interrupt when his boss was in full flow.

'I reckon that owner thought if he blamed the Germans he'd be able to claim on his insurance,' Hardacre went on. 'But a fireman died trying to put that fire out. In the end it was the owner's wife who turned him in – she thought it was disgusting, what he'd done. But he lied till he was blue in the face – didn't give a tinker's cuss about that fireman's life. Makes me wonder what we're fighting for, trying to protect people like that. Whatever happened to conscience, eh? That's what I'd like to know. How can a man like that not have a guilty conscience? Some of these people are as bad as the Nazis – even worse, I'd say, if they call themselves British.' He turned on Cradock. 'We need to get them off the streets and behind bars – understand?'

'Yes, sir,' Cradock replied meekly, feeling as though the detective superintendent's comment was some kind of personal reprimand.

'We'll definitely keep that in mind, sir,' said Jago. He judged that the detective superintendent's hobby horse had run its allotted course and that reassurance was now the best response.

'Right, well you do that. If you ask me, some of these good-for-nothings could do with a dose of Field Punishment Number 1, the way we used to do it in the army. That'd teach them a bit of respect. There's too much mollycoddling these days, you mark my words.'

'Yes, sir. All right if we carry on now, sir?'

Hardacre took a final look round the scene, as if checking that Jago had not missed something crucial to the investigation. 'Yes, very well – carry on, and make sure you get the maniac who did this locked up.'

'Yes, sir.' Jago replied, but Detective Superintendent Hardacre was already marching back the way he'd come.

CHAPTER THREE

'Mr Hardacre doesn't like people who set buildings on fire, does he, sir?' said Cradock as they watched their boss depart.

'That appears to be the case,' Jago replied. 'I can't say I do either. It sounds like we can add catching arsonists to our list of priorities for him – up there with the thieves. You should probably mark his words, as he said – and especially make sure you don't catch me mollycoddling you. Now, where's that special constable gone?'

He glanced around and beckoned Stone to rejoin them. 'I want you to stay here and make sure no one touches that body, all right? The doctor's going to send someone over to take it to the hospital, and after that you can resume your normal duties.'

'Yes, sir,' said Stone.

'By the way, are you a full-time special or part-time?'

'Part-time, sir – I've got a business to run.'

'What sort of business is that?'

'I'm a hairdresser, sir.'

'Really? Well, I just want to know where I can find you if you're not on duty.'

'I'll most likely be at one of my salons – I've got two.'

'And where would they be?'

'Not far – just down the road, really. One's in Catherine Street, round the back of the Theatre Royal, and the other one's in Maiden Lane, just by the south side of the market. That's the main one, and it's where I live too, in the upstairs flat. You can't miss them – they're both called Maison Charles.'

'Thank you – we may see you later. You can get back to that body now.'

'Yes, sir – thank you, sir.'

Stone returned to his post, while Jago and Cradock left the car in Drury Lane and followed his directions for the short walk to the market. As they made their way down Russell Street, the scene before them seemed to Jago like a vision of organised chaos. Vans, lorries and the occasional horse and cart were parked in apparently random fashion, while porters in flat caps and old overcoats pulled long and noisy two-wheeled market barrows behind them or pushed smaller, upright sack barrows before them, weaving their way through a maze of heaped-up crates and sacks of produce. Added to this, like ants scurrying to and from their nest, were men conveying their load in wicker baskets stacked six or more high on their heads. It was definitely a place to watch your step, thought Jago, as he took prompt evasive action to avoid a van edging its way through the crowd.

The inside of the market's main building, a large rectangular space under a soaring iron-vaulted roof, was a similar hive of activity. Long rows of what looked like traders' small shops or offices were fronted with boxes and crates of fruit and vegetables ranging up in carefully constructed displays to show off their wares to best advantage. What Jago took to be buyers were scrutinising the quality of the produce and getting out their order books, their relatively smart clothes differentiating them from the porters who bustled in all directions here too.

Jago judged it would save time to ask for George Radley's shop rather than push their way round the whole market in search of it, and the directions given by the first person they asked took them straight to it. The sign over the window said 'James Radley & Sons', and inside they found a cramped space where a middle-aged man sat hunched over a small office desk, conducting what sounded like a terse business conversation on a telephone. He gestured to them to sit down on a couple of wooden chairs that filled the space between the desk and the wall, and brought his phone call to an end.

'Good morning,' he said brusquely. 'I don't believe I've had the pleasure.'

'No,' said Jago. 'We're police officers. I'm Detective Inspector Jago, and this is Detective Constable Cradock.'

'Detectives, eh? And what are you detecting today? Nothing to do with me, I hope.'

'That depends. Are you Mr George Radley?'

'Yes.'

'In that case I'm afraid it is. It concerns your brother.'

'What, Roy? Is he in another scrape?'

'What do you mean?'

'Well, you know – he's always in trouble, that one. What people call a "colourful" character. If there's a scrape anyone can get in, he'll be in it.'

'He's in more than a scrape today, I'm afraid, Mr Radley. You may've heard that the Prince Albert Theatre was hit by a bomb this morning.'

'Yes, I did. You're not saying he was—'

'I'm sorry to have to tell you, sir, but your brother was in the theatre at the time. A police constable found his body.'

Radley slumped into his chair and swallowed hard. He closed his eyes and shook his head slowly. 'I'm sorry, Inspector, it's just a shock. You hear it happening all the time, don't you, what with the air raids and all, but you never think it'll be your own family.'

'Yes. I should note, though, that we don't believe it was the bomb that killed him – we're treating it as a suspicious death.'

'What does that mean? Someone killed him, deliberately?'

'We'll need to wait until the post-mortem's been done to be sure, but it's looking that way, yes.' Jago gave him a little time to adjust to this news before continuing. 'You say your brother was a colourful character – what do you mean?'

'Well, he was theatrical, wasn't he? You don't get to be successful on the stage unless you're colourful. He was larger than life, I suppose, and people like that sometimes leave other people a bit damaged along the way. Casualties of their success, you might say.'

'Can you think of anyone who might've wanted to harm him?'

'Not so much as to kill him, no. He probably annoyed a lot of people, and some of them might've hated him, but kill him? I don't think so.'

'Can you tell me where you were this morning, before nine fifteen?'

'What, am I a suspect?'

'No. I'd just like to know so we can eliminate you from our inquiries.'

'If you must know, I was here at work – and for several hours before that.'

'Right here, at your desk?'

'Not all the time, no. I was out and about round the market too.'

'Can anyone vouch for that?'

'You mean where I was at every moment of that time? No, of course not. But everyone in this market knows me – they'll tell you.'

'Thank you. And another question for you – I was told Mr Radley had family in this area. The person who told me mentioned you and your sister, but were there any other close relations?'

'No, just me and Joan – she's a bit younger than me. That's about it as far as family's concerned, unless you include Roy's wife. You know about her, do you?'

'No, I'm afraid I don't. So he was married, then?'

28

'Well, yes and no, really. I mean, he certainly got married, years ago, but they haven't been together for some time.'

'Were they divorced?'

'Not as far as I know, but something definitely happened. I don't know what, exactly – Roy never talked to me about things like that. I believe he walked out on her, but I don't know why.'

'Can you give me her name?'

'Yes, it's Doreen – Doreen Radley.'

'And do you know where we can find her?'

'I know what his address used to be, and if he left her, I imagine she's probably still living there. I haven't seen her since they broke up, though, so you'd better just try. They lived in Sussex Mansions, in Maiden Lane, next to the Bedford Head pub – Flat 22, I think.'

'So where was your brother living after he moved out?'

'Last I heard, he was in some theatrical lodgings in Goodwin's Court – number 16. Pretty basic sort of accommodation, I believe, thirty bob a week all found, but he never invited me there. He used to turn up here from time to time, but he never seemed to have much in the way of money – I think he'd fallen on hard times. Sometimes he'd ask if he could borrow a bit. Never paid it back, but it was never a lot, and I couldn't say no to my own flesh and blood, could I?'

'Do you have any idea what he might've been doing in that theatre?'

'No, I don't. I understand it's been closed since September. Judging by the state of his clothes when I last saw him, I wouldn't be surprised if he'd been dossing in there on the quiet. He probably knew everyone in the theatre business, so maybe someone let him sleep there. You'd have to ask the people at the theatre about that, I suppose.'

Jago nodded silently. 'I noticed on the way in that the sign over your shop says James Radley and Sons. So is it a family business?'

'Yes. James Radley was my father, God rest his soul, and that's what he called it. Of course, he was expecting Roy and I would both carry it on, but Roy had other ideas. He'd set his mind on going on the stage, and nothing my dad could say would change his mind. He just wasn't interested – always too much of a joker, he was, not cut out for business. So when Dad died, I took over running everything.'

'And your sister?'

'Well, as far as my dad was concerned, the business was always "and sons" – I don't think he ever saw Joan running anything. But she was more interested in flowers than potatoes and cauliflowers, so when she was old enough I gave the flower side of the business to her. She still runs it, over the other side of the market, and she's done well – turned out to have a flair for making money, like her dad.'

'Will you be telling her about your brother's death?'

'No. I'd rather you did it if you don't mind. I don't like things like that. Go round the other side and just ask anyone – they'll direct you. She's got her name over the stall too, so you can't miss it. She trades as Joan Radley – never married, see.'

'Very well, I'll do that. Thank you, Mr Radley – that'll be all for now. We'll be back when we know anything more about what happened to your brother.'

Radley made no response, as if lost in his thoughts, but after a moment he seemed to drift back to the present. 'Yes, right,' he said. 'Sorry, but I was just thinking about Roy. I can't believe he's gone – it still feels like he'll be in here any moment trying to tap me for a couple of quid for his rent. We didn't always see eye to eye, you know, and sometimes we may've got a bit steamed up about things, but now somehow it feels like none of that mattered, not really. It's just not going to be the same without him.'

Jago stood up to leave but paused when he noticed two framed portrait photographs on the desk: a young woman with a radiant smile and a man of similar age in army uniform with a more serious expression. 'Are these family too?' he asked.

'Yes, they're my two kids. They've not had the happiest of lives – my wife died in a road accident, you see, when they were both quite little. A drunken driver – he should never have been on the road. But they've grown up to be fine young people, and I'm very proud of them. That one's my son, James – named after his grandfather. He's a second lieutenant in the Royal Artillery now – the 5th London Field Regiment. He went out to France with the British Expeditionary Force. We heard from a pal of his who got back from Dunkirk that they'd been in some kind of last stand at a place called Cassel, up near the Belgian border. They tried to break out and get to Dunkirk, but only half the regiment made it home.'

'And your son?'

'He was reported missing, but now we've heard he's a prisoner of war. It's a relief to know he's alive, but as for when we'll ever see him again, well . . .' His voice trailed off into a poignant silence.

'And your daughter?'

'She's Patricia, and she's much closer to home, fortunately. She works for the BBC – doing very well for herself. She lives near Broadcasting House now.'

'I can see why you're proud of them.'

'Oh, yes, they've both done well. I wanted them to have opportunities, so I sent them both to private schools. You might be surprised at that, seeing me sitting here in this little office, but I don't mind telling you there's a bob or two to be made in fruit and veg if you're smart and run a tight business. My brother may've been the one with a name everyone knew, but I reckon I did all right for myself too. I'm no gentleman – I'm still rough at the edges – but I've worked hard all my life, and if that means both my kids've had better chances in life than I ever did, I'm happy.'

'What did your brother think of your children's success?'

'I'm not sure. He got on very well with them when they were little – I think they were both a bit in awe of him because he was famous – but I suppose when they grew up they had less time for him. My daughter still sees him once in a while, though – or saw him, I suppose I should say. I think she was a favourite of his.'

'Could you give me her address, in case we need to speak to her?'

'Yes, she's got a little place of her own. It's Flat 6,

Dunstan House, Hanson Street.'

'Does she have a telephone at home?'

'Yes, it's Museum 4293.'

'Thank you.'

'You'll probably find she's a bit posh now – you know, BBC and all that – but I don't think it's turned her head. She's still my little girl – I think.'

CHAPTER FOUR

Jago and Cradock took their leave of George Radley and made their way out of the market building. 'Now that we've discovered Roy Radley had a wife, I think we'd better see her before we do anything else, even if they were separated,' said Jago as they emerged into a cobblestoned area full of traders, customers and produce. Opposite them was a stone building with a grand portico and what looked like an entrance doorway that had been blocked up with white stone to match the surrounding wall. They walked a short distance down Southampton Street and turned right into Maiden Lane, where they soon found Sussex Mansions.

Doreen Radley was at home and seemed surprised to be visited by two police officers, but welcomed them into her flat. She looked in her late forties and was neatly dressed but not, to Jago's untutored eye, overdressed. The flat itself, at least what he could see of it, was similarly neat: tastefully decorated and furnished, but with no hint of extravagance or ostentation.

When Jago broke the news of her husband's death to her, he was intrigued by her reaction. He'd thought she might be distressed, but equally imagined she might even betray some sense of relief, given whatever acrimony might have caused their relationship to break down. But, in fact, if her response suggested anything, it was indifference.

'Oh,' she said. 'That's that, then – I'm not married any more. So this is what "until death do us part" means. I didn't expect it would be like this.'

'I'm sorry to bring you bad news, Mrs Radley,' said Jago.

'Yes, yes – thank you. I just thought I'd feel more than this, that's all. I suppose it's because I'd already lost him some time ago. Roy and I drifted apart, you see, and he left me.'

'But you remained married?'

'Yes. Some people said I should divorce him, but I'm a Catholic, and we don't believe in doing that. That's what I meant by "until death do us part" – that's the vow we take when we marry, and we're supposed to stick to it. No one can say I didn't stick to Roy, but people change, don't they?'

'And your husband changed?'

'Yes. I think he was too much in love with his work – and with the best will in the world, the kind of life you have if you're in variety's not good for marriage, unless perhaps you're both in the same act. When you're a performer you do a week in one place, then a week in another place, moving around all the time, living out of a suitcase in theatrical digs. That didn't appeal to me one bit – dragging myself round from pillar to post with him and staying in one miserable room after another, sitting there all alone every evening while he was out doing his show twice nightly, six nights a week? That's no life for a woman. I tried it for a bit, when I was young and in love with him, but I couldn't take it. At first, he was understanding, but, well, I think he lost interest in me – absence didn't make the heart grow fonder – or maybe he got more interested in someone else. I don't know for sure, and I suppose now I never will, but for whatever reason, he left me. Perhaps it was because he became successful. That can turn your head, can't it?'

'You think he left you for another woman?'

'I don't know. It's not unknown in his line of work, is it, to say the least. But if he did have some floozy hidden away somewhere he kept it very quiet. Listen, the straight answer is I haven't the faintest idea. I don't know who he met or who he spent his time with, I just know it wasn't with me, and in the end we were like strangers to each other. Then he left me. Since then, I've been living here on my own and I've hardly seen anything of him. We went our separate ways, and that's that.'

'Did he have any enemies?'

'Enemies? Why do you say that?'

'Because we're treating this as a suspicious death.'

'What, you mean someone killed him? In cold blood?'

'We won't be sure until we have the results of the post-mortem, but we think it's possible. So when I say enemies, I mean are you aware of anyone who might've wanted to do him harm?'

She shook her head. 'No, I'm not. But you never know, do you? Anything could've happened since he left me. Roy was a well-known performer, famous, really, and sometimes there are people out there who get funny ideas about you, and you don't even know. He might've made enemies without realising it. He was successful, and people can resent that, can't they?'

'But you can't think of anyone in particular.'

'No. All I'm saying is it wouldn't surprise me. Some people can't stand seeing other people doing better than them.'

'Although actually I've been told that your husband had suffered a bit of a downturn in his career of late.'

'Yes, so I've heard, but I haven't seen him or heard from him in quite a while, so I don't suppose I know any more about that than you do. If you want to know about how all that was going, you'd better ask his agent. She'll be able to tell you much more than me.'

'Ah, yes. Do you know her name?'

'Yes, she's Adelaide Mansfield – Miss, I believe.'

'And her address?'

'I've had no contact with her since Roy went his own way, but if she hasn't moved or been bombed out, her office is right next to the market – in Mart Street, behind the Royal Opera House. It's number 27, I believe.'

'Thank you. We'll pay her a visit.'

'Give her my regards, if she remembers me. I hope you

37

find out what you want to know, but to be honest, I'm not really interested any more. I've spent years feeling as though I had second place in Roy's life after his work, that I was just some sort of accessory. Once I stopped travelling with him, I was just sitting here at home, the faithful wife, waiting for him to pass through occasionally. Then one day he walked out and said he wasn't coming back. Do you know what that feels like? It felt like I was nobody and nothing, just a bit of his past that he'd left behind like an old suitcase – he might as well have killed me.'

CHAPTER FIVE

They left Radley's widow to her thoughts and took the short walk to the neighbouring flower market, another high-roofed building where they were directed down an aisle to a stall at the far end. Here they found a woman in her thirties tending a display of cut flowers.

'Miss Radley?' said Jago.

'That's me,' said the woman, looking up at the sound of her name. 'Can I interest you in some flowers?'

'I'm sorry, Miss Radley, but we're not here to buy. We're police officers – I'm Detective Inspector Jago, and this is Detective Constable Cradock. I'm afraid we've come with some bad news. It's about your brother, Roy.'

'Ah, I see. You've come to tell me he's been killed?'

Jago was surprised by her calm response. 'Yes,' he said, 'we have. We've just been with your brother, George, and he asked us if we could tell you.'

'Yes, that would be George – he's not one for talking about things like death. But I'm afraid you're too late – I already know.'

'How's that, if you don't mind me asking?'

'It's all right, Inspector, there's nothing for you to get suspicious about. One of my customers told me – she's a flower seller who buys a few blooms from me every morning and sells them on the street, mostly in Drury Lane and round that way. She's often up by the Prince Albert Theatre, and it was only by chance she wasn't caught by that bomb. She found out Roy had been killed and came straight back to tell me.'

'She knows that you and he are brother and sister, then?'

'Oh, yes – it's not a secret. I'm the youngest in the family, so most people round here know me either as George's little sister or as Roy's little sister.' She hesitated. 'And now I suppose I'm only George's sister. This war's a horrible thing, isn't it – never knowing whether the next bomb's going to miss you or kill you. I hate it.'

'We don't think it was the bomb that killed your brother, Miss Radley.'

'Oh – but I assumed . . . I thought it must've been. So what happened, then?'

'We won't know for sure until we have the results of the post-mortem, but we're treating it as a suspicious death.'

'You mean someone deliberately killed him? What kind of maniac would do that?'

'We don't know yet, but we will. For now, though, I wonder – can you tell me a bit about your brother Roy?'

'Yes.' She waited, breathing deeply as if to calm herself.

40

'So, what can I say? He was my brother. I suppose we were never very close – he was fifteen years older than me, so by the time I was born he was already working. It wasn't as if we grew up together – George could tell you far more about him, I'm sure. By the time I was old enough to take any notice of what Roy was doing, he'd already started his stage act, so he was off travelling all over the country to music halls and variety theatres trying to get his face known and make a name for himself.'

'That must've seemed very different to the world you lived in.'

'Oh, yes, definitely. At first, I thought it was all a bit glamorous – show business, I mean – and I used to tell my friends my big brother was a star. But when I got older, I could see it wasn't always a bed of roses, and when I did get to see him, he wasn't always as happy as he used to be. He never talked about it with me, though – I suppose to him I was still just a kid, even though I'm a grown-up businesswoman.'

'Yes, I understand you took over the flower side of the family business from your brother George.'

'That's right. There was a time when I thought I'd get away from London and travel the world and have adventures, but before I knew it, what I actually had was responsibilities and a business to run. So here I am still, living in Covent Garden the same as ever.'

'That reminds me, could you give me your home address, please, in case we need to speak to you again outside business hours?'

'Yes, of course. I live in Broad Court. You must know it

if you're a policeman – it cuts through from Bow Street to Drury Lane, right next door to the magistrates' court.'

'I am a policeman, but I'm not local – but I've probably walked past it.'

'Well, if you need to visit me, I'm at number 23. Top floor, Flat 12 – you just have to press the buzzer by the entrance.'

'Thank you. So, you were talking about taking over the flower business. I gather you've made a success of it.'

'Oh, yes? Who told you that?'

'Your brother.'

'Well, he should know. Kind of him to say so, though – I don't think I've done too badly. But these are very difficult times for my trade – the war's messed everything up. It used to be pretty regular – we'd get flowers from the Isles of Scilly just after Christmas, then from the Channel Islands, then Cornwall, then Lincolnshire, and so on. We used to get tons of daffodils from Guernsey, but that's all finished now the Germans are occupying it. We've got plenty of late-blooming chrysanths at the moment, but generally speaking there's just not so many cut flowers about, and when supplies are short it's difficult keeping prices down – but if you put your prices up too much, people aren't so keen to buy. It leaves traders like me in a bit of a pickle, and it's the same for the florist shops and flower sellers.'

'Yes, and by the way, the flower seller you mentioned who was near the Prince Albert Theatre – who is she?'

'Her name's Sal. She knows everyone and everything round these parts, and everyone knows her. What you might call part of the furniture. She's been a flower seller ever since I can remember – round Drury Lane mostly, and I think she used to do Piccadilly Circus.'

'What's her surname?'

'I don't know. She's just Sal, always has been. If you ask anyone round here what her full name is, they'll tell you it's Sympathetic Sal.'

'Why's that?'

'It's just what people call her. If you're in some kind of trouble, she's always full of it – sympathy, I mean. You've only got to look at her to know she must've had a hard life – you'd think she was knocking along a bit, but I don't reckon she's really any older than our Roy, and he was only fifty. I suppose maybe it's life that's made her what she is, though, for better or for worse. I mean, bad experiences can push you one way or the other, can't they? Make your heart softer or harder. With her I think it was softer. She was straight round here to tell me how sorry she was when she heard about poor Roy – which is more than our George did. Not that I expect to get a sympathy card from Sal – she wouldn't have the money to buy one. But she's like a kind of walking sympathy card – she'll always turn up and give you her condolences, be a shoulder for you to cry on. Never misses a funeral, and always puts a little flower on the grave. I sometimes wonder whether that's something to do with her own life too, as much as theirs.'

'What do you mean?'

'Well, she's a mystery to me, but there's a sadness about her. I've heard people say she had a bad experience when she was young, and it marked her for life. I don't know for sure, mind – it's just what people say, and I don't like to ask. But I think maybe when she does that, she's not just mourning for someone else who's died, she's mourning for herself in some way.'

'I see.'

Joan gave a little shudder, as if to shake off the burden of her own thoughts. 'Anyway,' she continued, forcing a brighter tone into her voice, 'that's probably more than you need to know about Sal. You should talk to her, though – she may look like just another poor woman trying to sell flowers on the street, but she's actually an interesting lady. She doesn't miss a trick. Tell her I sent you, if you do.'

'Thank you. Do you happen to know whether she was acquainted with your brother Roy?'

'No, I don't, but it wouldn't surprise me if she was. Like I said, she knows everyone.'

CHAPTER SIX

'It's time we went over to St George's,' Jago announced to Cradock as they came out of the flower market. 'I expect Dr Gibson will've finished his post-mortem by now, so we'll go to the hospital and see what he's got to say.'

They set off back to where he'd parked the car, but as they went, he glanced down a narrow side street and was distracted. It was Wellington Street, and it led to the Strand. They were probably just two minutes' walk from the Savoy Hotel, where Dorothy lived along with many of her fellow reporters in the American press contingent covering the war from London. He had a sudden desire to abandon Cradock and their investigation and call on her, but as soon as that wish came into his mind, he knew it was wrong and suppressed it. They still had work to do – it was his duty. For a quarter of a century now he'd been doing his duty in one way or another, his sworn duty to the King, first as a soldier and now as a policeman. If necessary, duty must come above life itself. But right now, he found himself wishing that sometimes duty might take second place to life.

They walked on, and his mind went to his recent visit to the cinema with Dorothy. When she'd said there was a film she wanted to see, he'd had a sense of dread that she had in mind *Pride and Prejudice*, the new Hollywood production starring Greer Garson and Laurence Olivier. Only a couple of days earlier she'd encouraged Cradock to take his young lady Emily to see it as a way of advancing his romantic relationship with her, so the possibility that she was going to suggest they did the same was intimidating. He'd read the book years ago, and all he could think of was its opening sentence, with its bold claim that a single man in possession of a good fortune must be in want of a wife. All very well in fiction, he thought, but he himself was a single man, albeit not one in possession of a fortune, never mind a good one. He couldn't imagine that this line wouldn't feature somewhere in the film, and while he wished Cradock good luck with it if he took Emily, the thought of sitting through it with Dorothy brought a blush to his cheeks even now.

As it turned out, he'd had to stop himself breathing an audible sigh of relief when he discovered that the film Dorothy wanted him to take her to was actually *North West Mounted Police*, about the Royal Canadian Mounted Police, the famous 'Mounties'. It sounded like safe territory, after all – a police story – so he'd taken her to the cinema to watch it. It starred Gary Cooper, an actor he associated with pretty rugged characters, playing a Texan on the trail of a Mountie deserter, but as the story unfolded it emerged that the Texan was in love with the deserter's sister, a young nurse, and his rival for her affections was another Mountie, Sergeant Jim Brett. After a trail of death and disappointment, the film ended with the hero losing the girl he loved to his rival because he put his duty first.

So it had turned out to be a romantic drama after all. And the ending? Was that supposed to be him? Only days before, Cradock had asked him whether duty came before love, and he'd replied that yes, sometimes it did. He'd be lying to himself to deny that the film had struck a chord, but would Dorothy knowingly have suggested they watch one that ended that way? That would be more devious than he believed she was. He dismissed the thought out of respect for her integrity and tried to divert his mind to a more immediate topic: the post-mortem. What could be more sobering than that? His well-established aversion to the gruesome clinical procedures of the pathologist, however, deterred him from dwelling on this for more than a few paces.

He turned for relief to another less taxing memory of their visit to the cinema: the chocolates. The box of Black Magic that he'd bought for the occasion had proved a hit with Dorothy, and he was pleased to have given her a present that she liked. Buying chocolates for women was not something he was used to. He remembered the adverts for Black Magic when they'd first been launched onto the market a few years before – the chocolates bought 'by men who understand women'. He shook his head at the thought of it: if there was anyone less likely to fit that description, it was him.

'You all right, sir?' said Cradock.

'Oh, yes – just an itchy collar,' Jago replied quickly, deploying the first excuse he could think of. He had to admit, albeit strictly to himself only, that there'd been something quietly thrilling about sharing those chocolates in the dark anonymity of the cinema, but he'd felt significantly out of his depth, and that was not something he enjoyed.

He walked on in silence beside Cradock, determined to focus on the job in hand. But there was one thought that wouldn't go away: the fact that the movie Dorothy had chosen was about the Mounties. And they, as everyone knew, 'always got their man'.

CHAPTER SEVEN

'Good morning, Detective Inspector, Detective Constable,' intoned Dr Gibson's lab technician and general assistant, the lugubrious and white-coated Mr Spindle, when they arrived at St George's Hospital. He glanced at his watch. 'Or should I say good afternoon? Welcome to our humble abode. Dr Gibson has asked me to escort you to the post-mortem room. I believe he's completed his investigation of Mr Radley's unfortunate departure from this vale of tears.'

Jago and Cradock followed him down the corridor to the room in question, where they saw Gibson seated at a small desk in the corner.

'The detective gentlemen are here, sir,' said Spindle.

'Yes, jolly good,' Gibson replied over his shoulder. 'Just finishing a few notes – be with you in half a tick.'

Jago stood beside Spindle, rubbing his hands together to

warm them. 'Always a bit chilly in here, isn't it?'

'Yes, sir. It's the way the bodies prefer it. We like to keep them comfortable.'

'I'm sure they appreciate that, Mr Spindle.'

'We get no complaints, sir.'

Jago smiled politely and tried to stamp his feet on the cold tiled floor as unobtrusively as possible to keep his circulation going. The presence of death in the room made him keen to feel warmth in his veins.

'I understand the deceased was a theatrical gentleman,' Spindle continued.

Jago suspected that the technician's idea of a theatrical gentleman might not stretch to include a variety comedian, but he had no wish to stop him in mid flow. 'That's right, yes,' he replied.

'A noble yet oft derided profession, in my view, sir.'

'Really?'

'Yes, sir. I once had thespian aspirations of my own, you see – strictly in the realm of amateur theatricals, of course, but from an early age I'd had a yen to tread the boards. Unfortunately, my career did not blossom – for some reason I was cast too often as the butler, and the more demanding parts eluded me. But I believe I'm a better man for the experience – to study Shakespeare and his language is to plumb the very depths of life itself, don't you think?'

'All the world's a stage, and all that, you mean?' Gibson interjected with a laugh as he put his pen down and got up from the desk.

'Indeed, Dr Gibson, sir, and all the men and women

merely players. You have your role to play in this world and I have mine, and these police officers have their own quite different roles, but together we make up the drama. And what better place to work than here, in a mortuary, to be reminded every day that no matter what our role in life, this is where we end up – as the Bard himself said, "sans teeth, sans eyes, sans taste, sans everything".'

'A profound thought indeed,' said Gibson. 'Mr Spindle is a man of hidden depths, Inspector. I think it's the cold in here that brings it out in him. Now, my stomach and my watch are both telling me it's lunchtime. Could I tempt you to a bite to eat in our refectory? It's a somewhat more congenial environment than this place, I think.'

'Yes, please,' Jago replied, not wishing to spend a moment longer than necessary immured in this tomb-like chamber.

They adjourned to the refectory, where Gibson treated them to ham sandwiches and a slice of fruit cake each and escorted them to a secluded corner of the room. 'I'm sure my medical colleagues can cope with anything I might describe as we discuss this case,' he said, 'but you never know when there might be visitors in our midst, and they might have less robust stomachs.'

Jago made no comment, unsure whether to be flattered by the implication that his own stomach was robust and not wishing to disabuse the good doctor. 'So,' he said, 'what can you tell us about Mr Radley's death?'

'Well, apart from the very evident presence of a weapon sticking out of his belly, you may be interested to know that I found some fresh bruising to the nose, the

51

face and various other parts of the body.'

'Does that mean he was in some kind of fight before he died?'

'If the bruises occurred close to the moment when he died, it can be impossible to say whether he got them just before or just after, so I can't be sure. They don't look inconsistent with the results of a brawl, but all I can say is that my professional opinion is that they occurred at about the time of death. I can't be more precise than that.'

'Thank you. And was it a screwdriver? I thought it was that, or perhaps a chisel, but of course we didn't attempt to remove it.'

'Quite right – I would not have been pleased if you had. It was indeed a screwdriver, but there's nothing unusual to report – it was the common type, with a six-inch shaft, a flat blade and a wooden handle. On the face of it, of course, a screwdriver wouldn't be an obvious first choice for someone planning to commit suicide or to kill – they'd be more likely to go for something sharper, like a knife. In a theatre, though, I imagine it's the kind of thing a carpenter or an electrician working there might leave lying around at the end of the day, if he knew the building wouldn't be in use overnight. If Mr Radley was in some kind of brawl, it's possible his attacker picked up the screwdriver as a random weapon and used it on him. Whether that actually happened, of course, I couldn't say – that's for you to establish. But what I can say is that the nature of the fatal wound would not be inconsistent with that.'

'So what was the actual cause of death?'

'When I opened him up, I found that the screwdriver had

penetrated the abdominal cavity and caused a laceration to his liver, with the result that he bled to death. The liver's well protected, tucked under the ribs, but an upward stab even with a four-inch blade would reach it.'

'Does that suggest this was someone who knew where and how to inflict a fatal wound?'

'Not necessarily. If you're attacking from the front an upward plunge into the abdomen would be quite a natural motion. This could have been intentional, but equally it could be what you might call the work of an amateur killer.'

'Can you estimate when he was stabbed?'

'Yes. It's helpful in that respect that we know exactly the time of his death, so we can work backwards from that. Having said that, if you suffer an abdominal wound like this, it all depends on what the weapon hits and how much damage it does – the interval between being stabbed and dying could be minutes or it could be a number of hours. The important thing to note in this case is that the laceration to the liver was only mild – the screwdriver just caught it as it went in – so he would have bled slowly. He would gradually have got weaker, with the loss of blood reducing the flow of oxygen to his brain until eventually he lost consciousness and then died.'

'So he died slowly?'

'Yes. Not just because it was only a slight wound to the liver, but also because he was lying on his back – the blood pressure falls more slowly than it would do if he were more upright. But once it fell to a certain point, he'd have a sudden deterioration and die. The other thing to note is that with him lying in that position most of the bleeding would have been into the inside of his body. Given the nature of the wound and the amount of blood lost into the abdominal cavity, I would estimate that he incurred that injury between one and two hours before he died. We know that he died at seven minutes past nine, so that would put the estimated time of the stabbing at, say, between seven and eight o'clock in the morning, although it could possibly have been a little later than that.'

'Thank you, that's very helpful. Mr Radley managed to speak to the special constable who found him just before he died, but unfortunately he was quite incoherent and didn't tell us who stabbed him or when.'

'Really? That is interesting, but not surprising given the slow nature of the bleeding. I should mention another relevant point, which is that I was of course paying particular attention to the liver, and I found evidence of cirrhosis, which would have contributed to his inability to stop bleeding. I also found a rather high level of alcohol in his blood, which suggests this man had been drinking more than was good for him quite regularly for some time, including not long before he died.'

'So he definitely had a drink problem?'

'That would be the colloquial term for it, yes. It also means it's likely that after he was stabbed he was too groggy to move, or even to be aware that he was bleeding. It would also explain the apparent incoherence of his last words to your constable.'

'Is there anything else for you to add?'

'No, except to say that my report will say that death was due to haemorrhagic shock consequent upon a penetrating injury causing a laceration to his liver.'

'And we should treat this as a case of suspected murder?'

'That would not be inconsistent with my findings.'

'Right, thank you, Doctor. We'll leave you to your next body now – unless you have any other questions of your own.'

'Well, actually, yes, a brief word would be in order – just a small private matter.'

Jago couldn't be sure, but he thought he caught Gibson making a discreet rocking motion with his hand in the time-honoured sign language for a drink. He remembered the Glenlivet pure malt with which the pathologist had entertained him when they were working on a case in Pimlico. That had been a month or more ago, plenty of time for him to have finished the bottle, but it had been a very convivial evening, and there might perhaps be a little left . . .

He took a key from his pocket and handed it to Cradock. 'Wait for me in the car, Peter – I'll be with you in a minute.'

Gibson watched as Cradock left the refectory. 'I was just thinking you might like to come round for a drink one evening. I enjoyed our chat last time, but I think for your young assistant it might not be such a treat to spend the evening listening to two old soldiers droning on about the last war.'

'Nor for us to have to try to explain things all the time,' said Jago. 'Peter's a fine young man in his way, but I spend rather a lot of time already explaining things to him, and it would be nice to have some time off in congenial company. When would suit you?'

'Not this evening, unfortunately. My neighbours are holding a cocktail party and I've said I'll go. Goodness knows what they'll be making their cocktails with – these days it might turn out to be a small glass or two of British sherry each, and that's your lot. But they're good neighbours, and it's kind of them to invite me. How about tomorrow evening at seven? I'll order some dinner.'

Jago's life had rarely, if ever, been disrupted by an invitation to a cocktail party, so he refrained from passing any comment on the engagement. 'Yes,' he said. 'That would be very nice, thank you, unless for any reason duty prevents it – that's always a risk in my line of work, I'm afraid.'

'Mine too,' Gibson replied. '*C'est la vie.*'

Jago might have been unfamiliar with the world of cocktail parties, but at least having had a French mother meant he wasn't flummoxed when someone came out with a few words in the language. '*C'est la vie,*' he replied, inwardly gratified that his accent was definitely better than Gibson's. 'I'll hope to see you at seven tomorrow, then.'

CHAPTER EIGHT

'Interesting what the doctor said about Radley's drinking, wasn't it, sir?' said Cradock, handing over the key as Jago settled into the Riley's driving seat.

It sounded to Jago as though his young assistant was eager to expound a theory, so he put the key in the ignition but didn't turn it. 'Yes?' he replied patiently. 'In what particular way were you thinking?'

'Well, it's just that I suppose it would've made it easier for someone to murder him if he was drunk,' Cradock continued. 'He might not've noticed them creeping up on him.'

'Yes, but stabbed in the stomach? That doesn't sound to me like his attacker was creeping up behind him, and it's a bit tricky trying to creep up on someone from in front. But you're right about the drinking – and the other interesting thing is that no one we've spoken to so far has mentioned anything about him being fond of a tipple, not his brother or his sister or his wife.'

'Maybe they don't want to give his secrets away now he's dead, or maybe they think they need to protect his reputation.'

'Perhaps, but if we're going to get anywhere with this investigation, telling us Radley's secrets is exactly what we need people to do. I think it's time we had a word with that agent of his – she must know a thing or two about him. We'll drop by on the way back.'

Number 27 Mart Street was an anonymous-looking building, with only an inconspicuous bell marked 'Mansfield Agency' beside the door to confirm that they'd come to the right place. Jago pressed the button, and within moments it was opened by a woman wearing a dark blue two-piece suit with a lace shawl draped round her shoulders. She peered at him questioningly over half-moon glasses, and he doffed his hat.

'Miss Adelaide Mansfield?' he said.

'Yes.'

'I understand you're Roy Radley's agent. Is that correct?'

'It is.'

Jago showed her his warrant card. 'We're police officers, Miss Mansfield – I'm Detective Inspector Jago and this is Detective Constable Cradock. May we come in?'

'Of course.'

She opened the door wider and led them up a narrow flight of stairs to a small and untidy office. 'I must say I don't usually have policemen calling – what's it about?'

'I'm sorry, Miss Mansfield, but we're here with some bad news. I'm afraid Mr Radley was found dead this morning.'

'Found dead? Oh, my goodness.' She put a hand to the wall as if to steady herself.

'Do you mind if we sit down?'

'Of course.'

As soon as they were seated, the agent reached for her handkerchief and gripped it tightly in her right hand. 'I don't know what to say – it's such a shock. What happened?'

'He was found close to death in the Prince Albert Theatre – it seems he'd been stabbed. A police officer sent for an ambulance, but unfortunately Mr Radley died within minutes, before any medical help could arrive.'

'And his family – do they know?'

'Yes, we've already broken the news to his wife and his brother and sister.'

She shook her head silently. 'The poor things. How is his wife?'

'Coping, I'd say. She asked me to give you her regards.'

'How kind of her. She's the one I feel sorry for – it can't have been easy for her, living with a man like him.'

'What do you mean?'

'Oh, nothing. It's just a general observation – in my experience comedians aren't always as much fun at home as they are on the stage, that's all. You marry the man, not the act.'

Adelaide thought for a moment, then seemed to pull

herself together with a little shake of her shoulders and reverted to a more serious and confident tone, which Jago assumed was her business voice. 'So, thank you for letting me know – I expect I'll hear about funeral details and so on in due course, and sadly there are no bookings for Roy that I'll need to cancel. Will that be all?'

'I would like to ask you one or two questions about Mr Radley before we go, Miss Mansfield.'

'Oh, by all means, yes. What would you like to know?'

'First of all, perhaps you could tell me how long you've been Mr Radley's agent.'

'Yes. Let me see now, that would be eight years – since 1932. I tend to specialise in comedy acts, and Roy was one of the most successful. The King of Comedy, that's what they called him – or at least, that's what he liked to be called. He wanted it to be his bill matter, but that might've been difficult.' She checked herself. 'Oh, forgive me, I should explain – bill matter is what we call the words the theatre puts under your name on the bill – you know, the placard outside saying who's on the programme.'

'Yes, I'm familiar with the term – my father was a music hall artist. But that was long ago, and his bill matter was just "popular vocalist".'

'Really? How fascinating. But anyway, Roy wanted "The King of Comedy" under his name, but the theatres wouldn't do it, because someone else had already used it, and bill matter's copyright – unlike a comedian's gags, of course. As they used to say when I started out in this business, there's no copyright in a joke. So Roy used his catchphrase instead – I expect you know what that is.'

'I'm sorry, I don't think I do.'

'Nor you, Detective Constable?'

Cradock's face was blank.

'It was "Mind yer backs" – like the porters shout in the market when they're coming through with a barrow or with those baskets piled up on their heads. You know he started out as a coster comedian, I assume?'

Cradock opened his mouth, but before he could speak Adelaide must have read the expression on his face. She gave him a motherly smile. 'Oh, dear, Detective Constable, you do look baffled – you've never heard of a coster comedian? It was before your time, I suppose. They used to do an act as cockney costermongers – you know, the men who sell fruit and veg from a barrow on the street – so there was an obvious connection for Roy, what with growing up here in the market. He told me once that when he was a young lad just starting out in the family business, his father made him work as a costermonger for a while so he could learn the tricks the men who bought produce from him got up to. They've always had a reputation for being a cheeky bunch, parking their barrows where they shouldn't and constantly dodging your boys in blue, so that experience came in very handy later for a comedy routine.'

Cradock nodded to acknowledge this piece of enlightenment.

'By the time I became his agent,' she continued, 'he'd adapted the act so he was a market porter, but basically doing the same sort of thing. He'd come on stage and say "Oi oi, mind yer backs," or sometimes it would be "Oi oi, oi oi, here comes Roy", and the audience would all join in on "here comes Roy". He was very popular then.'

'So it seems. But I've been told he'd fallen on hard times more recently,' said Jago.

'Well, yes, but the same could be said of nearly everyone who works on the stage. When the war started, all the theatres in London were closed down by the government, and that meant thousands of people were put out of work at a stroke of the pen. I know of one young actress who was reduced to addressing envelopes for thirty shillings a week and sleeping on a camp bed in a nine-bob-a-week attic just round the corner here in Covent Garden, and she was one of the luckier ones. It was a death blow to the whole industry. Things eased up for a while later, but then when the Blitz started in September there was no need for an order from the government – nearly all the London theatres and variety houses had to close themselves down because of the air raids.'

'Was that the reason for the change in his fortunes?'

'No – that was more of a personal nature. It was a tragedy. I don't want you to put this about, but when I started working with Roy, he was making up to a hundred and twenty pounds a week.' She paused, distracted – or so it seemed to Jago – by the dramatic bulging of Cradock's eyes. 'But later it all changed – something seemed to have knocked the stuffing out of him, and he lost his confidence. He began to act twitchy, as if he was afraid of something – something he didn't want to talk about.'

'Not even to you?'

'No – I don't know what was troubling him. What

I noticed, though, was that his bookings started going down.'

'And would I be right in thinking that's bad news for his agent too, if you're getting a percentage of his earnings?'

'Well, that's certainly one aspect of it, but my concern was more about the effect it was having on him – and Billy too, for that matter.'

'Billy?'

'Billy Barratt – he was Roy's straight man. It got to the point where Roy couldn't make enough money to pay for both of them, so that was the end of their partnership – Billy was out of a job.'

'Where could I find Mr Barratt?'

'Last I heard he'd retired and moved into Brinsworth House – that's the home for retired performers. It's run by the Variety Artists' Benevolent Fund, in Twickenham. If he's not there, I don't know where he might be.'

'Thank you. Just one more question – why were the bookings going down?'

She paused. 'If you want an honest answer, I'd say his work was drying up because he wasn't drying out.'

'What do you mean?'

'I mean he was having a problem with drink. It'd been getting worse in the last few years, and then when the war started and the government closed down all the theatres . . . well, what remained of his career crashed into the ground and burnt. That's why she got rid of him, I think.'

'Who?'

'His wife – she couldn't put up with it any more.'

'But I understood he walked out on her.'

'He may have walked out, my dear, or he may have been carried out on a stretcher, but whichever way he left, it was because she kicked him out. She's not a woman to mess with, that Doreen, and he wasn't the kind of man to stand up to her. He was happy telling jokes and making people laugh, but real life was something he couldn't get a grip on. He depended on her at first, and then later he depended on drink. He told me once she'd given him an ultimatum – either the booze goes or you go. In tears, he was, right here, sitting in that chair you're in. I told him he'd have to stop his drinking, but he said he couldn't, it was too late. I don't know what he said to Doreen, but next thing I knew she'd told him she'd had enough and sent him packing, and that was that.' She sighed. 'Poor Roy – to think of him having to sleep on the floor in a theatre. I never thought it would come to that.'

'Was that the Prince Albert Theatre?'

'Yes, of course it was. I thought you knew – you said that's where he was found.'

'Just checking.'

'Right, well . . .' She pulled back the cuff of her jacket and looked at her watch. 'My goodness, is that the time? I'm terribly sorry, Inspector, but would you mind awfully if I . . .'

'Of course,' said Jago. 'Thank you very much, Miss Mansfield – we'll see ourselves out.'

CHAPTER NINE

They shut the street door behind them and got back into the car. 'Well,' said Cradock, 'she was a bit keen to get rid of us, wasn't she? Do you think maybe she hadn't meant to let on that she knew Radley was sleeping in the theatre?'

'I'm not sure. She strikes me as an intelligent woman who's quite careful about what she says and doesn't say. But it fits with what George Radley said – he thought his brother might've been dossing there, didn't he? And the other things she said about him and his wife and the booze – that explains why he was living in the theatre. It must've been a choice between that or sleeping on the street in the middle of winter, under the stars – and under the kind attentions of the Luftwaffe too. Maybe drinking was the only way he could cope. I'd still like to know more, though.'

'What about Tipton, sir, the caretaker? He might know something.'

'You took the words out of my mouth, Peter – well done. I propose that we track him down at St Thomas's, then have a spot of supper at Bow Street nick, and then see if we can find Roy Radley's niece Patricia at home – I'll be interested to hear what she made of him. Run down the road to that phone box and see if it's still working, and if it is, call the hospital and see whether he's still there. If we promise to be good, they might allow him to have a couple of visitors.' He pulled a handful of loose change from his coat pocket and picked out a couple of pennies. 'Here you are – tuppence for the call. Have this one on me.'

'Thanks, guv'nor,' Cradock replied, and slipped out of the car, clutching the coins. He strode briskly to the red phone box, opened the door and disappeared inside, then moments later leant out again and gave a thumbs-up sign to Jago.

'Got through first time,' he said when he returned. 'Makes a change, doesn't it? They let me speak to the sister on his ward, and she said that's all right, we can visit him, as long as we don't stay more than ten minutes, don't disturb the other patients and don't get in the way of the nurses.'

'Just as well you didn't get a sister who's strict, then, isn't it?'

'Sir?'

'Never mind – let's go.'

* * *

66

The afternoon light was beginning to fade when they pulled up outside the hospital a quarter of an hour later. St Thomas's, hit by several high-explosive bombs since September, was still a sorry sight, as battered as the patients it did its best to care for. With some of its Victorian buildings on the Thames opposite the Houses of Parliament lying in ruins, it had now been designated as a casualty clearing station, and the ward where they found Tipton was one of the temporary ones rigged up in the basement. There was no natural light, but the white-painted walls made the most of the electric lamps that hung from the ceiling. The hospital seemed to have crammed in as many beds as possible, and there was barely room between them for Jago and Cradock to edge their way to Tipton's bedside.

The sister, as austere in person as she had sounded on the telephone, hovered nearby, keeping a watchful and suspicious eye on them. She'd already explained that it was not a normal visiting day, and they'd had to produce their warrant cards to gain admission to the ward. The fact that they were from the Metropolitan Police seemed to cut little ice with her: she reiterated the limit of ten minutes on their visit and gave the impression that rest was all that stood between her patient and his untimely demise. Only when Jago assured her of their compliance did she step aside and allow them to approach the bed where the theatre caretaker lay, propped up on pillows.

'We won't be long, Mr Tipton,' said Jago quietly once he'd introduced himself and Cradock. 'We just need to ask you a few questions about what happened this morning at the theatre. How are you doing?'

'Oh, mustn't grumble,' Tipton replied. His voice was weary, and his attempt at philosophical acceptance not entirely convincing. 'There's plenty in here worse off than me, judging by the noise some of them have been making. The doctor said they think I've got a touch of concussion because of that bomb, so they want to keep me in for observation for a day or two just in case. Apart from that, there's nothing broken, but I'm a bit bashed about.'

From the little Jago could see of him in his hospital pyjamas, that seemed indeed to be the case. His head was bandaged, but he had a couple of visible cuts to his face and a conspicuous black eye.

'I don't think there's much I can tell you about this morning,' Tipton continued. 'I was just minding my own business when there was this enormous bang and the ceiling fell in on me. Lucky I wasn't killed, I suppose, but the next thing I knew I was being whisked off in an ambulance and ended up here.'

'Have you heard anything more since then about what happened?'

'No, I've just been here, sleeping half the time.'

'In that case I'm afraid I have to tell you somebody was killed at the theatre – Mr Roy Radley.'

'Oh, that's terrible. Poor old Roy – I had no idea. That's what it's like with these bombs, though, isn't it? It's just a matter of luck – it hits one person but misses another, so one gets killed and the other doesn't.'

'It wasn't the bomb that killed him, Mr Tipton – we believe he was murdered.'

Tipton began to shake his head but then winced and moved a hand up to his bandage. 'I can't believe it. What makes you think he was murdered?'

'He'd been stabbed.'

'I see . . . I don't know what to say. So, is this what you wanted to ask me about?'

'It is. First of all, I've been told that you live on the premises – is that correct?'

'Yes, I do – I've been there about five years, since Sir Marmaduke gave me the job. You know he owns the theatre, do you?'

'Yes – carry on, please.'

'Well, when the theatres all got closed down at the beginning of the war, I thought he might be getting rid of me, but actually he said he wanted me to stay on. There's a lot of valuable stuff in there, see, and what with the blackout he was worried about thieves taking all the lead off the roof or breaking in. Some of those villains, they're like vultures, just waiting for the chance to pounce – they'd be in nicking the chandeliers too, I reckon, if they got half a chance.'

'Not a very enviable position for you to be in, then – on your own in a place as big as that, having to protect it?'

'It doesn't worry me. I'm an old soldier – I reckon I can look after myself if there's any funny business, and I know my way round in there in the dark much better than any intruders could. That theatre's my home.'

'And where exactly on the premises do you live?'

'I've got a little flat right up in the roof. Very cosy, but not the best place to be these days when there's bombs falling – doesn't matter whether they're high explosives or incendiaries, I still prefer to have something a bit stronger than a few old slates to keep them out of my bed. So when the air raids really got going in September I moved down a few floors and set up home in the basement – it's a bit spooky down there at night, but much safer.'

'I see. Now, we've been told that Mr Radley was sleeping in the theatre. Is that correct?'

'Yes, he'd been sleeping there recently – I think he was out of work and on his uppers, and Sir Marmaduke said he could, as a favour, like.'

'Which part of the theatre did he sleep in?'

'Just off the foyer, next to the gents' toilets. We've got a little room there, more like a cupboard, really, so I put an old mattress down for him, and it meant he could have a wash or whatever in the gents without having to roam round the theatre. I thought Sir Marmaduke would probably prefer it if he was tucked away, like.' He closed his eyes and yawned. 'Sorry, Inspector, I'm getting a bit sleepy.'

'We've almost finished,' said Jago. 'Can you tell me where I can get hold of Sir Marmaduke?'

'Yes – he's got an office over in Shaftesbury Avenue. The Prince Albert's not the only theatre he owns, you see – he's got a string of them. The address is Suite 3, Concordia House. It's up near Cambridge Circus, just a bit down from the Palace Theatre.'

'Thank you. And the phone number?'

'That's Gerrard 6839.'

Jago wrote the details in his notebook. 'Thank you. Now, can you tell me, please – did you see or hear anything unusual or suspicious between about seven and nine this morning?'

'No. The thing is, what with the theatre being closed down, I don't have as much to do as I used to. There's no performances, so I don't have to be on duty in the evenings, and I don't have to get up so early in the mornings either. There's generally no visitors around until well after nine o'clock in the morning, so I tend not to stir until about eight-thirty, and well, to be honest, I hadn't been up all that long when the bomb hit. Sorry I can't be of more help.'

'So was there anyone else at all in the theatre during the night or early this morning up to when the bomb landed? Apart from Mr Radley, of course.'

'No, not as far as I know – but it's a big place, so I couldn't swear to it.'

'Can anyone walk in off the street?'

'No, not unless there's a performance, and like I said, there aren't any of those at the moment.'

'How can people get in, then, if they've got business there?'

'Not through the front entrance – we keep that locked, so they have to ring the bell at the stage door round the back.'

'And who lets them in?'

'That'll be me – it's part of my job. Caretaker and

acting stage door keeper, that's what I am officially. Of course, if they've got a key they let themselves in, but anyone else has to ring.'

'And presumably no one rang the bell this morning?'

'That's right.'

'Who has a key?'

'Well, there's Sir Marmaduke, of course – he owns the place, so he comes and goes as he pleases.'

'Did you see him this morning?'

'No, but then I wouldn't necessarily, unless he wanted to see me about something.'

'Apart from Sir Marmaduke, are there any other keyholders?'

'Yes, there's the bloke from ENSA, on account of the props and all that.'

'Can you be a little more precise?'

'Oh, sorry. Well, you know what ENSA is, I expect.'

'The Entertainments National Service Association?'

'Something like that, yes – the people who put on variety shows for the forces.'

'So who is this man you mentioned?'

'Oh, sorry, he's called Reg White. He's something to do with their props – they've got their headquarters down the road at the Theatre Royal, Drury Lane, but they store some of their props at the Prince Albert, so he has to come round from time to time. He's got a key.'

'Anyone else?'

'Yes, there's Daisy, the cleaner. There's not so much cleaning to do now that we're closed down, but she still does it part-time.'

'What's her surname?'

'Greenway – Mrs Daisy Greenway.'

'Did you see either of them this morning?'

'No, but then I don't usually. They don't need to tell me when they're coming and going – they just let themselves in and out.'

'I see. So, is that all the keyholders?'

'Yes.'

'What about Roy Radley? He was living there – did he have one?'

'No. Sir Marmaduke's strict about who we issue keys to, so Roy didn't get one. The stage door's got a Yale lock, so he could let himself out that way any time, but he had to ring the bell like anyone else to get back in.'

'But if he was in the theatre, he could've let anyone in if he'd wanted to?'

'Yes, I suppose he could.'

'Thank you. We'll be off now, but there's just one more thing. I'd like to take a look tomorrow morning at that room Mr Radley used to sleep in at the theatre. How do I get in if you're still in here?'

The look on Tipton's face suggested this was too difficult a problem for him to focus his mind on. 'I don't know. I suppose you'd better take mine – it's in my coat pocket. Ask the nurse and she'll give it to you.' He paused, seemingly straining to concentrate. 'No, that's no good – I'll need the key to get back in when they let me out of here. Best if you get down to the theatre early tomorrow morning and ring at the stage door – if it's before nine o'clock Daisy should be there doing the cleaning and she'll let you in. She'll be able to show you that room too.'

'Thank you. That'll be all for now, Mr Tipton – goodbye.'

Tipton nodded as Jago and Cradock left. By the time Jago reached the foot of the bed and turned round for a parting glance back, Tipton was asleep.

CHAPTER TEN

Cradock was pleased and relieved that Jago kept his word and drove them straight back to Bow Street police station, and even more so when his boss paused only to phone Patricia Radley and arrange a time for their visit before heading straight to the canteen.

'She said we're welcome to call at her flat at seven o'clock, sirens permitting,' said Jago as they perused the limited options the canteen had to offer. 'She described the shelter where she lives as somewhat unsavoury, so I'm hoping we'll be finished before anything unfriendly flies over this way.'

Cradock confined his reply to a simple 'Yes, sir.' His own main concern was that no unfriendly aerial visitors should turn up in the next half hour and come between him and his supper, so he said nothing more lest he delay proceedings.

'I fancy sausage and mash with carrots and gravy,' said

Jago, 'followed by stewed apple and custard and a mug of tea. Would that suit you?'

Cradock concurred immediately and with enthusiasm. He felt intimidated at the thought of doing an interview with a young lady from the BBC, even if he wasn't responsible for conducting it himself, but he consoled himself with the thought that if he was in for an evening of mental strain, at least his stomach would be fortified for the task.

Having ascertained from the Bow Street desk sergeant that Hanson Street was only about fifteen minutes' walk away, Jago proposed that they go to Patricia Radley's home on foot and work off some of the stodge. Cradock knew that when Jago proposed something, at least when talking to him, it meant he'd decided. He wondered idly whether the same applied to his boss's dealings with the American lady journalist, but he had enough sense not to air the thought. Instead, he merely said, 'Sounds great, sir.'

They took detailed instructions from the desk sergeant on the recommended route, so as to be able to negotiate it in the blackout. The fact that when they set off they could see about three-quarters of the moon above, with not much cloud to obscure it, was a mixed blessing – helpful to them as pedestrians, but also potentially very helpful to German bomber crews in search of their targets. The immediate effect was that they walked a little faster than they might otherwise have done, and arrived at the flat in Hanson Street in more like ten minutes.

Patricia Radley opened the door and welcomed them

in. She was a smartly dressed and attractive young woman who looked in her mid or late twenties, with an air of intelligence and confidence that suggested to Jago she might well go far in her chosen career. Cradock's face looked as though he was at risk of swooning, so Jago threw him an admonitory glare as they sat down.

'Can I get you anything to eat or drink, gentlemen?' she said.

'No, thank you – we've just had something,' Jago replied quickly, before Cradock could open his mouth. 'As I mentioned on the phone, we're here in connection with your uncle, Roy Radley.'

'Yes, I know what happened – my father told me. It's very sad. But he said you were treating it as a suspicious death. What does that mean?'

'I'm afraid it means we believe he was murdered.'

She stared at him, as if trying to come to terms with the significance of his words. 'But that's terrible. I don't know what to say.'

'That's all right, Miss Radley. It's not an easy thing to take in. Were you and your uncle close?'

'We were very close when I was a child – I suppose because he was my only uncle. He used to make me laugh, and I have some very sweet memories of him from those days. I knew he was famous, because my parents had told me, but I didn't really know what famous meant – you don't when you're that age, do you? All I know is that he used to give me little presents, and I thought that was wonderful.'

'Have you kept in close touch in more recent years?'

'Not so much, no. Life gets more complicated when you grow up, doesn't it?'

'In what way do you mean?'

'Oh, you know, you get busy with work and friends, and in London there's always so much to do when you're not working – or, at least, perhaps I should say there was. The night life's not what it used to be, is it?'

'I'm afraid what most people think of as night life doesn't feature very much in a detective's life. In my experience the working day can be rather long and unpredictable.'

'I know what you mean. It's the same in the BBC nowadays. Ever since the Overseas Service got going, Broadcasting House has worked right round the clock, and the building seems just as busy at night as it is in the daytime. You may have noticed that when John Snagge or whoever it may be on any given day reads the news at nine in the evening and at midnight, he's on again at seven and eight the next morning, so obviously the newsreaders sleep there overnight. But now that we've got so many air raids, a lot more of us end up sleeping there too – the management have taken the seats out of the Concert Hall and made it into a dormitory, with mattresses on the floor and nothing but blankets on a sort of washing line hung from one side to the other to separate the men from the women. Still, it's no worse than what people are having to put up with all over the country, so we mustn't complain.'

'What's your own job in the BBC?'

'I'm an assistant to Stuart Hibberd, the chief announcer. I expect you know his name.'

'Ah, yes. He's the one they call the man with the golden voice, isn't he?'

'Precisely. It's interesting work, but not quite what I'd hoped for.'

'And what was that?'

'Well, my first job in the corporation was in the television service at Ally Pally – that's what we call Alexandra Palace. I was working for a man called Cecil Madden, who was in charge of programme planning. Before that, he'd been a variety show producer on the radio, and I think my surname caught his eye – at that time Uncle Roy was still doing quite well on the stage, so Mr Madden probably thought I knew something about show business, even though I didn't really. It was just a humble role to begin with, but I had my heart set on being trained to be a hostess-announcer.'

'What's that? I know the BBC has announcers, but why "hostess"?'

'They called it that because the job involved announcing the programmes but also looking after guests in the studio. They already had Jasmine Bligh and Elizabeth Cowell, of course, but there were high hopes of television catching on with the public and broadcasts being able to extend beyond the London area, so I thought there'd be opportunities for more, especially as they reckoned young women looked better than men on screen. The only restrictions were that they mustn't have red hair, because the cameras couldn't cope with that, and they couldn't be married women. Neither of those things applied to me, so I thought I had a chance. Unfortunately for me, though, the war came along, and the television service was shut down without even a closing announcement, so that was the end of that.'

'So you lost your opportunity to mingle with the stars?'

'I suppose so, yes, but that wasn't why I wanted to do it. In any case, Gerald says some of them can be a real pain in the neck.'

'Gerald?'

'Oh, he's a colleague of mine here. He used to be in the Variety Department but now he works in Talks, where they get famous people coming in to – well, to give talks on the wireless, so he knows what they're like. He and I were at Oxford together and we met through the University Dramatic Society – John Gielgud came up from London to do a production of *Romeo and Juliet* with us, and Gerald and I were both understudies. He was Mercutio and I was Lady Capulet, although neither of us actually got to play in a performance. Gerald was in his final year when I was in my first, so he showed me round the city and showed me the ropes, too, as far as university life was concerned. I was the first person in my family to go to university, you see, so I really didn't know what to expect.'

'Your father told us he was very proud of you.'

'I think perhaps he is, yes, but he's not a very demonstrative father, if you know what I mean.'

'How did you find it – studying at Oxford? I'd imagine it might've been unusual for a student there to have a father who worked in Covent Garden market.'

'Yes, it was. But don't forget, he wasn't just pushing barrows around or shouting out the price of his cabbages to passers-by – he was running a business. Not quite the same as being the managing director of the Anglo-Persian Oil Company, I grant you, which might be more the sort of thing you'd expect in Oxford, but nevertheless he's no fool – he's a businessman and he's very good at it.'

'And willing to pay for a good education for his daughter?'

Patricia laughed. 'He's good at running his business, but that doesn't necessarily mean he's rich. I did have a good education, yes – I went to the City of London School for Girls, down by the river, but my dad couldn't have afforded to pay the fees. I was a scholarship girl – it was London County Council that paid my bills.'

'He didn't mention that – I got the impression he'd paid for everything himself.'

'Well, he's a proud man, Inspector. If he gave you that impression, I expect he had his reasons – I was just grateful that he let me go. It was a lovely school – the girls who went there had to be academic enough to get in and had to pass the interview, but they weren't necessarily posh. The teachers were all spinsters and very dedicated – they wanted their girls to succeed.'

'And they got you into Oxford?'

'They did – Somerville College.'

'That must've helped get you into the BBC.'

She laughed again. 'I suppose so, although the elocution lessons I had when I was a girl probably helped too – it was Uncle Roy who suggested that, and he paid for them.'

'When was the last time you saw your uncle?'

'That was quite recently, actually, just a few weeks ago.'

'How did he strike you?'

'To be honest, I was shocked. He seemed to have gone downhill very rapidly – he always used to be smartly turned out, but now he was quite unkempt and hadn't shaved properly. I could smell drink on his breath, and I wasn't even sure he'd washed recently. Not the man I'd known as a girl at all. And now you say he's been murdered – I can't believe it.'

'Can you think of anyone who might've wanted to harm him?'

'What, kill him? No, I can't. But I was worried when I saw him – judging by the state he was in, he could have been mixing with all sorts of undesirable people, and that can be very risky, can't it? He might just have got caught up in some drunken brawl with a stranger – who can say? I don't think he would have confided in me about things like that – I was probably still a little girl to him.'

'What about your father or your Aunt Joan? How did he get on with them?'

'All right, I think, but when you're growing up they're just your auntie and your uncle, aren't they? They don't necessarily expose their soul to you. They're a different generation, and you really know nothing about who they were or how they got on when they were younger. I think my Auntie Joan had a bit of a soft spot for Uncle Roy – he was older than her, and I think she was proud of him. She seemed kinder to him than my dad was. But again, who can say? Perhaps that's just girls and boys for you.'

She glanced at the clock on the mantelpiece and looked back at Jago with a slight but meaningful rise of the eyebrows. It made him wonder whether she'd learnt her ability to send clear signals at the BBC.

'Well, Miss Radley,' he said, 'we mustn't take up too much of your time. But if you do think of anything else that might help us, please get in touch. The number's Whitehall 1212 – Scotland Yard.'

CHAPTER ELEVEN

The next morning Jago and Cradock made an early start in order to catch Daisy Greenway, the cleaner, at the Prince Albert Theatre. As the caretaker had predicted, when they rang the bell at the stage door it was she who opened it to them. She was a slim woman in her late forties and dressed for the part of cleaner, with dusters tucked into her apron pocket and a few wisps of hair escaping from her turban-style head covering, while the shadows under her eyes suggested she could do with a good sleep. Once they had identified themselves, she let them in, apologising as she moved a broom that was in their way. 'Mind how you go,' she said. 'It's a mess in here – that bomb only got the front of the building, but it's blown dust everywhere. I'm trying to clear up as best I can round the back here, but I hardly know where to start – I reckon it'll take me weeks.'

'We'll try not to keep you from your work, Mrs Greenway,' said Jago. 'So the rest of the building's still in use, is it?'

'Yes, that's right – I don't know anything about it, really, but they said I was to keep on cleaning the back, because it's still all right to use for offices and stores and that. I suppose they'll try and rebuild the front sometime so it can be a proper theatre again, but there's not much point doing that until the bombing lets up and they can put shows on. I suppose you're here about Roy Radley, though – terrible business, that.'

'Yes. We'd just like to ask you a couple of questions about it.'

'Feel free. People are saying he was murdered – is that true?'

'We're treating it as a case of suspected murder, yes.'

'Well, it's nothing to do with me, dear, I can tell you that. And I don't know anything about it, either. I'm just a cleaner – I can't see anything I say being of much help to you.'

'We'll see, Mrs Greenway. We've spoken to Mr Tipton, and he said you'd be able to show us the little room that Mr Radley had been sleeping in recently.'

'Oh, you know about that, then?'

'Yes. Could you show us?'

'Of course. Follow me.'

She grabbed the broom and set off ahead of them, walking slowly and unevenly. It looked to Jago like a touch of arthritis, which couldn't have made her cleaning job any easier, but she seemed to plod on patiently enough. 'Here it is,' she said when they reached the foyer. 'A bit of a mess still, as I said, but that's where he was sleeping.'

Jago and Cradock squeezed into the room. As Tipton had said, it was more like a cupboard, and a mattress occupied most of the floor space. Judging by what they saw, the blast must have blown the door in, because the single chair that seemed to be the only piece of furniture in the room was lying on its side, and a few clothes were scattered across the floor. There was nothing else of interest to be seen, except for three empty bottles. Jago blew the dust off their labels and identified them as whisky, from the cheaper end of the market.

'I wasn't required to clean in here,' said Daisy defensively, as if anxious that Jago might blame her for the state the room was in. 'It was up to him whether he kept it tidy. I wasn't responsible for his empties, either.'

'Don't worry, Mrs Greenway, we're not here to inspect your work. We just wanted to see where Mr Radley was sleeping. Did you see much of him while he was staying here?'

'No, I hardly saw him at all. I only come in to do the cleaning, and that means I'm working all over the building. Besides, I'm told he drank a bit, and I'm in here early in the morning and out again as soon as my work's done, so he was probably sleeping it off when I was in. That's why he had those bottles, I expect. I don't like men who drink – I think they should pull themselves together and do an honest day's work, like I do. We never used to have drunks sleeping on the premises before the war, you know.'

Jago completed his examination of the room. 'How long

have you been working here?' he said.

'Two years,' she replied. 'Stan Tipton got me the job – we go back a long way. He recommended me to Sir Marmaduke, the owner. The pay's reasonable, considering, and I only live just round the corner.'

'What are your working hours?'

'I start about half past five in the morning, unless there's an air raid on. If there is, I wait until the all-clear goes.'

'And when do you finish?'

'If I start at five-thirty, I've usually got it all done by about nine o'clock.'

'Were you here yesterday?'

'No, that was my day off. I used to work Monday to Saturday, but when we closed down Sir Marmaduke cut me back to three days a week – Monday, Wednesday and Friday. Without the audiences there isn't all the mess to clear up, you see.' She paused, then corrected herself. 'Unless we get bombed, that is.'

'Did Mr Radley ever say anything to you that might shed some light on why he was killed?'

'To be honest, I don't think I've exchanged more than a few words with him since he moved in. Like I said, I don't like drunks, and it wasn't my idea to let him bed down here. Besides, I'm not paid to stand around talking, and I like to get finished and off on time so I can make sure young Joe's had his breakfast.'

'You have a son?'

'Oh, Lord no, I haven't got any kids – he's my little brother. Joe Baxter – forty-two and still a bachelor. He moved in after my poor husband, Andy, died – that was a couple of years ago, just after I got the job here. Joe had lost his job and was skint, so I said he could come and live with me – I've always looked after him one way or another. I was on my own after Andy died, so it was company, and he managed to earn a few bob doing odd jobs here and there without having to worry about finding the rent. He needs his own place really, of course – I think it embarrasses him to depend on me – but he'll have to make a lot more money before he can afford that. Still, at least he's got a regular job now – the pay's not much, but every little helps, doesn't it?'

'What does your brother do?'

'He's an ARP warden – one of those new jobs we've only got because there's a war on. Every cloud has a silver lining – that's what they say, isn't it? It's local too, so he doesn't have to shell out money for bus fares.'

'What sector does he cover?'

'I don't know what the sector's called, but I know he does Drury Lane and some of the streets off it – I can't remember which ones, though.'

'Was he on duty yesterday?'

'Yes, he seems to be on duty all the time, as far as I can tell.'

'Do you know where he is now?'

'No, but he's usually at the ARP post down the road or at home – he doesn't have much of a social life.'

'I'd like to talk to your brother, Mrs Greenway. Can you give me your address, in case he's not at the ARP post?'

'Yes, it's a little flat in Long Acre, number 157.'

'Thank you. I hope to see you again soon.'

CHAPTER TWELVE

Daisy Greenway closed the Prince Albert Theatre's stage door behind them, and Jago glanced at his watch. It was a quarter to nine. 'I'm wondering whether Doreen Radley might be up and about by now,' he said. 'I think we should pop round to Maiden Lane and see if we can tackle her on a small matter of inconsistency.'

'You mean what she said about her husband walking out on her?'

'Precisely – it wasn't exactly borne out by Adelaide Mansfield's testimony, was it? Let's see if she wants to revise her account of what actually happened.'

They called at the flat in Sussex Mansions and found her in. She looked surprised to see them, although Jago thought this might be simply because her days normally got off to a slower and later start than his. Whatever the reason, she welcomed them in and sat them down.

'Have you come with news?' she asked. 'You said you'd know what happened to Roy when you got the results of the post-mortem.'

'Yes, I did,' Jago replied, 'and we can now confirm that we believe your husband was murdered. I'm very sorry.'

She nodded silently in response. 'Thank you, Inspector. I have to admit that's what I was expecting you'd say. Roy had a habit of rubbing people up the wrong way, especially people he worked with – I don't think they found him the easiest of colleagues. Maybe he just pushed someone too far this time.'

'Do you have anyone particular in mind?'

'No. I don't know who he's been mixing with in recent years – like I said, we went our separate ways some time ago.'

'Yes, I recall you saying so. But there's something else that's come to our attention that I'm interested in.'

'Oh, yes? What's that?'

'We've been told by your husband's agent, Miss Mansfield, that he'd developed a problem with drinking. But you didn't mention that – is it something you knew about?'

'Yes, I did.'

'So why didn't you mention it? It could be significant.'

'Look, Inspector, I'm sorry I didn't – maybe I should've told you. But the fact is there's a lot of gossip in the world Roy lived in. People were saying things about me that weren't true – they said his wife was such a nasty piece of work that she'd driven him to drink. Those were people who called themselves his friends, but they were no

90

friends of mine. I don't know why they did it, but it was horrible for me. I've spent years having to defend myself, and nowadays I suppose I don't like to draw attention to it. It was a mess he got himself into, and I couldn't do anything about it.'

'How long ago did Mr Radley's drinking problem start?'

'He was always a drinker, but it sort of built up gradually, and in the last few years it got really bad. Such a waste – he was a talented man. I mean, look at this place – it's not bad, is it? He bought this flat when he started doing well in his career and making serious money. Now I'm sitting here on my own, and he . . .' She shook her head slowly and sighed. 'Well, look how he ended up – a sad old failure drinking himself to death. What kind of epitaph will he have? Here lies Roy Radley – told some jokes, made people laugh, made some money, and drank it.'

'Was it the drinking that caused his career to fail?'

'Who can say? It's a bit like the chicken and the egg. You know – did the drinking get worse because he wasn't getting the bookings, or did his career take a dive because of the drink? All I know is he looked on top of the world when he was on the stage, but once he got off it he was helpless and hopeless. His basic problem was he lacked self-discipline – he'd got a lucky break and hit the big time, but he didn't realise you've got to work at success too. He was his own worst enemy. If it hadn't been the drink that brought him down, something else would've done. I think his career was doomed from the start, just like our marriage was.'

'I'd like to ask you about that too – your marriage. You told us that you and your husband drifted apart, and he left you – you said he walked out on you and said he wasn't coming back. But Miss Mansfield gave us a different account of what happened.'

'Oh, yes? What did she say?'

'She said you got rid of him.'

Doreen's eyes widened in an expression of angry disbelief. 'What? She's saying I killed him? The lying little—'

'No,' Jago interrupted. 'I don't think that's what she meant – she said you kicked him out.'

'Oh,' Doreen replied, calming herself. 'Well, so what if I did? I don't like that woman. She knew he was drinking himself to death and she should've told him – she's the professional who was supposed to be guiding his career, isn't she? He might've listened to her. But no – I think I was the only one with the guts to tell him the truth, and he didn't like it. I sat him down and told him the facts of life as far as his so-called career was concerned. But would he listen? Like heck he would. I think he was just too fond of the bottle – not to mention chasing round after girls half his age. He had a talent but he wasted it. He made everyone laugh except me – and he certainly wasn't funny to live with.'

'So what was his reaction when you spoke to him?'

'He just screamed at me and marched out of the room, banging the door. That did it for me. I told him he could either knuckle down, get off the drink and sort himself out, or he could pack a bag and get out.'

'What did he do?'

'He cried.'

'And what did you do?'

'I put some things in a bag for him and told him to go – so yes, I kicked him out, if that's the way you want to put it. I told him not to even think about coming back until he'd dried himself out and was ready to work. Then I got the locks changed – but he never came back.'

CHAPTER THIRTEEN

'She's changed her tune, hasn't she?' said Cradock as they came out of the main doors of Sussex Mansions and back onto the pavement in Maiden Lane. 'I wonder what else she might've kept to herself. And that brother of his, he's just the same – didn't breathe a word about our Roy's drinking. Do you think the whole family's trying to pull the wool over our eyes, sir?'

'It's beginning to look like that,' Jago replied. 'But if so, why? Let's look in at the market and see if George Radley's around.'

They took the short walk to the market and found Radley in his cramped office, the desk covered with a mess of papers. Seeing them arrive, he pushed the documents away with a sigh of frustration.

'Who'd run a business?' he said. 'Nothing but trouble – I swear it'll be the death of me.' There was a catch in his voice.

'I'm sorry, Inspector, that's not a good thing to say at the moment, is it? Take a seat.'

'Have we come at a bad time?' said Jago as he sat down.

'No, no, it's just this blasted paperwork – sometimes I wonder why I bother.'

Jago replied with what he hoped was a sympathetic smile. 'How's the business going? I don't suppose the war's made things any easier for you.'

Radley gave a bitter laugh. 'You could say that.'

'Taken a knock, has it?'

'Oh, yes – the war's hit us bad. The worst thing's getting the supplies in. We're still managing to buy in a lot of home-grown veg, like potatoes, carrots and turnips, so it's not a complete disaster, but on the fruit side we just can't get all the stuff we used to import, especially with those U-boats picking off the ships before they can even get here. We used to have apples from South Africa, oranges from Brazil, lemons from Spain, tomatoes from Morocco, you name it. That's what made the market what it is. But it's all stopped now. We're pretty much down to just English apples, and even they're only the ones that've been stored in gas to make them last longer. There's no knowing how it's going to work out in the future – there's just not enough to go round. There's even a shortage of mistletoe now. The whole world's gone to pot, hasn't it?'

'It certainly doesn't sound as though the war's done you any favours.'

'Too right it hasn't – we've had to completely change the way we work. Before the war started this place was open all day and all night. We'd be at work from two or three in the morning taking deliveries of fruit and veg from the growers, then selling it on to the retailers and suchlike, but you can't have all that sort of thing going on when there's planes coming over all night dropping bombs wherever it takes their fancy, can you? And lorries in and out all night and men running round all over the place with barrows of produce? You can't do that in the blackout. We've had to change the way we work and the hours we do it in.'

'How do you cope with the blackout, then?'

'Same as everyone else – we carry on as best we can and hope we won't get blown up. The worst problem was the roof – it's huge, and half of it's glass, but we have to comply with the regulations the same as any little house or office, so all that had to be blackened. But even so, we can't just work as normal, with lights blazing all over the place. It's the same in the other markets too. A mate of mine at Smithfield said the blackout caused them no end of trouble – they had about ten acres of glass roof over the market, and ten thousand electric lights to worry about. Their pitchers – that's the blokes who carry the meat – they start work at midnight, so all that had to be blacked out and dimmed and what have you.'

'It must be very challenging for you.'

'Yes – I know it's not like people losing their homes or getting killed, but even so . . .' His voice trailed away. 'Er, you said you'd come back when you knew about what happened to Roy – is that why you're here?'

'It is. We just wanted to let you know the doctor doing the post-mortem has confirmed that your brother's death was murder. I'm sorry to have to tell you that.'

'Thank you, Inspector. Yes, it feels worse – an accident's one thing, but the thought that someone deliberately killed him, that's terrible. What kind of person would do that?'

'That's what we intend to find out, Mr Radley.'

'Good. I suppose at least he managed to do what he wanted to do – go on the stage, I mean. That's more than I did. I wanted to be a doctor when I was a kid, but Roy was older than me, and by the time I grew up he was already off chasing his dreams.'

'That's quite a leap, isn't it, from selling fruit and veg in a market to performing on the stage?'

'Yes, but we've got a lot of theatres round here, and the Opera House, and you'd always get the toffs and the stars strolling back through here in search of a late-night drink, so maybe he got a glimpse of the high life and fancied a bit of it for himself. I don't know – but what I do know is he went, and I had to stay at home and work in the business.' He paused to reflect and shrugged his shoulders. 'Funny old thing, isn't it, life? You never know how it's going to turn out. I didn't get what I wanted, but at least I'm still here. Thankful for small mercies, that's what I am.'

'We met your daughter yesterday evening – she seems a very charming young woman. She said she'd seen your brother quite recently and was shocked by the state he was in.'

'Yes, she mentioned seeing him – it was something to do with some trouble she was having with the BBC, as I recall.'

'Really? Some trouble that involved your brother?'

'I don't know. She didn't seem to want to talk about it, so I didn't press her. She's grown up now and more than

97

capable of fighting her own battles – especially if it's trouble with the BBC. That's not exactly my area of expertise, but it is hers.'

'Of course. There's something else I wanted to check with you. Did you know your brother was sleeping on the floor at the Prince Albert Theatre?'

'What, every night?'

'Apparently.'

'No, I didn't, but like I said, it doesn't surprise me – I got the impression his whole life was going down the drain.'

'I see. Excuse me for asking a blunt question, but did your brother have a drinking problem?'

Radley gave a dismissive snort. 'What can I say? Roy didn't think so – he thought he could handle it, but he couldn't. He was trying to revive his career, but there were days when he could barely walk in a straight line, let alone perform on a stage. I told him to stop, but by then it was too late – once the booze gets its teeth into you, it doesn't let go. Why do you ask?'

'It's just that the pathologist found traces of alcohol damage to his liver. You didn't mention that he had a problem with drink when we spoke to you yesterday. Why was that?'

'It's what they call dirty linen, Inspector – you don't go round talking about it if no one's asking, and you didn't ask. I've got a business to run and a reputation to maintain, so it's not in my interests to go round telling everyone we've got a drunk in the family.'

'Did his drinking ever make him violent?'

'Not with me, but I don't think he would've tried it on

with me even if he was drunk. We grew up together, and I was always more than a match for him in a fight. As for other people, I probably didn't spend enough time with him to tell. Ask his friends, if you can find any.'

'Was your brother a religious man?'

'No, I don't think so. We're not that kind of family. His wife's a Catholic, though – maybe some of that rubbed off on him, but I can't say I ever noticed. I did hear he'd been seen going to church once or twice of late, and that was a bit of a surprise, but maybe he just wanted somewhere to sit out of the rain.'

'Which church was it?'

'St Paul's – it's right outside the door here, opposite the market.'

'Is that the building with a portico and what looks like a blocked-up doorway?'

'That's the one. Funny message for a church to give, isn't it? "This is the church but we don't want you to come in, so we've bricked up the door."' He laughed. 'Only joking – I think it was really because the bloke who designed it put the altar at the west end, and the bishop made them block the door and move it to the east end. So it wasn't anything to do with being unfriendly – they actually do very good work round here, and they've got a nice proper entrance at the opposite end of the building. But why do you ask?'

'It's just that before he died, your brother said something to the police constable who found him. He was struggling to speak, of course, but he seemed to be asking for forgiveness – he mentioned stealing, lying and killing. Our constable thought it sounded like a confession – the sort of thing he might say to a priest. Does that make any sense to you?'

'That doesn't sound like the Roy I knew, but being his brother doesn't mean I knew all his secrets. I'm certainly not aware of him killing anyone, though – I don't think he'd have the guts to do that. He was a soldier in the war, mind, but I think he spent all his time as a PT instructor, so he wasn't in the trenches or anything like that.'

'And lying?'

'Well now, that's a different matter. I can well imagine him doing that, if he stood to gain by it – and maybe even stealing too, if he had to. He wasn't the most upright of citizens, so who knows what he got up to? He might not've killed anyone, but I wouldn't be surprised if he'd put one or two noses out of joint along his way. If you're looking for names, though, I don't think I can help you – I didn't see enough of him to know.'

CHAPTER FOURTEEN

They left George Radley to his thoughts and his paperwork. As on their previous visit to him, the first thing Jago and Cradock saw on leaving the market was the building they now knew to be St Paul's Church.

'I think we'll drop in and see if the vicar's there,' said Jago. 'From what we've heard so far, Roy Radley doesn't sound like your average churchgoer, but maybe we can find out something about him here that other people didn't know.'

They made their way round to the other end of the building and went in. The church was a striking contrast to the market, so calm and silent after the busy commotion outside. It was a light and airy space, empty save for one elderly woman bundled up in a thick overcoat against the cold. She was vigorously polishing a brass candlestick on the altar, but looked round when she heard their footsteps approaching.

'Good morning,' she said, 'Can I help you?'

'Good morning,' Jago replied. 'We're looking for the vicar – is he here by any chance?'

'Yes, dear, he is, only he's not the vicar, he's the rector – same thing, really, but I always think it's polite to get these things right.'

'Quite – thank you for telling us. We're police officers, and we'd just like a quick word with him.'

'Ooh, policemen, eh? Well, just so's you don't get the wrong idea, I'm polishing this candlestick, not nicking it.' She gave a wheezy laugh. 'Just my little joke. I'm one of the parishioners, but I come in here once a week to keep things looking smart. I'm no good at flower arranging, but I do know how to polish.' She tucked her cloth into her coat pocket and set the candlestick back in its place. 'The rector's in the vestry, so if you come with me I'll take you to him.'

She led them back towards the entrance and off to the right, where she knocked on a door. It opened to reveal a tall, gaunt-looking man with grey hair and the dog-collar of his profession.

'Two policemen to see you, Rector,' the cleaner announced, and departed.

The rector welcomed them in and offered them seats at a table strewn with notepaper and envelopes. 'Forgive the mess,' he said. 'I'm catching up on my correspondence – there are so many needs in the parish these days, what with the war, that there are always letters to write.' He looked at them over the top of his glasses. 'I'm sorry, but I don't recognise you – I know the police here quite well, but have we met before?'

'No,' said Jago. 'I'm Detective Inspector Jago, and this is my colleague, Detective Constable Cradock. We're based at Scotland Yard.'

'Ah, that explains it. I'm the rector here, as you'll have inferred from Mrs Weller's introduction, and my name is Augustus Talbot. So, welcome to St Paul's Church – is this your first visit?'

'Yes, and it's a fine building you have here.'

'It is – we're very fond of our church. It was designed by Inigo Jones, although he's probably more famous as the architect of the Banqueting House in Whitehall, where Charles I had his head chopped off. Fortunately, this site has a more peaceable history. The whole area around here used to be a garden, you know – the ancient convent garden whose name evolved over the centuries into Covent Garden. Now the only bit of garden that remains is our little churchyard at the front of the building – we like to say it's the only garden in Covent Garden. Even that was actually a graveyard until Parliament put an end to burials in London in 1852. That meant all the graves and headstones had to be removed, and it was made into the beautiful garden you can see now. It's become a popular little oasis, or at least it was until we started getting those horrible daylight air raids.'

'It's actually one of those daylight raids that brings us here, Mr Talbot.'

'Really? How's that?'

'We're investigating the death of a man in Drury Lane.

He was in the Prince Albert Theatre when a bomb hit it yesterday – his name was Roy Radley.'

'The comedian?'

'Yes, that's him.'

'Ah yes, I heard about that this morning – very sad. Is it true that he'd been murdered?'

'Yes, I'm afraid it is. A constable found him at the theatre after it was bombed, and Mr Radley died at the scene shortly afterwards.'

'I see – poor man.'

'Did you know him? I've been told he came to church here occasionally.'

'I've met him – he came to our morning service a few times, and I got to know him a little. This church has been here for three hundred years, and we've always had a strong connection with the theatre because of the Theatre Royal in Drury Lane and the Royal Opera House both being in our parish. St Paul's is actually known as the Actors' Church because we have a special ministry to the world of theatre. So I've got to know a lot of actors and other performers over the years I've been here, and I've learnt something about the particular pressures and challenges they face in their professional and personal lives. It's a life that brings fame for some but poverty for others.'

'So what would you say it brought Roy Radley?'

'I knew more about his stage career than his personal affairs, but I'd say he had more than a taste of both. His life was on a decidedly downward trajectory, and judging by his appearance when he came to church, my guess is that he wasn't far from the bottom.'

'How was he coping with that?'

'Not very well, as far as I could tell. Sometimes he was the worse for wear for drink, and even when he wasn't, he was dishevelled and seemed to be struggling with life. He was a troubled man.'

'Troubled by his conscience?'

The rector responded with an inscrutable smile. 'By the time we get to his age – and mine too – we're all troubled by our conscience to one degree or another. Even inspectors in the Metropolitan Police too, perhaps.'

Jago smiled back. He wasn't about to reveal any of his own troubles to the priest. 'It sounds as though you actually knew him quite well,' he said.

'I don't think so. In this ministry one gets to understand people. You recognise familiar patterns in their lives. People tell you things they wouldn't tell their family or friends. But that doesn't mean I knew him well.'

Jago noticed the rector's quick glance at the mahogany clock on the far side of the room. 'We must let you get on with your work, Mr Talbot,' he said, 'but before we go there's just one more thing I'd like to ask you.'

'Of course, please do.'

'Thank you. It's just that our constable says that as Mr Radley was dying he was saying things like "God have mercy" and asking for forgiveness. It sounded more like the way a man might speak if he was making a confession to a priest, so I wondered whether that was something Mr Radley was in the habit of doing.'

'Well, I don't know whether it was his habit, but he did come to me once for that purpose. But before you go

105

any further, Inspector, I must remind you that I cannot divulge anything he may have said to me in the form of a confession.'

'Yes of course, sir – there's no need to worry. I'm well aware of the seal of the confessional, and I'm not about to ask you to break any confidences. I'm just trying to understand his circumstances and his state of mind. When did he come to see you?'

'It was about three weeks ago.'

'And what sort of state was he in?'

'He'd been drinking – the poor man could barely stay on his feet. He said something about wanting me to hear his confession.'

'So what did you do?'

'What I always do. I'm obliged to hear any man's confession, even if he's drunk and incapable, so I said yes, I would hear it. But in this case, even if I were willing to break the confidentiality of the confessional – which I'm not – I wouldn't be able to tell you anything. The fact is I could make no sense of the little he said before he passed out at my feet. All I could do was haul him onto a pew and fetch a couple of blankets for him until he'd slept it off. By morning he seemed to have no recollection of seeking absolution, and after I'd given him breakfast, he wandered off again. That was the last I ever saw of him.'

CHAPTER FIFTEEN

'Roy Radley's a bit of a puzzle, isn't he, sir?' said Cradock as they left the church. 'Nobody really seems to know what was going on inside his head.'

'Perhaps it's not surprising, though,' said Jago. 'You probably don't know what's going on inside my head, and I certainly don't know what goes on in yours. But you're right – I can understand the rector not knowing everything if he's only met him a handful of times, and his brother doesn't seem to have seen much of him for a long time, but I'd have thought his wife might've been more forthcoming. We'll have to see if we can get more out of her. The person I'd like to see first, though, is that man his agent mentioned.'

'What, Billy Barratt?'

'Yes – if he was Radley's straight man for all those years, travelling here, there and everywhere, he probably spent more time with him than Mrs Radley did. I want to know what he can tell us about the real Roy Radley. So I think we'll take a little drive out to that retirement home in Twickenham, and on the way we can stop by and visit those theatrical lodgings that George Radley told us about.'

Goodwin's Court, where Roy Radley had reportedly lodged after leaving his marital home, lived up – or perhaps down – to his brother's description of it as 'pretty basic'. The only access was through a passage barely three feet wide, so they parked the car in the neighbouring street and entered on foot. Here they found an alleyway not much broader, at about eight feet across, lined with little terraced dwellings and bow-windowed shops that looked as though they'd been there for centuries. Jago thought they might once have had a certain charm, but that was now buried beneath the accumulated black soot and grime of all those years. That and the evident disrepair of some of them suggested to him that these were the kind of places London County Council would be keen to demolish.

They found number 16, and when they knocked at its door they were greeted with a smile by a middle-aged woman.

'Good morning, Madam,' said Jago, doffing his hat. 'I'm afraid I don't know your name, but I'm given to understand that these are theatrical lodgings. Would you be the landlady, by any chance?'

'Yes, I am. My name's Ena Sandwell – Mrs. And who are you?'

'We're police officers, Mrs Sandwell. We're conducting inquiries concerning Mr Roy Radley, and we've been told that he used to live here. Is that correct?'

'Yes – you'd better come in.'

The house looked more cared for on the inside than it did on the outside, and Mrs Sandwell took them into what appeared to be her private living room and office on the ground floor.

'Can I get you a cup of tea?' she asked.

'That's very kind of you,' Jago replied, 'but we won't – we're just calling in on our way to Twickenham.'

'You said you're conducting inquiries about Roy Radley – is he in trouble?'

'No, it's not that kind of inquiries. I'm afraid Mr Radley is dead.'

She gasped, and her hand flew to her mouth. 'Oh, my goodness, that is a shock.' She breathed out deeply. 'What happened?'

'I'm sorry to have to say this, but we believe Mr Radley was murdered.'

'Murdered? Oh, my – that makes it even worse. Just give me a moment, please.' She took several deep breaths. 'All right, I'll be OK now – it's just getting news like that out of the blue, you know – it knocks you sideways.'

'I understand, Mrs Sandwell. May I just ask you a couple of questions?'

'Of course.'

'When did you last see Mr Radley?'

'I haven't seen him since he moved out, and that was a couple of weeks ago, nearer three.'

'What caused him to move out?'

'Well, it wasn't the usual reason. What I mean is, when you run theatrical lodgings your guests are always moving on – if they're in a show that's doing well they might be with you for a long time, but if they're touring, they usually only stay for a week. Roy used to tour, I know, but when he came to me, I think he was hoping to make it his home for a while. Unfortunately that didn't work out.'

'What happened?'

'I feel terrible having to say this, now that he's – you know. It's just that, well, the thing is, you see, he hadn't been paying the rent. I tried to be understanding – people say I'm too soft on that kind of thing – but it got to the point where I couldn't afford it. I told him I really needed the rent, and he said – bless him – he said he'd move out, said he knew where he could stay for next to nothing. So I said all right, and he did.'

'Did he say where that was?'

'No, he didn't let on, and it was none of my business to ask.'

'What sort of state of mind was he in when he left?'

'I think he was sad, mainly. He looked tired – it was like he'd been in a fight and lost. Things hadn't been going too well for him lately.'

'In what way?'

'He wasn't getting the work – that's why he couldn't pay, you see, and he was drinking more than was good for him, which can't have helped. It's a very difficult profession, being on the stage – you never know where your next job's

110

coming from, and it all depends on whether people like you. If the audiences decide they don't like you any more, or the producers, or even your fellow artists, you're on a slippery slope. I've had them all staying here over the years – variety performers, music hall acts, straight actors. Anyone who's theatrical, you might say. In Roy's case, it was probably the bookers – the people who book the acts. Some of them can be hard as nails – if they don't like you, they won't book you. Like I said, he looked tired – I think he was tired of life, and tired of having to be funny all the time.'

'Did he ever say anything about wanting to change, maybe turn over a new leaf?'

'Not to me he didn't, but he wouldn't necessarily want to have a heart-to-heart with his landlady, would he? The only thing I'd say is I sometimes got the impression maybe he'd have liked to be a straight actor, do proper plays, you know. I've no idea whether he could've made a go of it, though, or even whether he ever got the opportunity. But in any case, it's not for me to say, really, is it? I just make their beds and cook their breakfasts – I don't manage their careers. All I can say is, whether it was drama or his comic act, I don't think he was having to fight off the offers, if you know what I mean. Poor soul.'

'One last question, Mrs Sandwell. Can you think of anyone who might've wished Mr Radley harm?'

'You mean enough to murder him? What a horrible thought. It's a tough world, though, the stage, and everyone's competing for the work. It's all very lovely on the surface, but underneath, well, it's a bit different. You only get to the top in show business by climbing over the others, so who knows? One man's success means another man's failure, so he might've made an enemy or two in his time. There's a lot of jealousy, you know – a lot. But that's no reason to kill someone.' She looked at Jago uncertainly. 'Is it?'

CHAPTER SIXTEEN

The drive to Twickenham took them west through London and out into the greener suburbs of Middlesex. It wasn't an area Jago was familiar with: he knew Twickenham only for its rugby ground and as the home of the Metropolitan Police orphanage for nearly seventy years until its recent closure. After stopping to ask directions, however, they found Brinsworth House on the corner of a long tree-lined street leading off from the main road.

It could not have presented a more striking contrast to the theatrical lodgings from which they'd just come. A comfortable-looking Victorian mansion built in warm yellow brick, it stood in extensive grounds, and the only feature it shared with Ena Sandwell's home was its bow windows. Unlike those in Goodwin's Court, however, here they were imposing, solid-looking affairs in the same brick, flanking the front entrance porch, with elegant ironwork-railed verandas repeating their shape on the floor above. It seemed to Jago that for any variety performer who'd spent their life trekking from one set of miserable digs to another, retiring to a place like this might well feel like a foretaste of heaven. The broad smile on Billy Barratt's face when he met them in the entrance hall did nothing to challenge this theory.

'Policemen, eh?' he said when they had introduced themselves. 'Don't worry – I'll come quietly.' He laughed, but then his face sobered immediately. 'I'm sorry. Old habits die hard. Is this about Roy Radley?'

'It is, Mr Barratt. Is there somewhere we can speak privately?'

'Yes – you'd best come up to my room.'

They followed him upstairs and along a short corridor to a bedroom at the back of the house. He offered them the two-seat sofa beside a window overlooking the grounds and stood for a moment, staring out at the oaks and elms. 'Lovely view, isn't it?' he said. 'So tranquil – just the ticket for an old chap like me. I like to take a stroll through the trees in the clean air in the morning to wake me up and then come in for a nice cup of tea. Never been a big breakfast man – probably all those late nights in the theatre.' He sighed contentedly. 'Yes, I reckon I've fallen on my feet getting in here, you know. It's not an institution – it's more like a family. I've got my own key, I can come and go as I please, and if I get fed up with looking at trees, I can just toddle down to Strawberry Hill station and hop on the train, and in half an hour I'll be up in the middle of London looking round all the old haunts.' He turned away from the window and moved to the other side of the room, where he perched on the edge of his bed, facing them. 'Mind you,' he continued, 'nowhere's tranquil for long these days, is it? We had a terrible air raid here only about three weeks ago – people killed just round the corner, and another one over the back there, bodies being dug out for days afterwards. Looks like my quiet retirement might have to wait for a bit after all. Still, I suppose you've come here because of what happened to poor old Roy.'

'That's right,' said Jago. 'His agent's told us you were in an act with him for several years.'

'Ah, yes, dear Adelaide. She phoned me to pass on the news of his death – it's very sad. She told me I might be getting a visit from you, too. How can I help?'

'Well, first of all, could you tell me, please, how you came to work with Mr Radley?'

'I'm tempted to say "on the bus", but I'm afraid that's just the old comic in me – very sorry. No, the real answer is it was by accident, I suppose, as these things often are, although I've been an entertainer most of my life, so I was already in the profession. I actually started out as a bank clerk, if you can believe it, but I'd always had a yen for the stage, so I gave it up and joined a seaside concert party. People at the bank thought I was crazy, but I was young and I didn't care. We did little sketches and a bit of song and dance, the usual stuff, and I enjoyed it. Then the war came along, and I was in the navy for four years – that wasn't very entertaining, but I came through without a scratch. When I was demobbed, I picked up with the concert party again as a light comedian, and I started to think about going solo. To cut a long story short, I ended up being Roy's straight man.'

'What was he like to work with?'

'Well, being in a double act's a bit like a marriage – you spend all your time together and you depend on each other, but sometimes you can get on each other's nerves and it can be a strain.'

'Was that true of your working relationship with Mr Radley?'

Barratt paused as if weighing up the question before replying. 'We had our moments, but overall I think it was pretty good. The problems usually come when you've got two strong personalities working together and they both want to be top dog. That's when you get those "artistic differences" people talk about, which is the polite way of describing a major bust-up between two performers.'

'And you and Mr Radley managed to avoid that?'

'Yes, but that was because I knew my place. I soon realised Roy would never want to be anything other than the top dog – it was always just his name on the billing, for example, never "Radley and Barratt" or anything like that.'

'And you didn't mind, presumably.'

'No, I didn't – I needed the work. I'd been "resting", as we performers like to say, for about a year, and I didn't have a bean. I'd tried to make it as a solo comic, you see, but I just didn't have what it takes.'

'So what does it take?'

'Well, obviously you've got to have talent, but it's not just about that – it comes down to simple things like the looks you're born with. Roy's face was just made for comedy – the way he could bulge his eyes like that, and that chin of his. If we were out on the street together, people would stop us and ask for his autograph, because they recognised him, whereas I was just part of the scenery. If I was out on my own, no one ever noticed me.'

'Did that bother you?'

'I don't think so. Being in the public eye has its disadvantages too, you know. But I think that was the difference between me and Roy. To succeed in comedy you need to have warmth, personality – and it needs to be real, because people have to feel that they know you, that you're their friend. And even that's not enough – to be a real success you've got to have that special extra something that makes the audience love you. Roy had it back in those days, but I didn't. Have you ever seen a comic die a death on stage?'

'No, I don't think I have.'

'Well, take it from me – it's not a pretty sight. There's nothing worse than going out there and working through your gags and not getting a single laugh. That's what happened to me when I got booked for a week playing a little theatre up north on my own – I think it's a cinema now. It was my own fault, mind you – I should've known better. Southern comics don't usually play well in the north, and it's the same the other way round, especially in the smaller places – that's where you get the worst heckling, and even worse, the silence. I'm not kidding you – there was a boxing kangaroo act on the bill that night that got more laughs than I did. If you want to know what it was like, all I can say is this – I died in Doncaster. Twice nightly for a week, at the Empire.'

'But Mr Radley took you on?'

'Yes, he did. I might not have made it as a solo act, but as a straight man to Roy it turned out I was just what he needed. There are double acts where the straight man starts trying to get laughs of his own, and that spells trouble, especially with a man like Roy.'

'What do you mean?'

'I mean there was this thing about Roy – he was heading for the top and he didn't want anyone stealing his limelight. He knew I was safe on that score – I'd had my fingers burnt and was happy just to feed lines to Roy so he could get the laughs and I could get a regular pay packet.'

'What year was that?'

'We started the act in 1929, and we worked together until two years ago.'

'What happened then?'

'He sacked me.'

'Could you tell me why, please?'

'Simple – it was the drink.'

'I see. Tell me more, please.'

'Well, where to start? It was a gradual process, but I suppose it always is. For all I know, he may've had a fondness for the bottle for years, but that would've been before I knew him. If you want to know anything about what he was like before that, you'd better ask that pal of his at the theatre.'

'What pal would that be?'

'The caretaker – Tipton – I believe they used to work

together. What I can tell you is that before I started working with him, Roy was what I'd call a cheeky chappie comedian. He used to sing saucy little coster songs – you know.'

Barratt composed his face for a performance and sang in a rasping and laboured cockney voice:

Well, she knew the man who kissed her
said he loved her and he missed her,
but she never knew her sister
was her mum.

'He had a real gift for that sort of thing,' Barratt continued. 'And then there were the jokes, of course – like Max Miller's, but not as blue. His act got him into trouble with the theatre managements sometimes. I think they were worried they'd have the Lord Chamberlain's Office breathing down their necks. Some of the venues were starting to cancel, so he decided to tone it down a bit and switch to a double act. That's when he took me on. We did "a toff and a tough" act that he'd dreamt up – I was the upper-class idiot in evening dress, a bit tipsy on his way home from the opera or theatre, and Roy was a market porter, rough and ready, with a quick tongue and sharp patter. His jokes were still rather risqué, though. I don't think he could help it – it was just the way he was. The crowds loved it, and I think we were good, for a while at least. I don't think Doreen liked it, especially when people asked her if the "my wife" gags were all true, but I don't think she minded the money it brought in.'

'So when did it all start to go wrong?'

'When Roy got a bit of cash in his pocket, I think. Doreen managed everything, of course, including the money, but when he was making enough to hang on to a bit for himself, he started drinking more. Now, the odd drink now and then's one thing, but when it starts getting so regular that you can't go on stage without one, that's when the trouble starts. The thing is, you see, if you're a comic, your timing's everything. With the right material, if you get your timing right you can have the audience eating out of your hand. But it's got to be spot on – it doesn't matter how good your gags are, if your timing's off you fall flat on your face. That was the first thing I spotted with Roy – back in the days when we started working together his timing was brilliant, but the more he drank, the worse it got, and he started losing the audience. Then one night we were due to go on for the act and he turned up at the theatre blind drunk – he couldn't go on, and they had to say he'd been taken ill. But the theatre manager said he'd never work there again, and I suppose word got round. Bookings began to tail off, and Roy started hitting the bottle more and more. You know what it's like – you start sinking, and there's no way back up. In the end he sacked me and said he'd go it alone, but it didn't work. And then I think Doreen sacked him – booted him out, I mean. He was finished – no job, no home, no money.'

'And what about you?'

'I was fine, in one sense. When I was seventeen I signed the pledge – you know, "I promise to abstain from all intoxicating drinks" – so the demon drink's never got its claws into me. But when Roy was finished, so was I. The

120

closest I ever got to regular work after that was pantomime, and they only run from Boxing Day to February if you're lucky. But they were a lifeline – I got myself quite a reputation as a pantomime dame, and it certainly helped to keep the wolf from the door. Now we've got this blasted war, though, so this year there's only going to be one theatre in the whole West End putting on a panto – *Aladdin* at the Coliseum. There are still productions out in the provinces, of course, where there's less chance of bombs, but I'm too old to go traipsing round the country, and summer shows at the end of the pier have had it now because the army's blown lumps out of most of the piers to stop the Germans using them for invasion landings. So what with one thing and another I decided to throw in my hand and retire – a penniless old charity case – and that's why you find me here, enjoying the calm comforts of Brinsworth House.'

'And we shall leave you to enjoy those comforts, Mr Barratt. There's just one other thing I'd like to ask before we go. When we spoke to Miss Mansfield, Mr Radley's agent, she said that recently he seemed to be afraid of something but didn't want to talk about it. Can you shed any light on that?'

'No, I don't think I can.'

'He didn't mention anything to you about it?'

'Inspector, since Roy sacked me, I haven't exactly sought out opportunities for a friendly chat about old times. We haven't spoken to each other for two years.'

'I see. Well, thank you anyway.' He was about to turn away, but stopped. 'Oh, and by the way, can you tell me where you were between seven and nine yesterday morning?'

'Yes, I was having one of those strolls in the grounds that I mentioned. I don't recall the precise times, but I was up by about eight or so, went out for a walk, and was back having a cup of tea a bit before nine. Is that when Roy was killed?'

Jago didn't reply to his question. 'Thank you, Mr Barratt, you've been most helpful.'

'My pleasure, Inspector,' said Barratt. 'My pleasure. If there's anything else I can do to help, just ask. I've got plenty of time to spare.'

CHAPTER SEVENTEEN

It was only when they were driving up Piccadilly on their way back from Twickenham that Jago decided to make a diversion. 'I think we'll turn off here and go up Regent Street to the BBC,' he said. 'If Patricia Radley can spare us a few minutes, I'd like to ask her about this trouble her dad said she was having – a spot of trouble with the BBC that involved her Uncle Roy could be interesting, couldn't it?'

'Yes, guv'nor,' Cradock replied. 'I thought that was interesting too. And what about that thing Billy Barratt came out with? He said Stan Tipton used to work with Roy years ago, but Tipton never mentioned that to us, did he?'

'No, he didn't, although he did seem to be getting a bit sleepy by the time we left.'

'Slipped his mind, you mean, sir?'

'Hmm – possibly. We'll have to see if we can refresh his

memory. And while we're talking about Barratt, get on the phone to the station when you've got a moment and find out the train times from Waterloo to Strawberry Hill, will you?'

'In case he wasn't just out for a stroll in the grounds yesterday morning, you mean?'

'Yes – just to check.'

'Will do, sir.'

'Now then, we've still got two keyholders to talk to as well – Sir Marmaduke Harvey and that Reg White from ENSA that Tipton mentioned. At least he managed to tell us that before he nodded off, poor fellow.'

They turned into Regent Street and could see that this most elegant of London's streets had not escaped the attention of the Luftwaffe. Bombs had torn chunks out of its imposing Regency stonework, and several shopfronts were boarded over with sturdy wooden planks. There was no sign here, though, of the roughly chalked messages of cheeky defiance that the newspapers liked to photograph in the poorer parts of London after air raids. It made Jago wonder whether the denizens of Regent Street were too busy to indulge in the habit, or perhaps simply too refined.

They continued northwards, crossed Oxford Circus and entered Langham Place, home of the BBC. Broadcasting House was an arresting sight. It looked like an ocean liner that had cruised up Regent Street and berthed alongside the equally striking but much older circular portico of All Souls' Church. Both buildings, however, now bore the marks of the Blitz. Less than two weeks before, a landmine had blown the top off the church spire and shattered its doors and windows. One day the building would be restored, thought Jago, but not the life of the young police constable who'd been killed that night by the bomb's blast.

The neighbouring BBC headquarters had the doleful air of a battered veteran. There was extensive damage on its western side, and since Jago had last seen it the whole building, once so graceful in its white Portland stone, had been painted in a drab camouflage. The statue above the main entrance now presided over an ugly baffle wall added to protect the front doors from bomb blast, and the ground-floor windows to either side had been bricked up. He threaded his way through the gap at the end of the wall and heaved open one of the heavy glazed bronze doors to enter, followed by Cradock.

Inside, the austere art deco style of the entrance hall gave Jago the feeling of having stepped from one world into another, from the bedraggled chaos of London's streets into some kind of secular temple. Here they found a high ceiling, pinkish-grey stone walls and pillars, a mosaic floor, and facing them another modernist statue and a Latin inscription. They crossed the hall to the reception desk, where a man telephoned Patricia Radley for them.

'She'll be down in a minute, sir,' said the man. 'Do take a seat while you're waiting.'

They sat on a bench seat beside the reception desk, and a few minutes later Patricia came out of the lift and recognised them.

'Hello,' she said, 'I didn't expect to see you again so soon.'

'Yes, well, I hope it's not too inconvenient, Miss Radley,

but I would like to have another word with you.'

'Of course. I was just about to go for a quick bite of lunch with one of my colleagues. Would you like to join us?'

'I don't want to gatecrash your lunch engagement.'

'No, really, it's quite all right – it's my friend Gerald, the one I told you about yesterday evening. He'll probably be in the restaurant already. It's down in the basement – come with me.'

She took them down the stairs where, to Cradock's initial bafflement, each landing had a window.

'Aren't we underground now?' he said, staring at one.

She laughed. 'Yes, but not even the BBC fits underground windows – they're just pretend, illuminated from behind. An architect's fancy, I suppose, but you won't get a view of the worms.'

Two floors down, they continued along a corridor to the staff restaurant. This was a low-ceilinged room with small square tables and, after the grandeur of the entrance hall, surprisingly cheap-looking tubular metal chairs with canvas seats. It also featured floor-to-ceiling poles labelled with numbers and letters, which puzzled Jago, and even more so when the one nearest him lit up.

'What's that for?' he said.

'Oh, yes, that's rather clever – the numbers and letters are the studio numbers, and if you're required in the studio when you're down here eating, they light up its number to let you know. So there, you can see it's "8A" switched on, so someone's needed in Studio 8A, up on the top floor. Very modern, isn't it?'

'Very, although we have something similar in the police – if a constable's walking down the street on his beat and sees the blue light on top of a police box flashing, he knows the station wants him and he has to open it and answer the phone. The light doesn't tell him where to go, though – that would be too complicated.'

A young man in horn-rimmed spectacles who was sitting alone at a table on the other side of the room gave a discreet wave to Patricia as they approached.

'This is my colleague Gerald Scott,' she said when they joined him, 'and these gentlemen are policemen from Scotland Yard – Detective Inspector Jago and Detective Constable Cradock.' Scott nodded solemnly at the mention of Scotland Yard in a way that suggested he was impressed, but said nothing. He had a thin face and unruly dark hair, and his jacket looked a size too big for him. Jago was reminded of the young men who, twenty-five years ago, would have been handed a white feather by women who thought they ought to be in uniform. He didn't object to Scott remaining present during his conversation with Patricia Radley, but he did wonder silently whether for some reason she had felt the need for a chaperone.

'Food first, talk later,' Patricia continued briskly. 'Now then, gentlemen,' she said to her visitors, 'I recommend the cheese soup – it's good. They serve it with dumplings too, so it's filling, and if you've any room left after that there's bread pudding, the eating of which is a virtue since we're not supposed to waste any bread these days. Will that do?'

'Yes, thank you,' said Jago. He'd always liked flour dumplings in his soup, and he also hoped they might prevent Cradock from pleading weakness from starvation as the day went on, especially if they were followed by the extra ballast of bread pudding.

'You too, Gerald?' Scott nodded. 'I'll get yours, then, and you keep the table. Come along, gentlemen.'

She led Jago and Cradock to the serving counter, where they obtained their food, and she insisted on paying for them.

'Is this the first time you've been inside Broadcasting House?' she said, when they rejoined Scott at the table and began to eat.

'Yes,' said Jago, 'and I must say it all looks very smart. It's rather a sad sight on the outside, though – it looks as though it's been in a fight.'

'As indeed it has,' she replied. 'I expect you know about the bomb we had in October. It was one of those delayed-action ones – it hit the fifth floor but didn't blow up until later, while Bruce Belfrage was down here in a basement studio reading the nine o'clock news. I think the audience must have been very impressed – you could hear the explosion in the background, but he just kept on reading the news as if nothing had happened. He was an actor before he joined the BBC, so perhaps that helped, but even so, an example to all BBC announcers.'

'I heard some people were killed, though.'

'Yes, it was very sad – seven people in all. Four of them were members of our Monitoring Service, all working in Studio 3A. The rest of their operation was evacuated out of London some time ago – I don't think we're allowed to say where – but they'd maintained an information bureau here in Broadcasting House. A girl I know was working there, and when one of our wardens told her to get out, she did what she was told and survived, but four of them stayed at their posts and were killed. I keep thinking about it – if I'd been working in a different department, it might have been me, and I wonder what I would have done.'

'You mean stay at your post or leave?'

'Yes. They were both doing the right thing – the girl who obeyed the instruction and the four who stayed at their posts. They were all doing the right thing, weren't they? All doing their duty, but for some that's what saved them and for others it cost them their life. And it's happening everywhere now, every day, isn't it? Before the war started I had so many plans, but now I just keep thinking every little decision I make could mean the difference between life and death. We're all told we must do our duty, but now I'm not sure what's the right duty to do.'

Jago hoped she wasn't looking for advice. It was a question that had dogged him since he was sent to the front in 1916, and swearing an oath as a policeman when peace came hadn't resolved it in the way he'd perhaps hoped it would. He thought of the police constable killed on duty outside Broadcasting House: just twenty-three years old, he'd heard. She was right: it was happening everywhere, every day.

He was saved from having to comment on her remarks by Scott, who interjected his own view.

'You only have one duty, Patricia, and that's to look after yourself. Everything else is secondary.'

'Yes, but—'

'No buts. Just remember that one thing – you want to be here when the war's over, don't you?'

'Yes, of course I do, but . . .'

'Well, that means you have to look after number one – and let other people help you do that.'

There was a brief silence round the table, and Jago decided to move the conversation on. 'So, Mr Scott, what do you do here?'

'I work in the Talks Department, and before that I was in the Variety Department.'

'Really? Keeping up the nation's morale, eh?'

'Don't you start, Inspector. I suppose now you're going to tell me that when you were my age you were in uniform, fighting for the King.'

'I wasn't going to say that, actually. I imagine lots of men in the BBC are exempted from military service because of the work they do.'

'You're right – two thousand of us, apparently. That's why I've got this.' He pulled his jacket lapel forward so that Jago could see the small silver badge that he wore there. It was decorated with wings and streaks of lightning coming from a blue enamelled centre marked 'BBC'. 'The fact is, the services wouldn't have me because of my asthma, but you don't get a badge for that. This one was issued to me by the BBC. It's to show people on buses that I'm not in uniform because I'm doing something useful here – not that that stops the sarcastic remarks, of course.'

'People just don't understand, Inspector,' said Patricia. 'It causes no end of trouble for young men at the BBC.'

'I'm sorry to hear that, Miss Radley,' Jago replied. 'And

speaking of trouble, I've been told that there'd been some sort of trouble involving you and your uncle in relation to the BBC.'

'Who told you that?'

'It was your father, actually.'

'Ah, I see.

'He didn't go into any detail, but I wondered whether you might be able to.'

'Well, there's always trouble at the BBC, but I think he might have been thinking of something that happened fairly recently. It was all rather embarrassing, really.'

'I'd appreciate it if you could enlighten us.'

'Yes, well, it was quite simple really. My Uncle Roy was very keen to get on the wireless, and he'd got it into his head that because I work here, I could get him in, even just get him an interview. He thought he was an ideal act to have on *Music Hall*. Do you know that programme? It's on Saturday evenings at eight o'clock. But he wasn't really the type of entertainer the corporation wants, and the trouble was he couldn't see it.'

'Someone told me earlier today that his act used to be a bit like Max Miller's – and even after he toned it down it was still rather risqué.'

'Exactly, and that's definitely not what the BBC wants. I don't think there was the slightest possibility they'd give my uncle work, no matter what shade of blue his material happened to be. I mean, Clapham and Dwyer got banned for months for a gag that was nothing like as near the knuckle as that, and the BBC even broadcast a public apology. And in any case, comedians are engaged by the

Variety Department, and they're all down in Bristol now, because of the war, while I'm here in London working in a completely different part of the corporation. The idea that I, a humble assistant sitting in a tiny cubbyhole of an office deep in the entrails of Broadcasting House, could have any influence over the Director of Variety is ludicrous. I couldn't persuade my uncle, though – I think he imagined the BBC was a handful of chums all sitting in the same room and desperate to find artists willing to help them out by doing a programme or two for them. Well, maybe that's how it was in 1922, when it started, but not in 1940. He hadn't a hope in—Well, I should simply say there was absolutely no possibility. But he just couldn't see it – or wouldn't. I tried again and again to explain it to him, but my uncle was a difficult man.'

Scott stabbed his spoon angrily into the remains of his dessert. 'No he wasn't,' he growled. 'He was a scoundrel. He was making Patricia's life a misery.' He pushed the bowl away abruptly and stood up. 'I must get back to my work,' he said, and left them.

Jago raised his eyes inquiringly at Patricia.

'You must excuse him,' she said. 'He's rather sensitive, and he gets cross when the subject of my uncle comes up. But there's no need to worry, Inspector – I can fight my own battles.'

CHAPTER EIGHTEEN

A short drive from Broadcasting House took Jago and Cradock to Sir Marmaduke Harvey's office in Shaftesbury Avenue. It was less ostentatious than Jago had expected. He'd assumed that a successful theatrical impresario would work in plush surroundings, but Suite 3, Concordia House had an air of plain functionality. It made him think that perhaps Harvey was more interested in the daily grind of hard business than in making a splash, which might explain why he still had a string of theatres to his name. Whatever his motivation, he looked every inch the busy executive as he finished scribbling on a sheet of paper before striding to a connecting door and passing it through to an unseen person in an adjoining room.

'Very sorry to keep you waiting,' said Sir Marmaduke as the clacking of a typewriter began to sound faintly through the door. 'It's some changes to a contract that I need to get ready for the post. My London theatres may be closed, but I still have business interests in the provinces that are demanding my attention at the moment. Now, how can I help you? I understand you're investigating what happened yesterday – I visited Stan Tipton in the hospital yesterday and he said you'd been there.'

'That's right, Sir Marmaduke. Mr Tipton told us Roy Radley had been sleeping in the theatre with your permission. Is that correct?'

'Yes, it is. I knew Roy as a performer and I heard he'd fallen on hard times. When I made enquiries, I discovered his marriage had run onto the rocks and that things had got so bad he'd been thrown out of his digs. I don't mind telling you that I've made a lot of money out of the theatre – and I don't just mean the Prince Albert, I mean the theatrical business in general – and I don't take my artists for granted. You may not know it, but there are still too many bad eggs in this profession – I'm talking about unscrupulous theatre managers who hire performers and then don't pay them. We've got the Theatrical Employers Registration Act now, but I'm one of those who think it doesn't go far enough. Performers should have the full protection of the law, and if it takes the threat of fines or imprisonment to bring bad managers to heel, then so be it – we need to keep the crooks out of this business.'

'Indeed. Had you employed Mr Radley yourself in the past?'

'Yes. There was a time when he was very good for my business, and I couldn't simply abandon him when his life went in the wrong direction. I can't claim that what I did to help him was much, but I think providing him with shelter from the cold and a place to lay his head at night was the least I could do, especially at Christmas time. I make no claim to be a saint, Inspector, but I couldn't turn my back on him. You might say it was just a small gesture in memory of the good old days, when Roy was in his pomp and the theatres rocked with laughter because he was on the stage, entertaining them.'

'When did you last see him?'

'Oh, a week or two ago, I'd guess – I bumped into him in the Prince Albert.'

'How did he strike you?'

'To be honest, I thought he was a pitiful sight – a mere shadow of the man I used to know. It was sad to see him brought so low, although some would say he'd only himself to blame.'

'What do you mean?'

'Only that he had a considerable talent and a successful career, but he was the one who decided to spend his money on alcohol. I don't suppose anyone forced it down his throat.'

'Do you know why he took to drink?'

'No, I don't. I asked him, of course, more than once, but he was never forthcoming. There was only one time when he gave me anything like a straight answer – he said "Why does anyone drink? Isn't it always to forget?"'

'Forget what?'

'That's all he said. I assume it meant either he'd been hurt or let down or betrayed by someone, or maybe that there was something he'd experienced or done in the past that tormented him, but he never said anything that shed any more light on it. You may feel you're in the dark, Inspector, but if it's any consolation I am too.'

'So you can't think of anyone who might've wanted to harm him?'

'No, I'm afraid I can't. Obviously someone did, but I don't know who.'

'Are you aware of anyone Mr Radley himself may have harmed in the past?'

Harvey shrugged. 'I guess we all harm someone sometime, Inspector.'

'I'm talking about serious harm.'

'Do you mean physical harm? Financial? Emotional?'

'I don't know – what I'm thinking of is any form of harm serious enough to have been on his conscience.'

Harvey thought for a moment. 'No, I don't think I'm aware of anything like that – but I didn't know everything about him, and I certainly wasn't privy to the inner workings of his conscience.'

'Quite. Now, I understand from Mr Tipton that only a handful of people have keys to the Prince Albert, including yourself, of course. Were you there in the early hours of yesterday morning?'

'What hours, precisely?'

'Between seven and nine.'

'No – I was here in my office. I may be a wealthy man, and I can't deny that it was inherited wealth that got me into the theatre business, but I still have to work for my money, and I'm often here at my desk at seven or earlier.'

'Was anyone else here?'

'No – the only other person who's usually here is my secretary, but she doesn't come in until nine, air raids permitting.'

'And that was the case yesterday?'

'Indeed it was.'

'Have you lent your keys to anyone?'

'No – I'm quite strict about who has a key. A theatre's a very valuable piece of property, and I'll not let any Tom, Dick or Harry waltz in there without my say-so, and then only if they've got legitimate reason to be there. I wish I could apply that restriction to Mr Hitler too, but unfortunately my writ doesn't run to Berlin. Judging by what happened yesterday morning, his idea of visiting the theatre clearly isn't quite the same as mine.'

CHAPTER NINETEEN

'He seemed like a decent bloke, don't you think, sir?' said Cradock as they left Concordia House. 'Filthy rich, I suppose, but he looked after Radley a bit, so that was kind of him. A straight talker too, I thought.'

'I suppose so,' Jago replied, 'but was it all true? That's the question. Not much of it's verifiable.'

'Alone in his office, you mean?'

'Yes. And what he says Roy Radley told him.'

'But you can never get a dead person to confirm what someone says they said, can you?'

'I think that's a fair observation, Peter. Now, you mentioning kindness reminds me – Patricia Radley said something about her Auntie Joan being kinder to Roy than her father was, so before we see the ENSA man about his key, I'd like to stop off at the flower market and try to verify that. Let's see if we can find her.'

* * *

Joan Radley was alone at her flower stall and without customers when they arrived. She greeted them with a smile. 'Hello, Inspector. How are you today?'

'I'm fine, thank you. I just wanted to check something with you.'

'By all means. What is it?'

'We've been talking to your niece, Patricia, and she happened to mention that she thought you were kinder to her Uncle Roy than your brother George was. I thought that was an interesting observation – would you say it was true?'

Joan pursed her lips thoughtfully. 'I don't know. I suppose it's nice that she thinks that, but maybe it's just because of how I grew up. There's quite a gap in age between me and both of them – Roy and George, I mean. George is ten years older than me, and Roy was fifteen. So they were both my big brothers, and I think boys are often kinder to their little sister than they are to each other – more protective, I suppose. They both looked after me in their way, right from when I was a baby.'

'She also said she thought you were proud of him.'

She laughed. 'Yes, I think I was – but I was proud of both of them. That's only natural too – I imagine most little girls look up to their big brothers, and some still do even when they grow up. George and Roy were both out at work when I was still in pigtails, and both of them did well – George ended up running a business, and Roy was pulling in crowds on the stage. It's just a pity that things like growing up and working can come between people . . .'

'What do you mean?'

'Only that Roy and George were very close when they were boys, but it didn't seem to last when they were men. In more recent years, I think I've been closer to Roy than George has, but then Roy being on the stage hadn't affected me in the way it had George – that was a very sad business.'

'What, the fact that he was on the stage?'

'No, I mean what it did to George. But if you want to know about that, I think you'd better talk to George – I can't speak for him, and anyway, it's a personal matter.'

'You said just now that *some* girls still look up to their big brothers even when they grow up. Does that "some" include you?'

Joan's face crumpled. 'It did – it really did. But then . . .' She looked away and put a handkerchief to her eyes.

'Something happened?'

She nodded, not looking at him.

'Something involving George?'

She turned back to face him and shook her head slowly. 'No, not George. It was Roy . . .' She bit her lip. 'It was nothing . . .'

'I think you'd better tell me, Miss Radley.'

She took a deep breath. 'All right. It was just a little thing, but it really upset me. Roy came round here to see me last week – Wednesday, it was. I hadn't seen him for a while. He told me he'd been kicked out of his digs and was sleeping on the floor in the Prince Albert Theatre, but he made me promise not to tell George. Until I saw him that day, I hadn't realised what kind of state he'd got into. He always used to be so well turned out, but now his clothes were dirty, and he had stubble on his chin. I didn't know

140

what to say – all I could think of was to ask him how he was.'

'And what did he say?'

'Nothing. He just looked at me, and there was so much sadness in his eyes. I think he was ashamed. I wanted to give him a hug, but a customer called me over and I had to go and serve her. When I came back, he was gone.'

Jago could see that she was fighting back tears. 'Was that the last time you saw him?'

'No – that's not what it is. It was what happened next. I didn't have enough change for the customer, so I went to the little drawer where I keep my float. I'd not long been to the bank to top it up, and as soon as I opened it I could see there were two bank bags missing – two of the little brown ones for five pounds in silver. Ten pounds gone, and the only person who could've taken it was Roy. I was so upset – it wasn't losing the money, it was the thought of my own brother stealing from me. So if you're asking whether that "some" included me, the answer's no, not after that.'

'Did you report it?'

She looked shocked. 'What? Report my own brother? I couldn't do that.'

'And you said that wasn't the last time you saw him?'

'That's right. Later that day I decided to go and see him – I wanted to tell him he didn't need to steal from me, he only had to ask. So I went over to the Prince Albert, hoping I'd catch him there. I thought if I could see what conditions he was living in I might be able to bring some things to help him – blankets or whatever.'

'How did you get into the theatre?'

'Well, it was shut, of course, but I went round to the stage door and rang the bell, and a man came and let me in. He took me to Roy, who seemed to be camping in a kind of cupboard next to the gents' lavatories. It was horrible to see him reduced to that.'

'What did he say when you told him he didn't need to steal from you?'

'We didn't get that far. As soon as he saw me he told me to go away. He wouldn't let me speak, just told me I must go. He was getting angry, but I thought he was going to cry, too. I was so upset, I did what he said – I just went.' She paused at the memory. 'If I'd known what was going to happen, I'd have stayed, made him listen, found a way to help him, but . . . I never imagined I'd lose him like that. I'm just thankful that I managed to see him that one last time.'

CHAPTER TWENTY

After saying goodbye to Joan Radley and leaving the flower market, Jago found a telephone box and made a call to the Theatre Royal to confirm that Reg White was there and could see them. White met them at the stage door in Russell Street. He was a middle-aged man with a lean face and thinning hair. His tired-looking suit hung loose on him, giving him a generally underfed appearance, and his expression was that of what Jago's father would have called a man who'd lost a shilling and found sixpence.

He let them into the theatre and led them up the back stairs to what had, until its closure, been the dressing rooms. The one into which he ushered them still had its large mirror on the wall, and in one corner was a battered desk that gave the impression its owner was losing a decisive battle against an onslaught of paper.

'This is our office, if you can call it that,' said White.

'It's not much to write home about, but we have to make do – and it's a damn sight better than what some of our acts have to put up with when we send them out to the back of beyond to put on a show. But pull up a chair and tell me how I can help you.'

'Thank you, Mr White,' said Jago. 'We're here in connection with the death of Mr Roy Radley at the Prince Albert Theatre yesterday morning. I imagine you've heard about that?'

'Well, yes, I did. But I've heard he'd been murdered – is that true?'

'We believe that's the case, yes.'

'Terrible – what did the poor fellow do to deserve that?'

'We're not aware that he did anything to deserve it.'

'Oh, yes, of course – I didn't mean it that way. So, what do you want from me?'

'Just a little information. We're talking to everyone who holds a key to the theatre, and I'm told you're one of them. The caretaker at the Prince Albert said you have to go down there from time to time – something to do with props, I believe.'

'Yes, that's right. This place is ENSA's headquarters – we've been here since war broke out, but there was an air raid back in the middle of October and we had a couple of bombs through the roof. It was about midnight. A high-explosive one smashed through the grand circle and blew up at the back of the pit, and an oil bomb set the stalls on fire. The only good news was that no one was killed, and the safety curtain was down, so that took the blast and saved the stage and everything behind it. The offices survived, as you can see, such as they are, and we all just carried on working as usual the next day. We were short of space to store all our props, though, so the owner of the Prince Albert said we could keep some there.'

'Sir Marmaduke Harvey, you mean?'

'That's the man – not that I know him myself, of course. I expect he arranged all that with Sir Seymour Hicks.'

'The famous actor?'

'Yes, him – big theatrical producer too, of course. He's the Controller of ENSA now. Anyway, I pop down there from time to time because props are part of my job.'

'Which is?'

'My job? Oh, I'm what's called a mobile unit manager. I have to put together concert parties and send them out to entertain the troops all over the country, wherever they want us, really – aircraft hangars, searchlight batteries, barrage balloon sites, you name it. And it's my job to do whatever needs doing to make it happen. It's not exactly a picnic, I can tell you – we put on five hundred shows just in the first month of the war. And they all have costumes and props, so we end up storing quite a lot of them here – and now in the Prince Albert too. But we all have our part to play, I suppose.'

'Did you work in the theatre before you joined ENSA?'

'Yes, I was an assistant manager, at the Fortune in Bradford. It wasn't a big place like this or the Prince Albert, just a little number three.' He paused. 'Sorry – there's a sort of pecking order we have when we're talking about variety theatres in the profession. The number ones are the best – if you only ever play number one theatres, you're doing very well for yourself. If you play number twos, not so well – and if you only play number threes, well, that speaks for itself.'

Jago nodded. There was no need to mention that his father had explained this to him when he was a boy, from his own music hall experience, and besides, it was another sliver of education for Cradock.

'Anyway,' White continued, 'the Fortune got bombed at the end of August, so I was out of a job. Most of the provincial theatres are still open, of course, but there's too many people chasing the jobs now, and I couldn't get work, so really I suppose ENSA saved my bacon, just like it did for a lot of these acts we've got working for us now.'

'When was the last time you were in the Prince Albert?'

'That'd be yesterday afternoon – I went to see if that bomb of theirs had damaged any of our stuff.'

'And before that?'

'Oh, last Friday, I think.'

'And when was the last time you saw Roy Radley?'

'There wasn't a last time – I've never met the man.'

'Are you sure?'

'Yes – I'm sure I'd remember if I had. I met Robb Wilton once – now he's a real star, the best northern comic I've seen, I reckon. I got his autograph. He's on the wireless now too, isn't he?'

'I believe he is, yes, but were you not aware that Mr Radley was spending his nights in the Prince Albert Theatre?'

'No, that's news to me – but then I'm not there in the night, so I suppose I wouldn't have run into him. If I had I would've got his autograph too – I mean, he wasn't exactly Robb Wilton, but he was doing all right. Why was he spending his nights there?'

'We understand he'd fallen on hard times.'

'Really? Poor fellow. Down on his luck, I suppose. Still, even if you do well in this business the good days have to end sometime – I've seen it happen to plenty of performers. If I'd known, I might've signed him up for ENSA – there's so much demand out there, what with everything else being closed down, we've really had to lower the bar. You know what people say ENSA stands for, don't you – Every Night Something Awful. It's only a joke, but, well, many a true word's spoken in jest, that's what I say. Maybe desperate times call for desperate acts.' He began to smile wistfully to himself, as if wondering whether to laugh at his own wit, but his face immediately resumed its previous serious expression. 'The truth is, a lot of the shows we're sending out are full of old has-beens and second-raters. Still, Roy Radley's not available now, is he?'

'No, he's not.'

'Pity. Nothing's certain these days, is it? Doesn't matter who you are if a bomb's got your name on it.'

'Indeed. Now, about that key to the Prince Albert – have you lent it to anyone recently?'

'No. I've had no need – people who are in and out regularly on business have got one, and anyone else has to be let in by that caretaker you mentioned.'

'Right, well, thank you, Mr White – that'll be all for now.'

'Good – I'll see you out, then. Come back any time you

147

like if you think I can be of assistance. Just ring the bell at the stage door and someone'll come and show you up here if I'm in – you'll probably find me locked in combat with an even bigger pile of paper than I am today. Taking arms against a sea of paper – that's what Hamlet would say if he had my job, isn't it?' He looked at his desk and shook his head with an air of resignation. 'Well, time and tide wait for no man, and neither do audiences. Someone somewhere in His Majesty's Government thinks me sending out little concert parties to entertain a bunch of men stuck in a field with a couple of ack-ack guns in the middle of nowhere is vital to the successful prosecution of the war, so please excuse me if I carry on. I've got to get another show on the road.'

CHAPTER TWENTY-ONE

The two detectives left the Theatre Royal and took a stroll up Drury Lane, not for pleasure or exercise, but because Jago had decided that while they were there, they might as well see if they could find the flower seller that Joan Radley had mentioned. By the time they were halfway up the street he could see a woman ahead of them who looked as though she was engaged in that line of work. When they got closer, he could see she was a thin figure wrapped up in an old black overcoat against the cold, with a scarf pulled tight round her neck and a shapeless brimmed hat from a bygone fashion. She had a basket on her left arm, in which was arranged a small collection of cut flowers made up into posies and buttonholes. The basket was not full, which suggested either that she'd made a few sales already or that she'd come out not expecting to make many.

'Excuse me,' said Jago. 'I'm looking for a lady called Sal.'

'Well, you've found her,' she replied. 'How can I help you? A nice buttonhole for you and your friend?'

Jago glanced at Cradock, who shook his head. 'Just one for me, then,' he said, handing over a sixpence as the woman fixed a red carnation in his coat lapel. 'Thank you,' he added with a smile. 'I wonder if we might have a brief word with you too. We're police officers.' He noticed the guarded look that flashed into her eyes. 'We're plain clothes – here's my warrant card.' He pulled the card from his pocket and offered it to her.

'Thanks,' she said, holding it at arm's length and squinting at it for a few seconds. She handed it back with a disappointed shake of her head. 'Not that that makes much difference – I'm short-sighted, or is it long-sighted? The one where you can see things over there but you can't make out what's under your nose.'

'I think that's long-sighted.'

'Right, well, that's what I am . . . Story of my life, that is.'

'I'm sorry?'

'Oh, nothing – take no notice. So what do you want me for? Am I in trouble? If you've come to move me along for selling flowers here, I'll have you know this is my pitch and I've got a licence. I know my rights.'

'No, don't worry, you haven't done anything wrong – but we were told you might be able to help us with a little information.'

'Who told you that, then?'

'Joan Radley.'

'Oh, that's all right, then. I know her. And what's your name?'

'I'm Detective Inspector Jago, and this is Detective Constable Cradock. Could we take you for a cup of tea somewhere and have a chat?'

'If it's a brief word you want, I'd rather stay here if it's all the same to you. I don't want to miss a sale. What is it you want to know?'

'I'm told that you were near the Prince Albert Theatre yesterday morning when it was bombed. Is that correct?'

'Yes, that's right, and it's a miracle I'm here talking to you now, I reckon. If I hadn't had to pop away for a moment I'd have been killed, as like as not. God moves in a mysterious way.' She paused, as if waiting for Jago to concur with her explanation.

'I'm also told that you know everyone and everything in this area,' he said.

'Maybe I do. I don't think people take much notice of me, not unless they want a flower, but I take an interest in what's happening around me.'

'A sympathetic interest, by all accounts – I gather you're known as Sympathetic Sal.'

The beginnings of a smile played at the corners of her mouth. 'That's what they call me, yes.'

'And why's that, do you think?'

'It's because I feel sorry for people – I care about them. This world's a rotten place – sufferin' and shame, that's what it is. And strife – always strife. And all these bombs now, as if we didn't have enough trouble already. Anyway, if they call me Sympathetic Sal it's because when life kicks you in the teeth, I know what it feels like.'

'And what's your surname?'

'I don't know. If I had one once, I don't remember it now. Who cares, anyway? Sympathetic Sal's good enough for me.'

'Really? What about your identity card?'

'Never had one. I don't think the people who make them even know I exist.'

'So you don't have a ration card either?'

'Don't need one. I go down the market every day and I pick up whatever old bits of fruit and veg are lying around on the stones, and the traders there sometimes slip me a cotchel too.'

'A cotchel?'

'Yes, that's what they call it in the market – they'll give you a bit of this and that for nothing. A couple of cabbages and a bunch of carrots, a few apples maybe – whatever they've got handy, like a little present to take home. They're very good like that – mostly it's the people they work with who get a cotchel, but some of them give me one too, and when I get home I boil it up into a very nice drop of soup. People who know me care about me, see, like I care about them. Anything else I need, I buy it with the few bob I make from selling the flowers – I don't need much, and there's always ways of getting a bite to eat if you've got the right friends. I don't steal nothing, mind, so don't you go getting the wrong idea about me, Mr Inspector. It's just that I don't do things like identity cards and ration cards and all that official stuff – I like a simple life. I can't read or write, I sleep on the floor of my old pal's room round the back of Long Acre, I live on odd scraps of food, and I sell flowers. I'll be doing that till the day I die, and then I'll be gone. And if the government doesn't know I exist, that's no skin off my nose. I've got no complaints.'

Jago could think of one or two people employed in His Majesty's Civil Service who might well have complaints about her, whatever her name was, but he was disinclined to let that distract him from the focus of his investigation. 'I'd like to ask you one or two questions about that incident at the Prince Albert Theatre,' he said. 'The bomb.'

'Yes – what do you want to know?'

'Are you aware that a man was found dead in the theatre?'

'Yes, of course – I came running back when I heard that bomb go off, and I could see it had hit the theatre. Someone said Roy Radley had been killed. Is that right?' There was concern in her voice, but it fell short of any obvious anguish or distress.

'It is. Did you know him?'

'A bit. When he was young, but that was a long time ago. People change, don't they? And not always for the better. I'm told he was a big success – made pots of money and then drank it all away. Well, more fool him, that's what I say. There's only two sorts of people I don't feel sorry for – that's them that ruin other people's lives, and them that ruin their own. There's no excuse for that.'

'So that's what Mr Radley did? Ruined his own life?'

'Of course he did.'

'And other people's lives – did he do that too?'

'I reckon he did, yes.'

'Anyone in particular?'

'I don't know about that – but people like him, they don't get to the top without treading on a few people on the way up, do they?'

'Did he tread on you?'

'Me? No, not me. No one treads on me, luv. Like I said, I don't think they even notice me.'

Her eyes shifted almost imperceptibly to her right, and Jago realised she was looking over his shoulder and farther down the street.

'Excuse, me dearie,' she said. 'There's someone I've just noticed down there – one of my regular gentlemen. I'll just go and see what he wants.'

She slipped away before Jago could speak, and he watched as she headed towards a well-dressed young man who appeared to know her and bought a posey of flowers from her before going on his way. Jago hurried down the road, followed by Cradock, lest she should escape the rest of his questions.

'Just a couple more things I want to check before you go, please,' he said.

She gave him a patient smile. 'Of, course, Inspector – always happy to help a policeman. What else do you want to know?'

'What time did you get to the Prince Albert yesterday morning?'

'About eight o'clock, I think.'

'And did you see anything suspicious?'

'I don't think so – it was just Drury Lane on a Tuesday

morning. Same as any other day – apart from a German plane screaming down the street a bit later and dropping a bomb on the place.'

'No one acting suspiciously?'

'Not apart from the pilot of that plane,' she cackled. 'I could see he was up to no good.'

'And what about the previous evening? Were you near the theatre then?'

'Yes, I was – in the early evening. That was always a good time for business before the war started and the theatres got closed down.' She paused, as if reflecting on those past days. 'Time was, I'd stand here in the mornings and see all the stars going in for their rehearsals and whatnot, and some of them even used to say hello. They were the ones I liked, not the snooty ones who strolled past with their noses in the air like you was some bit of dirt on the street. And in the evenings, well, I used to see all sorts of goings-on – I reckon some of those toffs with young ladies on their arms would've paid me a bob or two not to tell their wives what I'd seen. Not that I've ever done anything like that, of course – but I can't say I haven't been tempted, especially when they won't even buy a flower or two. Most of that evening business has gone now, of course, what with the theatres being shut and the blackout, but you still get people going to the clubs and restaurants and what have you, although nothing like the number there used to be since we've had these bombs every night.'

'You said you were there on Monday in the early evening – could you be more precise?'

'Well, I was walking round the area for most of the

afternoon, not just standing on the same spot all the time, but the only particular time I remember being near the theatre would've been about five to half past five or so. It's getting dark by then these days, so I packed it in then because I don't like to be out when the air raids start.'

'Did you see anyone coming in or out of the theatre while you were there?'

'One or two people came out late afternoon – people who had business there, I suppose. But I don't recall seeing anyone going in.' She thought for a moment. 'Mind you, there was one, about five o'clock I'd guess.'

'Going in?'

'Yes, that's right. In through the front entrance – that was before it'd been bombed, of course.'

'Did you recognise who it was?'

'No, sorry.'

'Male or female?'

'It was a bloke.'

'Can you describe him?'

'Just a pretty standard-looking bloke, really. Medium height and build, nice smart overcoat, hat like yours.'

'Would you recognise him again?'

'I might.'

'Did you see him come out again?'

'No, I didn't – but like I said, I didn't stick around once it got dark, and in any case he might've left by the stage door, round the back, so I wouldn't have seen him then.'

'Was he carrying anything?'

'Just an umbrella, I think.'

'And was there anyone else with him?'

'No – he was on his tod. And he didn't buy a flower.' She smiled at Jago. 'But you did, so thank you. And now you'll have to excuse me – time's getting on, and these flowers won't sell themselves. Bye, now.'

Before Jago could reply, she was off down the street in search of a customer.

CHAPTER TWENTY-TWO

Cradock waited until Sal was out of earshot before speaking. 'She's a bit of a character, isn't she? I mean, won't give us her proper name, doesn't have an identity card? What's she hiding?'

'I don't know,' said Jago, 'but people refuse to give their name and address to policemen every day, and if I have no reason to believe she's committing an offence, I really don't mind. If we discover she has, then of course we'll pursue it, but in the meantime, I think we've got more important things to worry about.'

'But what about her ration card – can she really be living like she said, without even a ration card?'

'There are people who do, you know. I heard about one just the other day – he was an old fellow living in some kind of dugout in the woods, scraping by on a few odd jobs for locals, and he'd actually refused to have a ration card. He just didn't want to be part of what the rest of us call normal life.'

'Like tramps, you mean?'

'I suppose so, yes – people who don't like to be tied down.'

'Or who don't like people like us to notice them. She seemed to be quite keen on not being noticed, didn't she? And all that business about not knowing her surname – that's ridiculous, isn't it?'

'Possibly, but she probably has her own reasons for not wanting us to know. It seems a bit extreme to claim she doesn't know her own name, but if she's living without an identity card and doesn't want to disclose her full name, she could just as easily have given us a false one. Perhaps she's just eccentric.'

'Off her rocker more like, I'd say.'

'That's your medical judgement, is it?'

'Well, no, but I'm not convinced she was being entirely straight with us. There was that thing she said too, about Roy Radley. She said he'd trodden on other people on his way up, but she was a bit cagey when you asked her if she was one of them, wasn't she?'

'I'm not sure I'd call her response cagey,' Jago replied. 'She said "No one treads on me", and after all the years she's been working on these streets that might be just a plain fact. She strikes me as the sort who can look after herself.'

Cradock was silent for a moment, wrestling with a thought. 'Here,' he said, 'what she said about ruining other people's lives – do you think Roy Radley could've had something to do with that bad experience Joan said Sal had

159

when she was young? She said Sal and Roy were about the same age, didn't she?'

'It could be, Peter, but only in the same way that it could've been any one of a million men. Do we have any evidence that it was him?'

'Er, no, sir.'

'Let's wait until some evidence turns up, then, before we jump to any conclusions.'

'Yes, sir. There's one thing we have got some evidence for now, though, isn't there? What Joan Radley said about that money her brother nicked from her – he was a thief, wasn't he? So if he was confessing to lying and stealing and killing when he died, at least that might explain the stealing bit.'

'That would appear to be the case, yes,' said Jago. He pulled his cuff back and checked his watch. 'Right, time for one last call. I'd like to check with Daisy Greenway whether she's lent her key to the theatre to anyone. Let's nip up to Long Acre.'

They continued their stroll up Drury Lane in silence. When they got to the junction with Long Acre, Cradock stopped.

'I was just thinking, sir,' he said, 'about what Mr Hardacre said.'

'Yes? What in particular?'

'About that bloke who set fire to his own warehouse in Southwark – he said he paid an air-raid warden to go in and start the fire, didn't he?'

'Yes.'

'So it made me think about that Mrs Greenway's

brother – he's a warden, isn't he, and she's got a key, so maybe—'

'I see your reasoning, Peter, but there are many ARP wardens, and I'm sure very few are crooks.'

'But it's possible, isn't it?'

'Anything's possible.'

'So would it be worth talking to him, sir?'

'All right, then – although if he's on duty we might have to wait till tomorrow.'

They soon found Daisy Greenway's flat. She was at home and let them into a narrow hallway where they squeezed past the coats hanging on a row of hooks on the wall. At the far end of the hallway was an open door. Judging by the familiar but not entirely pleasant smell of boiling washing coming from that direction, Jago assumed the room it led to must be the kitchen. Three more doors, all closed, marked the rest of the accommodation, and from one of them came the muffled sound of dance band music.

'Come in and make yourselves comfortable,' she said, opening the first door. 'There's not a lot of room in this place, but I'm sure we can squeeze you in.'

The living room they entered was indeed small, but she seemed to have crammed as much furniture and knick-knacks into it as possible, and the inclusion of a small dining table with two chairs suggested this was also where she ate. She edged awkwardly round the table and moved some knitting from the sofa so that Jago and Cradock could sit.

'It's not much, but it's home,' she said. 'Not a bad area, either – I've lived here all my life. I remember when Long Acre was all coachbuilders, from one end to the other, but

161

it's all changed now. The last proper old traditional one closed down four or five years ago, and they'd been here for a hundred years or more. Now it's all firms making bodies for motor cars. And lots of greengrocers' shops too, now, on account of the market getting bigger and needing more room – they make a right mess, some of them. Still, I suppose that's what they call progress.' She sighed. 'Everything changes, doesn't it? More's the pity. But what's gone is gone, and there's nothing we can do about it. Anyway, what can I do for you? Is this more about that terrible business at the theatre?'

'Yes, it is, Mrs Greenway. Before I forget, though, is your brother at home? We'd like to have a quick word with him if he is.'

'Yes, that's him with his music on the gramophone – he loves his bands. Shall I fetch him?'

'Yes, that would be helpful.'

She left the room, and they heard her knocking on a door. 'Pop into the front room for a moment, Joe,' she said, raising her voice over the music. 'Couple of policemen want a word.'

The sound of the dance band stopped abruptly, and moments later she returned with her brother. His hair was ruffled, and his face looked tired and wary. 'What is it?' he asked. He rubbed his chin. 'Pardon my not being shaved yet – I've been sleeping off last night's shift.'

'That's all right, Mr Baxter. Your sister mentioned to us that you're an air-raid warden, and that your sector includes Drury Lane.'

'That's right.'

162

'And you were on duty yesterday.'

'Yes, I was.'

'I see. We're making inquiries into the death of Mr Roy Radley yesterday, and you may be able to help us, since it occurred in Drury Lane.'

'Ah, yes – Daisy mentioned that. What would you like to know?'

'First of all, were you anywhere near the Prince Albert Theatre when it was hit by a bomb?'

'Not when the bomb actually hit it, no. I was on the night shift, so I'd gone off duty and come home.'

'What time would that be?'

'Well, the all-clear went at ten to seven, so things were quiet after that, and I knocked off a bit after eight. I got home about twenty past eight and crawled into bed upstairs.'

'Did you hear the bomb?'

'Oh, yes – I'd barely nodded off. It sounded close, so I jumped out of bed and put my clothes back on in case I was needed. I ran to my post, and they said it had hit the Prince Albert, so I went down there.'

'What time did you arrive at the theatre?'

'It was five and twenty past nine. By that time the heavy rescue party had arrived, and a fire engine too, and the day shift people had everything under control, so they stood me down. I came home and went straight back to bed again.'

'Did you see anything that might be relevant to the death of Mr Radley?'

'No, sorry, can't say I did.'

'And you, Mrs Greenway, I suppose you heard the bomb too?'

'Oh, yes, it was a terrible noise, but I didn't go out to have a look. Joe's useful in situations like that – he knows what to do with air raids and all that, but I'm not, so I decided to stay put.'

'Thank you. There's just one more question I'd like to ask you, Mrs Greenway – about your key to the theatre.'

'Yes?'

'Have you ever had to lend it to anyone?'

'No – anyone who needs to get in and out of the theatre either has a key or gets let in by the caretaker when they knock on the door. Who would I lend it to?'

Jago gave a casual shrug. 'A fellow employee? Friends? Family?' He glanced inquiringly at her brother, whose face was impassive.

Daisy Greenway's was not. 'Here,' she said, 'I saw that. What are you getting at? Are you suggesting I'd let Joe have my key to the theatre? What's your game? Trying to pin that murder on my brother?'

'No, I'm not, Mrs Greenway – I'm just trying to rule out anyone who might've been able to get their hands on your key, even without your knowing.'

She made a show of calming herself down. 'Right, then, just so's we know where we stand. My Joe's a good man who's doing his duty and risking his life for other people, and I won't have anyone making baseless accusations against him.'

'It's all right, Daisy,' said Joe. 'There's no need to make a fuss – they're just doing their job.'

'Yes, well, that's as may be,' she replied. 'Anyway, Inspector, if you're trying to find out what happened in that theatre, you'd be better off talking to that other bloke – he's a shifty piece of work if ever there was.'

'Who are you talking about?'

'That other bloke in the theatre. I don't know his name, but I've seen him there once or twice early in the morning when I'm doing my cleaning. I wouldn't be surprised if he was dossing there too.'

'What did he look like?'

'Scruffy. Dirty clothes – like a tramp. Youngish.'

'Have you ever spoken to him?'

'No. He seemed a bit shy, wrapped up in himself, if you know what I mean – I've never been close up to him. I saw him once standing in a corner with his eyes closed, and it sounded like he was saying numbers, over and over again. Then he opened his eyes and saw me, and ducked away, like he didn't want anyone to see him.'

'What were these numbers?'

'I don't know – I didn't write them down, did I? It just sounded like some long number, again and again.' She screwed her eyes tight. 'Hang on, it's coming back. That's it – it was eight three double-one five double-eight.'

'Did that mean anything to you?'

'No, of course it didn't. Anyway, that's about all I can tell you – the only thing I can say is he didn't look like he belonged there. And before you ask, I didn't lend him my key, all right? Now, is that all you need? Only I've got things to do.'

'Yes, that will be all, thank you. And thank you too, Mr Baxter.'

CHAPTER TWENTY-THREE

By the time Jago arrived in Knightsbridge that evening the blackout had been in force for nearly two hours. Not the slightest crack of light showed from any of the windows in Gibson's apartment block, which suggested to Jago that its residents probably had enough cash to buy made-to-measure blackout curtains. He couldn't imagine anyone in Knightsbridge relying on nailing a piece of old carpet over the window.

He parked the car on the road outside the flats and, mindful of the regulations, he locked it. This was something he'd never been that bothered about before the war: the Riley Lynx was a convertible after all, so when the roof was down there was nothing to stop anyone getting in, and even with the roof up, it would only take a thief with a sharp knife a few seconds to do the same. Needs must, however, and it wouldn't do for a detective inspector to be fined in court for omitting to immobilise his car. He raised the bonnet and did his best to position his flashlight beside the engine so as not to attract the attention of any marauding German bombers overhead, nor, for that matter, of any belligerent ARP warden on the ground. He removed the distributor cap, pulled the rotor arm off the shaft and popped it in his pocket, then closed the bonnet. As a finishing touch he placed inside the windscreen a small card that said 'This vehicle is immobilised. There is no need to deflate the tyres'. The card had been given away by a tyre company, and he hoped it would dissuade any passing policeman from taking overzealous action. If he'd still been on his home turf in West Ham, some of the local uniform men at least would know his car, but there was no chance of that here in the middle of London. There were many things already in his mind to be thankful for when the war was over, and being free to abandon this little ritual was prominent on his list.

There were steps up to the entrance, and he was grateful that someone had had the sense to paint the front edges white. It seemed as though since the outbreak of war, white paint had been liberally applied not just to vehicles but also just about every kerbstone, roadside tree and lamp post in London. He imagined they'd probably saved a good number of lives, and quite possibly brought comfort and joy to paint manufacturers too.

He greeted the commissionaire in the entrance lobby and took the lift up to Gibson's flat, where within moments he'd been relieved of his coat and hat and allotted a comfortable chair. The flat was pleasingly warm after the street, but he couldn't help rubbing his hands together to dispel the cold.

'Chilly outside, is it?' said Gibson.

'Just a tad,' Jago replied with an involuntary shiver.

'In that case I have just the thing for you.'

Gibson crossed the room to the cabinet standing against the opposite wall and produced a bottle. 'Do you recognise this?'

Jago laughed. 'You must've been reading my mind. I must confess I was wondering whether you might have a little of that Glenlivet left, but I didn't know what your drinking habits are or how many other people you'd entertained in the meantime.'

'My drinking habits are restrained and selective,' said Gibson, 'especially where pure malts are concerned. And as it happens, not too many guests have darkened my doors these last few weeks, so demand has been low. And if we're confessing, then I have to tell you that since you last came here, I've acquired another bottle, so we have a reserve.'

'I'd better not ask you how you got it – as a policeman I'm technically never off duty.'

'Oh, don't worry – your job's not at risk. I was given it by one of our consultants. Can you believe it? He's a Scotsman with no taste for whisky – said it was a gift from a grateful patient, but he was only too happy to find a good home for it.'

Gibson poured a measure each into two glasses and handed one to Jago. 'Cheers,' he said, 'and here's to a quiet Christmas.'

'Cheers,' Jago replied, and took a sip. 'Excellent.' He placed his glass on the small table next to his chair. 'So, have things been quiet round this way since I was last here?

You'd had a few bombs over the road in Hyde Park at that time, as I recall.'

'Yes, that's right. They messed up some of the grass, of course, but I don't think there were any casualties. Nothing much since then – I suppose they've got better things to aim at, although I must confess I've no idea how good their aim is anyway.'

'And St George's?'

'Yes, the hospital's been spared too, I'm pleased to report. That place is so old, I fear that if even a small bomb hit it the whole bang shoot would come down round our ears. We did have quite a near miss a few weeks ago, though, and the place the bomb actually hit was what you might call a celebrity target. You know we've got the Wellington Monument across the way from the front entrance here? A high-explosive bomb hit a house over the road from the monument, at the end of Piccadilly. It was number 145, just three doors down from Apsley House, that grand place where the Duke of Wellington lives – the house people used to call Number One, London.'

'Isn't number 145 where the Duke of York used to live with his wife and the two little princesses before he became the King?'

'It was, yes – so if we hadn't had the abdication they might still have been living there and perished. It was a big place, and I believe it was being used as the headquarters of some sort of relief and comforts fund, but now all that's left is the stone facade – the inside's all destroyed.'

'A close shave for them, then – saved by the abdication.'

'Indeed. Now, in case you're feeling hungry, I should

just mention that dinner will be here shortly. I've spoken to the people downstairs in the kitchen and ordered savoury meat roll, with carrots and potatoes – I had to choose in your absence, unfortunately, because apparently it takes a couple of hours to cook, but I hope you'll find it adequate. And for dessert I've gone for something seasonal – mince pie and custard.'

'That sounds just fine, thank you.'

'Good. So now tell me, how are you getting on with your inquiries?'

'Well, Mr Radley seems to have been a bit of a character – but you'd expect that with a performer, I suppose. And he did have a drink problem, as you correctly pointed out after the post-mortem, but people have been quite cagey about that.'

'Perhaps they want to protect his reputation – that can happen when someone dies, can't it? He was in the public eye, after all, and when you're a celebrity like that, I imagine you have to be careful to make sure you only get your picture in the papers for the right reasons. I remember reading once that he was trying to get into serious acting – Shakespeare, of all things – and I don't suppose people take you seriously if all they've read about you in the papers is that you're a drunkard. Had the drinking affected his career?'

'It seems so, yes. And not just his career – his whole life. It seems to have put paid to his marriage – his wife told us he'd left her, but later on she admitted she'd kicked him out, and it was because of his drinking.'

'Do you know why he started drinking, or perhaps I should say why it got out of hand?'

'I'm not sure. No one's really explained it, but then why does anyone start drinking too much?'

'If you ask me, I'd say it's often because strong drink's a comfort that becomes a tyrant. But why some people can keep it under control and others can't, that's a mystery.'

'His wife says he lacked self-discipline – that can't have helped, if it's true. The man who owns the theatre said he'd asked Radley himself why he'd taken to drink, but he never got a straight answer – except that it was to forget. He might've just been saying that, of course, but even if it was true, he never explained what it was that he was trying to forget. So that leaves us a bit in the dark.'

'What a sad story. He must have had a talent, but I expect you and I have both seen what too much of this stuff can do to that.' He eyed his glass cautiously and put it down. 'Moderation in all things, eh?'

'Absolutely,' said Jago. 'If I had a pound for every policeman who'd lost his job because of drunkenness, I could retire tomorrow.'

'I must admit it's not an unknown problem in my own profession too, but some people think the medical authorities are too lenient towards alcoholic doctors, and far too few are struck off, even for repeated convictions.'

'Really? Is the public aware of that?'

'I couldn't say, but it was in the *British Medical Journal* last year, so in principle it's public knowledge. These days, of course, we need every doctor we can lay our hands on, but I for one rather baulk at the idea of being operated on by a surgeon with an unsteady hand.' He was interrupted by a respectfully muted knock at the door. 'Ah, that'll be our meal,' he said. 'Take a seat at the table while I let him in.'

He opened the door, and a man in a white jacket brought their dinner in and placed it on the table. He inclined his head in the slightest of nods and left.

They began eating, and Jago was pleased to find it more than adequate. The only time he'd ever eaten in a serviced flat before was on his previous visit here, so he was no judge, but he assumed that if you paid for the kitchen service, as Gibson did, you were entitled to expect decent meals. In wartime, however, such things were not to be taken for granted.

'That was delicious,' he said. 'Thank you.'

'Thank the kitchen staff, not me – I'll pass that on to them. I'm glad you enjoyed it – I was brought up to clear my plate as a matter of duty, and I expect you were too, so it's not always easy to tell whether your guests are merely being polite.'

'Ah, yes, another duty. I've been feeling recently as though my whole life's been just one duty after another. Do you ever feel like that?'

'I do, but I think that's because of where I grew up.'

'Where was that?'

'In East Africa – I was born there. You couldn't imagine anywhere more unlike West London, and I don't just mean the weather was better. But as a child I knew nothing different – it was my home.'

'How did that come about?'

'My father was a clergyman, and he was appointed chaplain to the Bishop of Eastern Equatorial Africa, so I spent my childhood in Mombasa. We lived in a place called Freretown, which I don't suppose for a minute you'll have heard of.'

'I'm afraid you're right. Was it a big place?'

'No, not at all. It was barely a town, really. It was set up back in the last century as a home for freed slaves.'

'Freed by whom?'

'The Royal Navy – back then they had warships doing anti-slavery patrols off the African coast for years, and a man called Sir Bartle Frere bought some land for the people they'd rescued from the slave-traders. It was an unusual community, because the slaves who'd been freed came from all over Africa, and they'd been through terrible experiences at the hands of the traders. You can imagine that growing up in a place like that, where everyone had suffered so much, had a profound effect on me. I think that's one reason why I wanted to become a doctor. I feel it's a calling, but it's also a duty.'

'And does duty always come first in your life?'

'That's an interesting question. I'm not a paragon of virtue, but if I take an objective look at my life, I suppose apart from eating and sleeping all I do is work, so I guess in practice most of the time it does, yes.'

'Do you think there could ever be circumstances where you might choose not to do your duty?'

'Oh, certainly. I mean, for example, let's say we're invaded next week, and the Nazis take over running the country. They might be German Nazis or the home-grown variety, but either way, from the little I know of their views on matters like eugenics and the Jews, I suspect it wouldn't be long before their definition of my duty was in serious conflict with my own convictions. In that case I'd be unable to do my duty – or to put it another way, I'd choose not to do my duty if it would violate my conscience. You'd be in the same situation too, wouldn't you? I don't suppose you'd be too comfortable if it was suddenly the Gestapo you were working for instead of the Home Office.'

'Too right I wouldn't. We're supposed to think that could never happen, but look at the Channel Islands – what a shock that was. Who'd have thought they'd end up being occupied, with the police getting their orders from the German army? I wouldn't like to be in their shoes – sometimes you can only do one duty at the expense of another, and how do you choose?'

'More difficult for a policeman than a doctor, I'd imagine. But even so, it's a problem I don't think we can ever avoid altogether, even if we're not caught up in a war. Let's take a more everyday example – and perhaps a more agreeable one. I happen to be a bachelor, so I can give myself wholeheartedly to the duties of my profession, but if I met a wonderful woman and married her, my heart would belong to her, and I'd no longer live entirely according to my own priorities.'

'Maybe, but you couldn't just stop doing your duty to your patients, could you?'

'No, but I might have to reorganise my life so that my devotion to duty was not at her expense or to the detriment of our marriage.' He laughed. 'But look at us, two middle-aged confirmed bachelors debating the challenges inherent in marriage. What do we know about it?'

'Yes,' said Jago with a smile, 'but it's still an interesting question. Let me put it like this – if you were married and you found yourself torn between your duty to your work and your duty to your wife, and there was no way of reconciling the two, which would you choose?'

'Well, like you, I'm sure, I'm not overly fond of hypothetical questions, if only because life isn't a hypothetical matter, but I'll tell you how I'd settle it. As far as I'm concerned, the marriage contract – should I ever enter into it – is something that lasts until one of us dies, whereas my employment contract is subject to three months' notice on either side. I know it's not quite as simple as that in the realities of life, but I find that perspective helpful in assessing the relative importance of my duties. I suppose what I'm saying is sometimes it's your duty not to do your duty.'

'So you would've abdicated, would you?'

Gibson laughed again. 'Now we are being hypothetical, aren't we? No one's ever offered me the job of king.'

'But when it boils down to it, the King put the woman he wanted to marry before his job, so that means he followed the same priorities as you would.'

'I suppose so, yes, although some people might think the job of king involves a duty to God too, so that might complicate the issue.'

'Yes – but I'm no judge on the question of duty to God, so I'd have to pass on that one.'

'And I'm no judge on the question of whether the King should have renounced the throne for love of a woman either. Perhaps we should both be thankful we don't have his job and that we don't have wives, eh? It keeps life simple.'

Jago said nothing. He wasn't so sure he wanted his life to be quite as simple as that.

CHAPTER TWENTY-FOUR

Thursday morning was another early start, and Jago was glad he'd followed the doctor's advice of moderation and not overindulged in the Glenlivet. He'd woken with a clear head, and thought he'd probably need it for the day to come. Joan Radley's apparently passing remark that her brother Roy's stage career had affected George Radley more than her had lodged in his mind, and he was intrigued to know what that effect was and why she'd described it as a sad business. He would talk to George, as she had suggested.

He'd arranged to meet Cradock at seven o'clock, and out of pity for the young man's constitution had offered him the reward of breakfast. He parked the car at Bow Street police station and sought advice from the desk sergeant regarding a suitable place to eat. The sergeant's first recommendation had also been the closest: the Kemble's Head, on the corner of Bow Street and Long Acre, one of a small number of pubs in the immediate neighbourhood of the market that were specially licensed to open between five and nine in the morning. The justification for this was to allow all-night and early-morning market workers to slake their thirst, but no landlord was going to object to a couple of police officers joining them.

Jago found a table that was relatively secluded: it wouldn't do to be overheard as they combined a sturdy sausage sandwich with a recap of the previous day's findings. 'So, did anything particular stand out for you yesterday, Peter?' he said.

'Yes, sir – that bloke Daisy Greenway mentioned. Shifty, she said – that sounds suspicious. And Tipton never said there was someone else dossing in the theatre, did he? Why's that?'

'We don't actually know there was – all she said was she wouldn't be surprised if he was, because he looked like a tramp. That doesn't necessarily mean he was sleeping there.'

'Oh, yes,' Cradock conceded. 'But she'd seen someone in there, hadn't she? Early in the morning, too, so it's possible whoever he was saw something of interest to do with the murder, isn't it?'

'Yes, you're right.'

Cradock took confidence from the relatively rare experience of being told he was right. 'And that number she mentioned,' he continued, taking his notebook from his pocket. He thumbed through it to find the page he was looking for. 'Here it is – eight three double-one five double-eight. I was thinking about it last night – do you think it could be significant?'

'It could be – there must be some reason why our mystery man was saying it, unless he's just in the habit of muttering random numbers to himself. Does it mean anything to you?'

'Not in itself, no – it's just a string of numbers. But it reminded me of something.'

'Yes?'

'My mum's Co-op number, sir – for the dividend. When I was a kid, I had to learn it so that when she sent me down the shop for something I could give the number and then she'd get her divi twice a year. A shilling in the pound, I think it was, so that probably came in very handy. Anyway, it was a long number, but I said it so many times I can still remember it – two three five, seven double-eight.' He paused. 'Mind you, I can't see why a bloke would stand around in the shadows in some old theatre reciting his Co-op number.'

'Neither can I, Peter. My mum used to have a Co-op number too, but when Daisy Greenway said what she'd heard, it reminded me of something different. When you're a soldier, you're given a number that you have to learn and never forget. In my day it was a regimental number, but nowadays it's just called your army number. I'm wondering whether that young man's been a soldier at some time – we must look into that.'

'Yes, sir. And that reminds me, sir – about Billy Barratt. I called the railway station last night, like you said, and asked them about trains from Waterloo to Strawberry Hill.

Turns out there's one in the morning that leaves at seven forty-three and gets in to Strawberry Hill at seven minutes past eight. Back in plenty of time for a nice cup of tea, I'd say.'

Fortified by their breakfast, Jago and Cradock left the pub and walked down Bow Street, where the evidence of recent air raids was clear. They passed the bombed-out remains of what might have been a pub, and a building with a sign indicating that it had once been a wine and spirit store. Here they crossed the road into Russell Street and made their way into the market.

As they approached the door to George Radley's shop, they had to step abruptly to one side as a man with an angry scowl on his face came out and stormed off, banging the door behind him.

'Sorry about that,' said Radley when they went in. 'Just the usual trouble. You know – people. Business would be fine if you didn't have to work with people. He'll get over it – he just thinks I ought to pay him more because of the bombs, and I sent him away with a flea in his ear. I told him we're all getting bombed, and business is bad, and if I paid everyone more there'd be no business left and he wouldn't have a job to complain about.'

Jago made no response: how Radley ran his business was no concern of his unless it involved infringements of the law, and generally speaking, fleas in ears did not constitute an offence. He did wonder, however, what it must be like to work for Mr Radley.

'So, what can I do for you gents today,' Radley

continued, 'or have you come here to tell me you've found out who killed my brother?'

'No, I'm afraid we haven't established that yet, Mr Radley. I'd just like to ask you a bit more about your brother's decision to go on the stage. You mentioned before that your father was expecting you and your brother to carry on the family business after him, but you ended up running everything.'

'Yes. By rights that sign outside should say James Radley and Son now, not sons, because Roy's not involved, but that's what the business was called when our dad set it up and that's the name it's known by, so it didn't seem right to change it.'

'Was your brother ever involved in the business?'

'Oh, yes, very much so when he was younger – he started out working as a porter in the market, same as me. Dad fixed up those first jobs for us – probably thought it'd knock some sense into us if we had to do some hard graft for a while and find out how the whole place worked before he took us into the business. But Roy packed it in for the stage when he was nineteen – that was back before the last war. Dad took it very hard. It's a long tradition in the market, you see – businesses are handed on from father to son, and you get generations of the same family working here. It's just the way it's always been. I reckon it would've broken my old dad's heart if neither of his sons kept the business going. But anyway, Roy scarpered off to the theatre as soon as he was big enough and bold enough to stand up to Dad, and that was the end of his time in the market. Dad died a few years later, so I've been running

181

the business since then. I had no choice.'

'That must've caused a certain amount of resentment in you, I would imagine.'

'Yes – Roy had swanned off for the bright lights, and I was left here to be the dutiful son. But would I kill him? Of course not. You need to look elsewhere for that.'

'And where might that be?'

'How would I know? You're the detective. But you know those theatrical types – very highly strung and impetuous, aren't they?'

'Do you have anyone in particular in mind?'

'Lord, no – I'm just a jumped-up greengrocer, aren't I? Roy got the life he wanted, much good it did him, and I got nothing.'

'But you had the business.'

'I did, but don't go thinking that just fell into my lap. It didn't come free, you know. Dad had left it to the two of us, fifty-fifty – still hoping, I suppose – so I had to borrow a lot of money and buy Roy out. That stuck in my throat, I can tell you, but I suppose it kept him going while he got on with his clowning about on the stage. And he did all right for himself in the end – at least for a while. Pity Dad didn't see him being successful, I suppose, but that's life.'

'And later on, when your brother was down on his luck in the theatre world, did you ever offer him work in the company?'

'No. You make your bed, you have to lie in it, that's what I say. He had his chance of earning an honest living and he chose to throw it away, chasing his dream. You say he was down on his luck, but it was his drinking that ruined his career in the end, and a man who's drunk is no use in a business. Besides, I don't think he'd ever have wanted to work here again – all he wanted was money for nothing.'

'Which you weren't prepared to give him.'

'No. Helping him out with his rent once in a while was one thing, but letting him sponge off me for everything was a different kettle of fish. I'd never asked Roy for money in the old days when times were tight for me. Besides, he'd made far more money than I ever have, and he'd thrown it all away, so to be perfectly honest with you I didn't feel I owed him anything. I'm sorry if that sounds harsh, especially with him dead now, but life's hard, and if we think the world owes us a living, sometimes we just have to take the consequences. There was a time when I'd have done anything for my brother, but when he went on the stage it was . . . well, for me and our dad it was like he'd spat in our faces and said goodbye for ever. There's no coming back from that in my book. If you ask me, there was some kind of weakness in Roy's character. He just didn't seem to have enough backbone – like with that girl of his.'

'Girl?'

'Yes – the one he jilted. Years ago it was – she was called Sal.'

CHAPTER TWENTY-FIVE

'Interesting connection there, guv'nor,' said Cradock as they emerged from Radley's shop. 'With Sal, I mean. Plenty of water under the bridge since then, though, I dare say – I can't imagine anyone falling for Sal now.'

Jago gave him an admonitory look. 'Really, Peter. How can you say such a thing? We've no reason to believe she's anything other than a charming lady. Just because you don't have eyes for any woman over twenty-five, it doesn't mean there isn't someone out there who'd find her the perfect soulmate.'

'Sorry, sir. Yes, I do appreciate that an older man than me might find a, er, more mature lady irresistible – I know that can happen, but, er . . .'

Cradock seemed to be regretting the turn his argument was taking, and Jago was alarmed by the thought that if the boy was having a stab at subtle irony, he himself might be the target. He decided to nip it in the bud.

'Quite. We'll track her down later and see whether she's willing to tell us the story, if there is one, but in the meantime I want to take up that suggestion of Billy Barratt's and ask Stan Tipton about the time he used to work with Roy Radley – and why he didn't mention the fact when we spoke to him.'

'Do you think he'll still be in the hospital?' said Cradock, relieved that their conversation had returned to safer waters.

'We'll have to check. Let's pop into Bow Street nick and use their phone. You call St Thomas's, and I'll have a little think.'

They retraced their steps the short distance back to the police station, and Cradock went off to use the phone while Jago sat in the front office and waited for him. Cradock returned a few minutes later.

'Right,' said Jago. 'Did you get through?'

'Yes, sir – eventually. They say they've still got Stan Tipton on the ward and we can visit him, but we mustn't stay long or tire him.'

Jago smiled. 'I'm sure a little harmless reminiscing about the good old days won't be too tiring for him. I think we'll run down to St Thomas's straight away – but mind your Ps and Qs when we're there, or we'll both be in trouble with those nurses, and that won't be a pretty sight. They don't like visitors cluttering up their wards, and if we weren't policemen on a murder inquiry I very much doubt we'd get through the door.'

To travel to the hospital by car meant contending with the London rush hour. Jago felt reluctant in principle to regard the war as having brought any benefits, but it was undeniable that it had thinned out the traffic – everyone was short of petrol, and many private cars had been laid up for the duration by their owners. On the other hand, of course, there was the damage the air raids were doing to the roads, and on this occasion it was a burst water main south of the river that delayed them. Time was precious, but he was consoled by the fact that Tipton was unlikely to be far from his bed whatever time they arrived.

When they were admitted to the ward they found the patient indeed propped up in bed and looking rather more alert than when they'd last seen him.

'Good morning, Mr Tipton,' said Jago, pulling up a chair to the bedside. It appeared to be the only chair available, so Cradock remained standing.

'Morning,' said Tipton in a businesslike tone.

'How's your head?' Jago inquired, noticing that it was still bandaged.

'Much improved, I think. I'm hoping I'll be out of here soon – I just need the doc to give me a clean bill of health.'

'I'm glad to hear that. Now, we won't stay long, but I'd be grateful if you could tell us a bit more about your working life – the days before you became a caretaker, that is.'

'Certainly – there's not much to tell, though.'

'I'm told that you were a performer once. Tell me about that.'

'OK, well, it was nothing sensational, but I suppose you could say I was born to it – we were a music hall family and we had an acrobatic tumbling act. You've probably seen that sort of thing – half a dozen of us on stage together, all running around doing fast flips, back somersaults and the like. I used to enjoy that, showing off what I could do and getting applause. Then the war came along – the fourteen war, that is – and I ended up in the army, but I came through with all my arms and legs intact. When it ended and I was demobbed, I would've gone back to the old act, but my parents had had to retire – old age, you know. I wanted to stay in the profession, though – it was the only thing I knew, apart from soldiering, and I'd certainly had enough of that for one lifetime. So I took a change of direction.'

'I see. Now, a little bird told me that you used to work with Roy Radley – was that your change of direction?'

'Oh, right – well, yes, it was, actually.'

'Tell me more.'

'Well, he was putting a new act together and he was looking for someone like me. This was early in 1919. It wasn't a tumbling act, like I'd been used to – it was a comedy acrobatic act. There were three of us, so he called it Lock, Stock and Barrel – Roy was Lock, I was Stock, and we had a fat bloke as Barrel. That's what made the act stand out, and we went down very well, especially with our teeter-board routines. That's the one where the heaviest bloke jumps down onto a board like a seesaw and makes the lightest one – that was me – shoot up into the air, turn a somersault or two on the way up and land on the catcher's shoulders. We'd start with Barrel as the jumper, but then we'd decide to switch places, so now you've got this fat bloke trying to do the somersaults and landings. He wasn't as fat as he looked, of course – it was mainly padding – but it meant we could do a few tricks. He'd do some comic falling about and failing on the easy jumps, but then of course when it came to the most difficult one to close the act, he did it perfectly, landed straight on Roy's shoulders.'

'I wish I'd seen it.' Jago paused. 'I didn't know Mr Radley had been an acrobat.'

'No, well he wasn't originally, he was a comedian, but he ended up in the army when the war came along, like me. He told me he joined up in 1914, and they put him in the Army Gymnastic Staff as a PT instructor at Aldershot. That kept him out of the fighting, I think, but he was discharged in 1917 on medical grounds – kidney trouble, I think he said it was.'

'So Lock, Stock and Barrel was a new departure for both of you?'

'Yes. I was a better acrobat than Roy, although all that time doing gymnastics meant he could pick it up pretty quickly, but he was the one who came up with all the comedy ideas, and he was the leader.'

'Why didn't you tell me the two of you had worked together?'

'Because it's not all happy memories, I'm afraid. It's all in the past now, though, and I've put it behind me, so I don't like raking it up for nothing.'

'But we were told you and Mr Radley were pals.'

Tipton shrugged. 'We were back in those days.'

'But not more recently?'

'Well, people change, don't they? Especially when they drink too much. Roy could be fun when he was sober, but when he was drunk he was a pain in the neck.'

'But you got along all right with him living in the theatre with you?'

'I didn't kill him, if that's what you're thinking. It wasn't a matter of getting along with him – mostly I avoided him. Don't forget it was Sir Marmaduke's idea to let him stay there, not mine. As far as I was concerned, it was a case of put up or shut up – so I just put up with him being there, and I didn't talk about it.'

'By the way, is there anyone else sleeping in the theatre at the moment?'

'What makes you ask that?'

'Oh, nothing in particular – I just wondered whether Mr Radley was the only one, or whether there might possibly be someone else who'd taken up temporary residence there.'

'Well, the answer's no.'

'Are you sure?'

'Unless they've moved in since I've been in this hospital, yes, I am.'

'I see. Now, when I asked you just now about the days when you and Roy Radley worked together, you said it's not all happy memories – so when did the unhappy memories start? Was it when you were in Lock, Stock and Barrel?'

'No, things were pretty much OK then. We kept going for a few years, but then Barrel got ill and decided to pack it in. The act was getting a bit tired anyway, so Roy came up with an idea to give it a new lease of life. It was a great idea too, to give him his due – he replaced Barrel with a slim girl and changed the name to Lock, Stock and Beryl.'

'Ah, yes, very good.'

'We were still a comic acrobatic act, but now we had

different routines. That kept us going for a few years until we had to slow down a bit, so then he changed us again, to an adagio act.'

'That's dancing, isn't it?'

'Yes, it's a sort of slow acrobatic dance, two men and a woman in our case. Beryl was what we called the flyer – we'd fling her around and catch her, and she'd stand on our shoulders and strike artistic poses. She was as light as a feather and great to work with, and we had a pretty good act. Not quite up there with the likes of Karina, Vadio and Hertz perhaps, but we didn't do too badly. Unfortunately, though, it didn't last very long.'

'What happened?'

'Roy happened, that's what. It was one of the throws – I'd send Beryl flying through the air with her arms stretched out to her sides in a graceful pose, and Roy would catch her in his arms. Only this one night in 1928 at the Clapham Grand he didn't. He dropped her. She broke her leg, and that was the end of her career – she never danced again. It was the end of our act too.'

'So what did you do then?'

'Not a lot, to be honest – acrobats tend not to have long careers. That's how I ended up being a caretaker, and I'm grateful for my two quid a week.'

'And Mr Radley?'

'He went back to being a comedian – less energy required, and if you're lucky, more money.'

'And presumably he was lucky.'

'He must've been, I reckon – he did quite well. The only one of the three of us who landed on his feet, you might say.'

Tipton's face suggested he was pained by the irony of his own joke. He simply sighed and raised his eyebrows to Jago in a 'What can you do?' expression.

'Thank you, Mr Tipton, that's been very helpful.'

'You're welcome. I think that's enough ancient history for today, though, if you don't mind.'

'I understand. But there's just one more thing I'd like to ask you. Daisy Greenway told us you got her the job as cleaner at the theatre. Is that right?'

'Yes, that's right.'

'So were you and she pals too?'

'Well, I knew her.'

'When you were a performer?'

'Yes.'

'Was that in the days when you and Roy Radley were working together?'

'It was, yes.'

'So did she know Mr Radley back then?'

'Is that what she said?'

'She didn't actually say anything about it. I'm just wondering.'

'Well in that case you'll have to ask her yourself. She's a fine woman, and I'll not hear a word said against her. When I was a kid, if I told tales I got a clip round the ear from my dad, so I've never done it since, and I don't intend to start now. If you want to go raking up her past you can, but it won't be me who helps you. Go and ask her.'

CHAPTER TWENTY-SIX

Getting back from St Thomas's Hospital proved easier than their journey to it: the flood from the bomb-damaged water main had subsided, and with it the jam of vehicles. Jago fancied that somewhere in London there was a man standing by a big tap who could simply turn off the supply, but conceded that the reality was no doubt more complicated. He had no idea how the unseen and unknown system might work, but as far as water was concerned, London seemed to live in a permanent state of feast or famine. For every day when the roads turned to rivers because of the air raids, there was another when even the Thames couldn't be drained fast enough to put the fires out. He didn't envy the London Fire Brigade and the men of the Auxiliary Fire Service: the police weren't the only people working under severe duress in the Blitz.

He parked the car at Bow Street police station on their

return: the next few calls he was planning to make would all be within walking distance. And the first destination on his list was Adelaide Mansfield's office in Mart Street.

They found her in, and a glance at her desk suggested to Jago that she was either very tidy or not very busy. Judging by what she'd told them on their previous visit about the effects of the war on the world of theatre, the latter explanation seemed the more likely.

'Did you manage to track down Billy Barratt?' she asked as they sat down.

'Yes, we did, thank you,' said Jago. 'It was a very helpful visit.'

'Good. I'm sure you won't want to tell me what he said, though, so I shan't ask.' She gave Jago a conspiratorial glance from the corner of her eye. 'I hope he didn't say anything too compromising about me, though.' Her tone was jolly but forced, with a hint of nervousness.

'You can rest assured, Miss Mansfield.'

'That's a relief. So, what brings you back here?'

'There's just a couple of things we'd like to check with you concerning Roy Radley.'

'By all means. Have you heard the news, by the way? There's a rumour going round that Roy had all his money stashed in the Prince Albert. Everyone knows he was rich, and now that word's got out that he was dossing in the theatre, people are saying he still had a bag stuffed full of fifty-pound notes and he'd hidden it in the theatre.'

'Do they say where in particular? It's a big place.'

'Yes, I think they're saying it's under the stage, hidden in a big basket. But no one's allowed in, of course, so they're wondering whether somebody might break in and find it – or whether that's what happened on Tuesday morning, and it might be why Roy was murdered, so someone could steal his treasure.'

'It's an interesting idea, but rumours aren't evidence, unfortunately, and this might be just the product of someone's overworked imagination. It would be strange if Mr Radley had so much money in his hands but still chose to live in squalor on a theatre floor.'

'I agree. He enjoyed his comforts, and I think he held on to them until his money ran out.' She gave a regretful sigh. 'You know, I still can't believe Roy's gone. I keep thinking of him as he was in the good old days – successful, popular, going from strength to strength, always looking for a new challenge.'

'So I gather. Someone told me yesterday that he'd once tried his hand at Shakespeare. Is that right? It sounds intriguing.'

'Yes, he did, actually, but it was his idea, not mine, and I tried not to get too involved. I wanted him to keep building his career in variety, and I thought this Shakespeare thing would be just a flash in the pan. I mean, it's a different world, isn't it? It may all be performing on a stage, but people like him in variety are always "artistes" – they never claim to be actors or actresses. Still, to give him his due, in the end he did persuade a touring company to take him on, but I've always had a sneaking suspicion they only did that because they thought his name would sell tickets for curiosity reasons, not because he had a talent for it. Besides, as far as I could tell he knew next to nothing about Shakespeare, but the rest of the company had trained and studied his works for years.'

'Did you go to see him?'

'No – as I said, it was a touring production, so the performances were all too far away, and I was busy. But if you want to know how it all went, I suggest you talk to a lady who lives just round the corner from here. She's an actress, and she played with him in the same production – Miss Constance Merivale.'

'That name rings a bell, unless I'm mixing her up with someone else.'

'No, you're probably thinking of the right person. She became something of a star when she got into films in the twenties, but then unfortunately the talkies came along. There were lots of actors and actresses who came to grief then because they didn't quite have the right voice for the new technology, and she was one of them. She struggled along for a bit, but the talkies swept the board. By the end of the twenties, something like two-thirds of our cinemas were equipped for sound, and her movie career was over. She managed to find some work on the stage, but I think she was regarded as a has-been and couldn't get the parts she used to. Still, as they say, that's show business.'

'It does sound rather a sad story.'

'It was, but similar things happened to much more famous people than her – look at Mary Pickford. One of the biggest stars in the world in the days of silent film, but things were never the same for her once we had talkies.'

'Can you give me Miss Merivale's address?'

'Yes – she's not one of my clients, but I think I've got it in here.' She pulled open the drawer of a card index on her desk and rifled through the cards, then pulled one out. 'Here it is: Flat 1, 16 Hanover Court.'

'And you say it's just round the corner?'

'Yes – turn left as you leave here, turn right when you get to Floral Street, and then take the first on the left. Her place is about halfway up on the right-hand side. And just one word of warning – she's not what you might call run-of-the-mill.'

Jago smiled. 'Thank you. That sounds suitably intriguing – I shall look forward to meeting her.'

'She should be able to tell you a bit about what Roy was like in the days when he was on the crest of a wave.' She shook her head slowly. 'He was so full of life back then, you know, a real live wire, and always working. I don't think he ever had a day off with sickness.'

'Presumably that changed, though, when he took to the bottle?'

'Of course, yes, and that made it all the more tragic – he was incapacitated because of his own decisions and actions.'

'Talking of sickness, did he have much trouble with his kidneys?'

'His kidneys? I wasn't aware he had a problem with them – what makes you think he did?'

'It's just something that someone mentioned. He said Mr Radley was discharged from the army in 1917 on medical grounds, and his understanding was that it was because of some unspecified kidney trouble. Mr Radley never mentioned it to you?'

'No, he didn't. I know he suffered from back pain, so perhaps it was to do with that.' She stopped for a moment, lips pursed in thought. 'But no, that was a horse, and it was much later.'

'A horse?'

'Yes. He told me he was injured. There was a horse van standing here in the market, and a stray dog started barking at it and frightened it – frightened the horse, I mean – and it bolted, still hitched up to the van. Anyway, it took two policemen to stop that horse and get it under control, and they both got a reward for doing it. But that was only after it had knocked poor Roy down. He hurt his back, and after that he was often in pain.'

'When did this happen?'

'It wasn't long before he started his double act with Billy Barratt – and before I became his agent, so I didn't know about it until he told me much later. I'd asked him why he always did his act with a barrow. It wasn't one of the big costermonger's barrows, just one of those two-wheeled things they call a sack barrow, I think, but even so, when you have to get a train to your next week's booking every Sunday it must be a bit awkward taking a prop like that with you. He said he used the barrow because it fitted his character as a market porter, but it was mainly so he could have something to lean on while he did his act – to relieve the pain.'

'I see. I wasn't aware of that.'

'Neither was I until I asked him about the barrow – he never talked about his past. To be honest, I did wonder whether the pain might have been what drove him to drink – I've heard of that happening. I've even wondered sometimes . . . well, whether as time went by he started to need something to lean on because of the drinking more than for the pain. We'll never know that now, though, will we?'

'Possibly not, no. I understand what you're saying about him never talking about his past, but is there anything at all you can remember that might shed some light on his earlier days?'

'There's only one thing. Last year, when the war started and ENSA was set up, I asked him just casually whether he was going to get involved. It was a perfectly innocent inquiry, but his reaction was quite strange – he didn't say anything. I asked him whether perhaps he'd done his bit entertaining the troops in the Great War – I didn't know he'd been in the army, you see, until you mentioned it just now, so I thought he might have kept on working on the stage. He just looked at me, and . . . well, I won't repeat the precise vocabulary he used, but he told me in no uncertain terms that he had, out of the kindness of his heart, and that if that was gratitude, they could something well keep it.'

'And you've no idea what provoked that response?'

'No, I haven't a clue, but I certainly touched a raw nerve. If I inadvertently reminded him of something unpleasant, it must have been a deeply personal matter. Perhaps you should try asking his wife – she might know.'

'Yes, thank you. One last question, if I may. You mentioned before your impression that there was something he was afraid of, something he perhaps didn't want to talk about. Could it have been linked with something in his past, do you think?'

'I don't know – I guess a man can be afraid of lots of different things.'

'You said he'd lost his confidence.'

'Yes, but I don't know whether that was because of any particular experience he'd had. I think it was more like a nervous thing – you know, something that was happening in his head. It was as if he'd seen a ghost. I don't mean literally, of course, although performers can have rather vivid imaginations, and a ghost can be very good for a theatre's business. The Prince Albert says it's got one, but I think they may have invented it to compete with the Theatre Royal – their ghost's a very famous one, an eighteenth-century gentleman in riding coat and top boots, and before the war people came from far and wide in the hope of seeing it, so it was good for ticket sales.'

'But you think Mr Radley was haunted in a different way?'

'Yes, I do.'

'What makes you say that?'

'It's just that the way he was behaving made me wonder whether he thought someone was after him – out to get him. So I asked him.'

'Really? And what did he say?'

'He just looked at me – as if he was looking through me, really – and after a bit he said "The hound of heaven" and walked away. Not another word.'

'Do you know what he meant?'

'No – I've no idea. He never said anything more about

it, and I never asked. It felt as though I'd be opening up an old wound, and I didn't want to do that. I'm his agent, not his priest. But now I think maybe I should have pressed him a bit more – there was something going on under the surface with poor Roy, and it wasn't good.'

CHAPTER TWENTY-SEVEN

Jago had never had occasion to visit a film star before. This wasn't an omission that troubled him, but he feared that for Cradock the prospect might have the allure of a life-changing moment. His fear was confirmed before they reached Constance Merivale's door.

'Just wait till I tell my mum,' said Cradock. 'A real film star.'

'Have you seen any of her films?' Jago asked.

'Er, no – but I bet my mum has.'

'That's nice. I hope she's impressed. But just one word of caution, Peter – don't gawp. She may or may not be famous, but we're police officers, and to us she's just the same as any other member of the public.'

He glanced up and down the street while they waited for a response to their ring of the bell. He didn't know what to expect the residence of a film star, albeit a fading one, to look like on the inside, but the surroundings were not auspicious. Hanover Court was an easily missed alleyway, narrow enough, he thought, to present an element of hazard for two bicycles to pass, and the side opposite the flat was entirely taken up by Hazell's printing works. But perhaps this was only Miss Merivale's pied-à-terre in London. For all he knew she might also have a country house in the Chilterns – handy for escaping the bombs – and perhaps even a villa in Cannes, although that would be decidedly less handy now that the South of France was labouring under the collaborationist regime of Marshal Pétain.

The door eventually opened, revealing not a maid, as he'd half expected, but a pale-faced woman with a Marcel wave hairstyle who identified herself as Miss Constance Merivale. When he introduced himself and Cradock as police officers who were making inquiries into the murder of Roy Radley, she seemed to take it in her stride as if it was the sort of thing that happened to her every day. Jago thought she was surprisingly calm, but then he reminded himself that she was, of course, an actress.

Miss Merivale invited them in and took them to what she called the drawing room. It was tidy and well furnished, but its walls and curtains were in such overwhelming shades of pink that he couldn't help thinking 'boudoir' would have been a more appropriate designation.

She herself was decorated with a pale blue chiffon dress in layers that floated around her as she glided ahead of them. With a long cigarette holder that she seemed to be using more as a theatrical prop than as a means of smoking, she presented, he thought, a picture of elegance, and an artfully contrived picture at that. Close up, he suspected that beneath her powdered face she might well be older than himself, and the fact that Adelaide Mansfield had mentioned her career in silent films before the advent of talkies lent weight to that suspicion.

She motioned them to a pair of delicate armchairs and arranged herself decorously on a softly upholstered chaise longue. 'Welcome to my humble home,' she said. 'It's not a mansion, but I'm semi-retired from the stage now . . .' She paused in such a way that Jago thought perhaps she was giving him a cue to express incredulity that one so young should have considered retirement of any degree, but he had no inclination to play along. He was a policeman, not an actor. 'And I wanted a place I could manage easily,' she continued, not put off by his silence. 'There's something very special about the Garden – Covent Garden, I mean – and I love living here. It is the very heart of the town. I have the Opera House on my doorstep and the Theatre Royal round the corner, and a treasury of rich memories wherever I go.'

'I understand the Opera House has been turned into a dance hall now, though.'

'Yes – it's sacrilege. We must all insist that it be restored to its original purpose the very minute this ghastly war is over. The theatre must rise from the ashes, and so must the opera.'

'You said just now that you were semi-retired. What does that mean in your profession? Is it the same as "resting"?'

'It means, my dear, that I'm still working, but only

doing half the work I should be. These are unspeakably difficult days for the acting profession, even for an actress of my, er . . . experience. One has numerous expenses – one's fans expect one to maintain certain standards. But it pains me to tell you, Inspector, that I have been dragged before the court for a debt. Debt, Inspector! All for the sake of a measly ten pounds two and sixpence. But I'm not ashamed – it's the act of a perfidious tradesman, and the world must know. I've used the same firm of dressmakers – intermittently, I grant you – since 1928, and just because it wasn't convenient for me to settle my account when they demanded payment, they hauled me up before the bench at Bow Street magistrates' court – in front of my neighbours! And that beast of a magistrate ordered me – ordered, if you please – to pay them three pounds a month until the debt is cleared.'

'I'm very sorry to hear that, Miss Merivale. I—'

'Prating knaves and mountebanks, every one of them,' she steamed on, regardless of his attempt to stem her tirade. Her performance, he thought, was positively Shakespearean. 'This war has been devastating for the profession,' she said, 'and for the stars more than anyone else. As soon as it started, theatrical salaries were literally cut to the bone – players were only getting three pounds a week plus a percentage of profits, if there were any, and that was if you were lucky enough to get work at all. Just a few weeks ago, even I was only offered four pounds a week to tour the provinces in something I'd never even heard of, and with income tax at eight and six in the pound that leaves barely enough to pay for my manicure and facials.

The only people who haven't reduced their payments are the BBC, bless them, but unfortunately, so far for some misguided reason they haven't called on my services.'

Jago recalled Adelaide Mansfield's remark about how the advent of films with voices had affected Miss Merivale's career. Perhaps the erstwhile star ought not to be too surprised, he thought, if the radio, which offered only voices with no pictures, was not beating a path to her door.

There was a silence: she'd stopped. He seized his opportunity. 'You have my sympathy, Miss Merivale. Speaking of performances, I was told that you once appeared in a play with Roy Radley. Is that correct?'

'Oh, yes, I shall never forget it. Dear Roy. That was before the war started, when the world was a kinder place. It was in one of Conrad Fordley's touring productions. I know people always think of dear Donald Wolfit as the man who takes Shakespeare to the provinces, but Conrad's were well received too.' She looked down into her lap and then up again at Jago, the faint hint of defiance in her eyes making him suspect that those in the know might not have considered Fordley, of whom he'd never heard, in the same league as Wolfit, of whom he had.

'It sounds like quite a leap,' he said. 'From variety to Shakespeare, I mean.'

'Indeed it was – one minute they're sharing the bill with Vesta the Tap-Dancing Xylophonist, the next they're tussling with the world's greatest playwright.'

'Do you know what made him want to take on a change like that?'

'Why do any of them, my dear man? It seems to

be something that just happens to these comedians – they achieve some success telling jokes on a stage, and suddenly they develop a desire to try their hand at what we thespians call the legitimate theatre. It's as if every comic wants to play Hamlet. I don't know why – usually they have no experience or training, and often they have no ability, but they seem to have a strange compulsion to prove to the world that they can be straight actors or actresses. Roy seemed to have caught the same bug, poor thing. I think he would have had no rest until he'd tried his hand at it.'

'What was the play he appeared in?'

'It was the Scottish play.'

'Ah, yes – I know. We're not supposed to say the name, are we?'

'Actually, it's all right here in my flat – it's only bad luck if you say it in a theatre. Unless you're in a performance or a rehearsal, of course – it would be awkward if you couldn't say it then.'

'OK. So you were in *Macbeth* together.'

'That's right. I played one of the three witches and had some excellent notices in the local press.'

'And Mr Radley?'

'Hmm . . . What can I say? It was perhaps a less successful experience for him, I'm afraid.'

'I meant what role did he play.'

'Ah, yes. Well, it goes without saying, really – he was cast as the porter.'

'I suppose that was a part where he could claim some background knowledge.'

She gave a tinkling laugh. 'Yes, indeed. He told me about his time working in the market, and of course I've seen the men at work here for years, although Shakespeare's porter is actually a gatekeeper. I don't know how familiar you are with the play, but the porter has just one scene, when Macduff and Lennox knock at the gate of Macbeth's castle. On the face of it, it was the perfect role for Roy – after all, he'd made his name as a comic market porter. In theory, I suppose, he might have turned in an absolute pippin of a performance, but I think in the end he . . . How can I put it? I think he struggled with the subtlety of the character.'

'You mean he played it as if he was still doing his old comedy act?'

'I don't like to sound critical, but you may be right. People often think Shakespeare wrote scenes like that into his tragedies just to provide a moment of comic relief. They were certainly funny, but they could be deadly serious too. In this case, the porter's also effectively keeping the gates of hell, because of the terrible murder Macbeth has just committed, and while we laugh, we're also aware of a great underlying darkness to the scene.'

She rose from the chaise longue and crossed the room with the same dramatic use of the cigarette holder, as if addressing a literary salon.

'The porter's not a clown in the way that, say, Falstaff was, and to combine the darkness and the comedy is no mean challenge, even for an experienced actor. It's a very subtle balance to maintain, and I think if the role's played by a man who's famous as a variety theatre comic, he has to have a rare talent to pull it off. If the audience only knows him as a wisecracking joker, it's difficult for them to accept the character, and I think those provincial audiences struggled with Roy's performance. It didn't help that one of the porter's lines as he stands at the gate is "Knock, knock – who's there?" I don't know whether Shakespeare's original audience took that as a serious question or not, but now of course it's just the opener to a corny gag that makes you groan. I don't think Roy ever found a way of delivering that line in a way that worked for the play – the director was tearing his hair out. The critics weren't impressed either – they said his performance should have been Mr Radley being transformed into the porter, but in fact it was Shakespeare's porter becoming Mr Radley, and they had a fair point.'

'You mean they "panned" it? Is that the correct term?'

'It is, precisely. The thing is, to be a successful actor you have to become the character you're playing. It's not like a masquerade, where you just hold up a mask in front of you and your audience has to assume that's who you're representing – you have to actually *be* that character, and that's what Roy never quite managed to pull off. In the end I think they judged his appearance in the play as a distraction and a weakness rather than a strength, and in due course some pretext was found to remove him discreetly from the production.'

'That must've hurt.'

'Yes, it must. One critic was particularly cruel – he said Roy's performance was characterised neatly by Macduff later in the same scene in just four words – "O horror,

horror, horror!" I suppose the critic thought that was funny, but I believe Roy never tried for a part in the legitimate theatre again.'

'So how do you think the experience left him?'

'It's difficult to say. He must have been disappointed, and he may well have been devastated, but he never discussed it with me, and I don't recall anyone telling me he'd talked about it with them either. That doesn't surprise me, though – I've had some disappointments in my own career, and it's not the sort of thing one necessarily wishes to discuss with all and sundry. I suspect it may have embittered him, judging by the turn his life took later.'

'You mean his drinking?'

'Yes, I do. Looking back now, it's ironic that the porter's often played as a drunkard – I didn't know then that Roy would get into the state he did. It's the porter who has that famous line about drink – "It provokes the desire but it takes away the performance." This isn't what Shakespeare meant, I know, but if you took the word "performance" to mean Roy's stage act, that line would just about sum up the effect drink had on his ambitions. And of course, if Roy was murdered as you say, the irony of him playing this part begins to look grotesque. The scene he was in comes immediately after Macbeth has murdered the king in order to get the throne for himself. Roy used to call himself the King of Comedy, but now I suppose someone else will be scheming to take his place on that throne.' She paused, but whether for reflection or for dramatic effect Jago couldn't tell. 'Fame and success are fleeting, Inspector,' she continued. 'As Macbeth himself says in Act 5, "Life's but a walking shadow, a poor player, that struts and frets his hour upon the stage and then is heard no more." It's a sobering thought – and a suitable epitaph for poor Roy, perhaps? Who knows?'

Perhaps her question was rhetorical, Jago thought, but rhetorical or not, he declined to answer it.

CHAPTER TWENTY-EIGHT

As they left Constance Merivale in the seclusion of her home and her memories, Jago found himself reflecting on how her whole career had been unexpectedly upended by something as mundane as a technical advance in the process of film production. Then there was Roy Radley's accidental back injury, as recounted by Adelaide Mansfield, and how a random event as trivial as a dog barking at a horse could have affected him for the rest of his life. It wasn't just war that made life vulnerable, he thought, it was the nature of life itself. Gibson's suggestion that he might find himself under the direction of the Gestapo if events took a turn for the worse had unsettled him more than he'd cared to show at the time. He'd realised that he'd made some complacent assumptions about his future as a policeman. The reality was that the job could change beyond recognition in the years to come, and he might not be up to it – and goodness only knew what it might be like by the time Cradock reached the age he was now.

It was the barking of a dog as they neared the market that brought him back down to earth. Two dogs, in fact. They were fighting over what appeared to be a cabbage, both gripping it tight and growling angrily through their teeth. Strays, he thought. Thousands of dogs had been put down by their owners when the war began, but even so, now there seemed to be more roaming about unleashed than ever. Some, he supposed, must have got loose when their owners' homes were bombed, but it seemed many were being let out at night and simply getting lost in the blackout. The regulations said they had to wear a collar with their owner's name and address engraved on it, but these two were evidence that this order, like others he could think of, wasn't being universally obeyed.

He looked round. Cradock had stopped. 'All right, Peter?' he said.

Cradock couldn't move: he was frozen, his feet rooted to the spot. Nor could he speak. He didn't know what scared him more, his fear of the dogs or of Jago finding out about it.

Jago's voice was patient and gentle. He'd seen this before, and far worse. Strong young men armed with rifle and bayonet, yet paralysed with fear, unable to move when ordered even though they knew the penalty for disobedience was a firing squad. Battle-hardened soldiers with their nerves strained to breaking point whimpering in a foxhole under an artillery barrage. And he knew what it was to be crippled by fear himself. 'It's all right, Peter,' he said. 'Nothing to worry about. I'll just stand between them and you, and then you'll be OK.'

He positioned himself in front of Cradock and kept a watchful eye on the dogs. 'Now just go over to the side there, by that shop – they won't bother you there.'

Cradock forced himself to move, and Jago joined him.

'I'm sorry, sir,' Cradock blurted out, dejected. 'I don't know what . . . I just couldn't help myself.'

'That's OK,' said Jago. 'Was it a memory?'

'It was, yes, sir. It was when I was a kid – a dog went for me, bit me on the hand. I've still got the scar.' He pulled off his glove and showed his hand to Jago. 'It's faded now, but you can still see it, can't you?' He sounded anxious to prove his case.

'Yes, I can see it.'

'I really am sorry, sir, I mean it. What kind of policeman am I, scared of a dog?'

'Two dogs, Peter – and dogs who were fighting. I think even an experienced dog handler would think twice before trying to get between them. There's no need for you to apologise.'

'Thank you, sir. I want to be braver, though, really – I can't be like this again.'

'I'll help you not to be. The first time I was up in the front line in France the sergeant in our platoon helped me. He was a seasoned old soldier, and he could see I was scared. He didn't shout at me. He just said it's all right to be afraid – it's natural and it's normal. But he said courage is about doing your job even when you're scared to. You have to decide – again and again. Take my advice – just

213

face up to it and be honest. I can tell you that wasn't the last time I was scared, and that's what I've had to do.'

Cradock looked thoughtful. 'OK, sir, I'll try.'

'Good – and take it easy. In your own time, all right?'

'Yes, sir. But those dogs over there.' He still looked wary. 'Isn't it our job to do something about them? I mean, I know it's not like stopping a runaway horse, but aren't we supposed to take them in?'

Jago smiled. 'Strictly speaking, yes, but on this occasion I think we can safely leave that to the uniform boys. We've got bigger fish to fry.'

The mention of frying fish seemed to take Cradock's mind off his troubles. Jago assumed this was not so much to do with getting his work priorities right for the rest of the day but more with the reminder that lunch might not be far off.

'So,' said Cradock, doing his best to brighten up, 'I suppose you mean let sleeping dogs lie, right?'

Jago sighed. 'I suppose so, yes. But if you think those two are sleeping, you'd better get down to Woolworth's with Sal and buy yourself some glasses. Now come along.'

They left the dogs to their cabbage and continued walking, weaving their way through the chaotic traffic and skirting the main building of the market.

'Talking of dogs, sir,' said Cradock, when they were at a safe distance, 'that reminds me.'

'Reminds you of what?'

'What that agent was saying – Miss Mansfield. Do you know what she was talking about? You know, that thing about Radley being afraid of something and saying it was the hound of heaven. I've been wondering what that meant. Could it be something like the *Hound of the Baskervilles*, in that Sherlock Holmes story? There was a film of it on last year, but I, er . . . well, I didn't particularly fancy going to see it. It was a big sort of phantom dog that killed people, wasn't it, and everyone was terrified of it.'

'Indeed it was, but I'm not so sure about the hound of heaven, and I've no idea what it might've meant to Radley in the state he seems to have been in.' He glanced at his watch. 'But look, the church is just over there, and we can spare a few minutes. If it's something about heaven, that rector ought to know the answer. Let's go and see if he's in – if he is, you can ask him.'

They walked round to the church and went in. They could see the rector sitting near the front, deep in conversation with a man they didn't recognise, so they waited just inside the door until he'd finished. After a couple of minutes the visitor left, and the rector came over to them.

'Good afternoon, gentlemen,' he said. 'Have you come with news about poor Mr Radley?'

'Not exactly, Mr Talbot,' Jago replied. 'There's just something we'd like your advice on. Something more in your line of business than ours, I suspect.'

'By all means. Would you like to go to the vestry, or will here do?'

'Here's fine – we won't be long. Detective Constable Cradock has a question for you.'

Cradock gulped, a little nervous at having to ask a rector a question about something to do with heaven, especially in front of his boss, but he thought maybe this was Jago trying to help him be braver, so he took the plunge.

'Yes, Mr Talbot,' he said, doing his best to sound more confident than he felt, 'it's just a little thing I was thinking about. You see, we've been talking to someone who knew Mr Radley, and she said he'd seemed afraid of something, as if someone was out to get him. She asked him what was the matter, and the only thing he said was "the hound of heaven", and then he just walked off without another word. I reckon you must know everything about heaven, so I wondered if you might have any idea why he said that.'

The rector laughed. 'You flatter me, Constable. I can't claim to know everything about heaven, but I was brought up on a farm, so I do know a little about dogs. I'll do my best. Are you familiar with the origins of the term?'

Cradock looked blank and shook his head.

'It's the title of a poem by a man called Francis Thompson. I don't suppose you know of him?'

'No, I don't, sir.'

'Well, that doesn't matter – I don't think he was what people call a household name. He died before the Great War, and he had a rather sad life. He studied for the priesthood, but the seminary decided he had no vocation. Then he studied medicine but failed the exams. After that, things went downhill – he suffered from tuberculosis and became addicted to laudanum. From what I've heard, the poor fellow ended up pretty much destitute, selling matches and living in cheap common lodging houses in London.'

'He didn't have any connections with the theatre by any chance, did he?'

'I'm not sure. I have read somewhere that when he was a boy he had a toy theatre that he loved playing with, so he may have retained an interest in the stage. I couldn't say. All I know is that he was a poet.'

'And this poem of his – what's it about? I mean, why would Mr Radley say that when she asked him what was the matter?'

'I don't know why he said it, but I can tell you the poem's about the way God pursues us – that's why Thompson chose that title, I suppose. So perhaps Mr Radley felt that the Almighty was pursuing him.'

'Like a hound, you mean?'

'Yes.'

Jago had a question of his own to ask. 'But a hound's a hunting dog, isn't it?' he said. 'So is the poem about God pursuing someone in love, or in judgement?'

'It's more about the fear of the man being pursued, really, but in the end I think it's about both – you'll have to read it for yourself. I'd like to hope that if Roy Radley referred to it, he was thinking of love, but if the lady you mentioned said he seemed afraid, then perhaps it was judgement. He may have picked it up from one of my sermons, actually – I mentioned the poem one Sunday morning recently when he was in the congregation. I remember it clearly, because while I was still speaking, he suddenly got up and walked out. I know some people have a low threshold when it comes to sitting through sermons, but mine are short – always ten minutes and no more. Be that as it may, he got to his feet and pushed his way past the people sitting beside him as if he was desperate to escape. I naturally wondered whether it was something I'd said.'

'Can you remember what you were speaking about?'

'At that particular moment I'd just referred to Luke chapter 12, where Our Lord warned his disciples not to be hypocrites, because whatever they might try to hide would be revealed, and things they might have kept secret would be shouted from the rooftops. That's a pretty terrifying thought for most of us, I'm sure.'

'But I imagine people don't usually walk out like that.'

'You're right. And the theme of my sermon was actually comforting, not condemning – it was the story of the Prodigal Son, whose father welcomed him home despite all the bad things he'd done.'

'So love rather than judgement?'

'Precisely. But I can't say what Mr Radley may have been thinking – fear and guilt are powerful emotions, but they're things we usually keep secret.'

'I'm not going to ask you to reveal anything confidential, Mr Talbot, but do you think Mr Radley had secrets?'

'We all have secrets, Inspector.'

'Yes, but there are secrets and secrets, aren't there?'

'Of course, and I'd said that in my sermon. There are innocent secrets, like when you buy your children the presents of their dreams for Christmas but you keep it secret so their joy will be complete, and there are guilty secrets, the ones you most dread being exposed, because they're things you've done that are wrong. The first type is motivated by love, and its result is joy. The second is motivated by evil, and it leads to fear.'

'I'm afraid it's the second type that concerns me. I'm just wondering whether Mr Radley might've had some guilty secrets – some very guilty secrets, in fact. The woman we spoke to said she thought there was something going on under the surface with him, and it wasn't good.'

'Then you must do your job, Inspector, and I can't say I envy you. As the book of Jeremiah says, the heart is deceitful above all things, and desperately wicked. I think in days like these we see that very clearly – so many wicked things happening. We look at animals and think nature's cruel, but we're much more cruel because we can decide whether to harm others or not.'

'But not everything people do is wicked – some people do great acts of kindness, especially at times like this.'

'Absolutely. My own predecessor here was killed doing precisely that.'

'Really?'

'Yes, he was outside, helping people to safety during an air raid, when a bomb landed and killed him.'

'Quite recently, then?'

'No, not at all – it was in 1918.'

'Ah, in one of those Zeppelin raids?'

'No – I think they stopped sending the airships over in 1917. This raid was aeroplanes. Nothing like what we've seen in the last three months, but they still killed hundreds of people. The Odhams printing works in Long Acre was being used as a shelter, and a bomb landed on it. It must have been awful.'

The rector turned to Cradock. 'All before your time, I suppose, Constable, but people here still remember it. So yes, your Inspector's right, there are always people doing good in the darkest of times, and I would say the love of God goes on pursuing us in those times too. But you know, I still think we can learn a lot from dogs. Do you like dogs?'

Jago waited to see whether Cradock would answer this question: it would be good for him to try.

'No,' said Cradock. 'Not when they turn nasty. They scare me then.'

Good for you, thought Jago.

'You should spend some time getting to know sheepdogs, then,' said Talbot. 'My father kept sheep, and there's nothing a sheep farmer fears more than having a loose dog getting in among his sheep and worrying them. Sheep die because of that. They're what I call bad dogs. But sheepdogs are gentle and never harm a sheep – they're good dogs. But it isn't really a matter of good and bad dogs – it's more about the difference between trained and untrained dogs. A sheepdog is trained – it does exactly what the shepherd tells it to, and it never gets aggressive or angry. If only we could be like that.'

'Does anything ever make you angry, Mr Talbot?' said Jago.

'Yes,' the rector replied. 'Bullying. I hated it at school and I hate it now, when bad people bully other people who can't fight back, like the way the Nazis are with the Jews.

And I hate it when a bad man like Hitler forces good men from one country to fight against good men from another and kill them.'

'Is that what we call righteous anger?'

'I don't know, but I don't like to see any kind of anger in myself. It's too easy for it to make you lose control. How many people have been murdered because of anger? I tell you, if you want to find out who killed Roy Radley, my advice to you is to look for where the anger is.'

'Thank you, Mr Talbot. Now, before we go, there's just one more thing I'd like to ask you.'

'By all means. What is it?'

'When we spoke to you before, you told us about the time Mr Radley came to you wanting to make confession. I know you can't tell me what he said, but I wonder what your impression was of his motivation.'

'In what sense?'

'I mean do you think he was sincere?'

'Given the condition he was in, it's difficult to say. But I always take such a request seriously. If a man wants to confess, he confesses, and God hears him even if he speaks a foreign language to me – or in this case if his speech is impaired by alcohol. My responsibility is to listen to him, offer him absolution, and give him such advice as I believe may help him.'

'Did you give him any advice?'

'Yes – the next morning, when I gave him some breakfast before he left. I told him, as I always do, that whatever he'd done, he should try to put things right with anyone he may have harmed or offended by his actions.

Whether he was in a fit state to take it in, however, let alone act on it, I can't say.'

'What exactly do you mean by "put things right"?'

'I mean apologise to them, seek their forgiveness, and if there's anything you can do to make good the wrong you've done them, do it. I think he was searching, and the thing he was looking for most was forgiveness.'

CHAPTER TWENTY-NINE

Jago and Cradock came out of St Paul's and into its garden, which was neatly laid out in an old-fashioned formal way and, Jago noticed, still fitted with equally old-fashioned gas lamps. It was as calm and peaceful as the rector had said, but they didn't stop to sample the comfort of its benches, not least because of the chilly temperature.

Jago was reflecting on what the rector had told them, and also on their chat with Stan Tipton, which had been revealing, but only up to a point. Tipton had confirmed that it was he who'd got Daisy Greenway her cleaning job at the Prince Albert, and then admitted to having known her in the days when he was a performer, but he'd been more coy when it came to the question of whether he and Daisy had been friends. Jago's main concern was to establish whether Daisy might have been part of Roy Radley's world in those days. Nothing she'd said had suggested that was the case, but he was curious. If she'd known Tipton when he was performing, and Tipton was an old pal of Radley's, it was possible that she'd known Radley too. But if so, why not mention it? Tipton clearly didn't want to 'tell tales' about Daisy's past, so he'd have to take the caretaker's advice and ask her himself.

They strode on through Inigo Place and into the hubbub of Bedford Street, then headed up past the Garrick Club to Long Acre and Daisy Greenway's flat. She'd said she only did her early morning cleaning job on Mondays, Wednesdays and Fridays, so there was a reasonable chance she'd be at home.

This assumption proved correct. As on their previous visit, when they arrived at her flat they found a strong smell coming from the kitchen, but this time it was the much more agreeable aroma of baking. As they installed themselves on the now-familiar sofa in the living room, Jago hoped that Cradock would not swoon at the smell of it.

'I hope we're not disturbing you, Mrs Greenway,' he said. 'We'll try not to take too much of your time.'

'Oh, don't worry about that – it's my day off, so there's no rush.'

'Is your brother in today?'

'No, Joe's out – it's just me. Can I get you a cup of tea?'

'That would be very nice, thank you.'

'And I've just taken some jam buns out of the oven. They would've been rock cakes, but I couldn't get any dried fruit, so I've tried a recipe I saw in the paper.

Basically, it's just the plain dough, but with a drop of jam on top.'

Jago answered quickly, anxious to forestall an overenthusiastic response by Cradock. 'That's very kind of you. Just one each, though, please – we mustn't eat you out of house and home.'

She worked her way round the table again, as before, and left the room. Jago cast an eye over the clutter that surrounded them and noticed a small photograph propped on a shelf. He crossed the room to peer more closely at it. The photo showed what looked like a family in their Sunday best – mother, father and two children – standing stiffly for the camera, none of them smiling. The style of their clothes suggested it might have been taken when Daisy and her brother were children, and he wondered if it was indeed a childhood picture of them. He returned to his chair just as Daisy came in with a tray.

'I was just looking at that photo over there,' he said. 'Is that you and your family?'

'It is, yes,' she replied, putting the tray down on the table. 'That's me and Joe when we were kids, and our old mum and dad. They've both passed away now, sadly. Dad did the same job for fifty-one years, then retired, and died three weeks later. Poor Mum was devastated, but I think when he stopped working all the heart went out of him. He loved that job.'

'What did he do?'

'He was a lamplighter – for the Gas Light and Coke Company. That was in the old days, of course, before everything went electric, but there's still a lot of gas lamps 'around even now, especially in Covent Garden.'

'Yes, I've just seen some a few minutes ago in St Paul's Church garden.'

'That's right – nice ones, they are. My dad used to have a hundred and twenty lamps to look after. He'd go out every afternoon in the winter and light them all with his stick, and then he'd be out again at six the next morning to turn them all off. Same beat every day – five miles in the morning, five in the evening. I think I'd have got bored stiff doing that, but he didn't. He used to say everyone knew him, and he was so regular, they used to set their clocks and watches by the time he passed their house. And when it got to this time of year, the butcher used to give him a pound of sausages – they wouldn't do that now, would they, unless they wanted the food inspector breathing down their neck.'

The mention of the word *beat* had taken Jago back to his own early days as a uniformed constable in the Metropolitan Police. There had been some dull night turns, but at least being a policeman meant dealing with people, who were always different. The idea of dealing only with the same street lamps every day and night – even with the possible bonus of a pound of sausages at Christmas – made him think he was definitely of one mind with Daisy Greenway on this point.

'It's always good to hear of a man who was happy in his work,' he said, doing his best to draw something positive from the picture in his mind. 'So how old were you and your brother in that picture?'

'I was twelve and Joe was ten. We looked sweet and innocent then, didn't we?'

'I expect we all did at that age, Mrs Greenway.'

'Was it Joe you wanted to talk to?' she said, handing them their drinks and buns.

Jago thanked her and took the cup and saucer she was offering, while balancing the plate with his bun on the arm at his end of the sofa. 'No, it was you, actually. We're still trying to find out more about Roy Radley, and I'm particularly interested to know whether you were acquainted with him in the past. But first, I must ask you something else. I've noticed that you have a little difficulty walking – I wondered how you got that limp.'

'Oh, that was years ago. I broke my leg, and it didn't quite heal right – but it doesn't stop me working, so I can't complain.'

'I'm glad to hear that.' Things were beginning to fall into place in Jago's mind. 'Did it stop you dancing, though?'

'Dancing? Why ever would you say that?'

'Because when we first met you, you said you and Mr Tipton went back a long way, and since then he's mentioned that he was in a dance act with Roy Radley. Were you part of that act too?'

She gave him a shy look. 'You're a good detective, aren't you? All that's so long ago I don't really talk about it now – it feels like it was a different world. But as a matter of fact, I was, yes.'

'Lock, Stock and Beryl?'

'Yes, wonderful name, wasn't it?'

'And you were Beryl?'

'Yes. It was lovely while it lasted, but sometimes it only takes one little slip and you've had it. In my case it was a broken leg, and that was the end of that.'

'The end of your career, you mean?'

'Unfortunately, yes. I used to love dancing – just like my dad and his lamplighting. I think loving your job must run in the family. I still might've had to retire by now, of course – dancers don't go on for ever – but if I'd been able to carry on, I probably wouldn't be sitting in this little flat now and working as a cleaner. I might even have been able to help Joe set up in business or something. But you know what they say – if ifs and ands were pots and pans there'd be no work for tinkers' hands.'

'Indeed. But here's the thing that's puzzling me, Mrs Greenway. You gave me the impression that you hardly knew Mr Radley, but you were part of the same act as him. Why didn't you mention it?'

'I don't know. I suppose it's because it was all such a long time ago, and I've tried to forget. The thing is, Roy was supposed to catch me, but one night he dropped me. I don't know what he thought about that, and maybe he didn't think about it at all, but it was his fault, and it took away the thing I loved most in the world, my dancing. Besides, life moves on – it hasn't been easy for me, but friends have been kind.'

'Like Mr Tipton?'

'Yes, him especially. He knew what my dancing meant to me, and how terrible it was for me when Roy did that – I think they might even have had a fight over it.'

'Were you close to Mr Tipton?'

She hesitated. 'He's always been a friend, and there was even a time when I think he would've liked to marry me,

228

but it didn't work out like that. It doesn't always, does it? Not when it's more on one side than the other. He was a good man, and he still is, but I don't think we were meant for each other – I realised in the end there was never going to be that special magic between us, even if I tried. And then I met my Andy and fell in love, and that was that – we had a wonderful marriage until he passed away, bless him. I don't think poor Stan ever married, so I feel a bit sorry for him, but I know I made the right decision. I hope he's happy.'

'Thank you, Mrs Greenway. And what was your relationship with Mr Radley like after that incident?'

'Him dropping me, you mean?'

'Yes.'

'Well, you know what they say – forgive and forget. Like I said, I tried to forget, because I didn't want it on my mind all the time. But it's difficult when you used to be an acrobat and a dancer and now you can't even walk straight.'

'And forgive?'

'That's not as easy as it sounds either. It's all right when someone says they're sorry – then you say that's all right, dear, you couldn't help it. But if they don't say sorry, well, you can't do that, can you?'

'So Mr Radley didn't apologise?'

'I can't say he did, really, no. He just never mentioned it – as if it was just something that had happened but was nothing to do with him. I never understood that – how can you ruin someone's life and not even say sorry? He packed in the adagio act and went off to be a big-shot comedian, and I ended up as a cleaner and Stan as a caretaker. All right for some, I suppose you might say.' She stopped, gazing towards the window as if into the past, then snapped her attention back to Jago. 'But here, don't get me wrong – I didn't kill him or anything. I couldn't do that to anyone.'

CHAPTER THIRTY

'That's put a new light on it, don't you think, sir?' said Cradock as they retraced their steps down Long Acre from Daisy Greenway's flat. They were passing a theatrical costumier's premises as he said it, the third he'd seen that day, but he supposed he shouldn't be surprised, what with there being so many theatres nearby. It just wasn't something he was used to: in the places he'd grown up in and worked in he'd never seen one. The whole area felt odd to him. Daisy Greenway had talked about her show business past as a different world, but to him, that was what Covent Garden felt like. With its actors, actresses, agents, variety artists and even an actors' church, it was like a foreign country. It even had its own language: words like 'teeterboard' and 'adagio' that he'd never heard before. He'd never been abroad, but he felt increasingly disinclined ever to try. And now it turned out the theatre cleaner was a one-time acrobatic dancer with a lamplighter for a dad – and even she used words like 'adagio'.

'What's that, Peter?' said Jago. He was in a different world of his own, thinking of Dorothy. He didn't know when he'd see her next and he was missing her, but now Cradock required his attention.

'New light on the case, sir – Daisy Greenway and that business about Radley dropping her. Bit of an eye-opener, that, wouldn't you say?'

'In what way?'

'Motive, sir. Plenty of it there, I'd have thought – you know, revenge.'

'Perhaps, yes, but she came out with it quite freely, didn't she? I didn't have to press her very hard to reveal it. She didn't claim to have forgiven him, but she'd tried to forget it. We all have setbacks in life, and we're all let down by people, but that doesn't necessarily mean we murder them.'

'Yes, sir, but even so . . .'

'I'm not saying you're wrong, Peter. But I'm not saying you're right, either. All I'm saying is that she's another person whose association with Roy Radley didn't end happily, but that could be more a reflection of his character than of hers.'

'Right. Yes, sir, I see what you mean.'

'What I'd like to do now is have a word with another lady whose life doesn't appear to have been excessively enriched by knowing Mr Radley.'

'Sir?'

'I mean someone else who was fed up with him.'

'Oh, I see, sir. Who's that?'

'His wife, Peter. The long-suffering, estranged and now widowed Mrs Radley. I want to see if she can tell us about whatever it was that put her husband off entertaining the troops so suddenly.'

'Thank you for sparing a little of your time for us, Mrs Radley,' said Jago when he and Cradock were ensconced in the comfortable surroundings of her Sussex Mansions apartment. 'There's just a small matter you might be able to help us with.'

'I'm always happy to help if I can, Inspector,' she replied, sitting straight-backed on the edge of an armchair. 'What is it?'

'There was something you said when we were here before – you said your husband Roy had a habit of rubbing people up the wrong way.'

She laughed dismissively. 'If you're in any doubt about that, I suggest you ask anyone who's ever met him – you'll probably have a dozen witnesses to corroborate it within an hour.'

'I don't think that'll be necessary. No, the reason why I mention it is that earlier today someone told us about an incident that probably comes under that heading.'

'I see – so you want me to do the corroborating, do you?'

'Possibly, yes. When we were talking before, I didn't ask when you and Mr Radley got married. When was it?'

'It was in the summer of 1911. I was only nineteen and should have known better – he was two years older than me and a lot more charming than he turned out to be later.'

'I understand he served in the army for the first part of the Great War and was then medically discharged. Is that correct?'

'That's right.'

'Some kidney trouble?'

'That's what he told me, yes. Why do you need to know about that?'

'I'm only asking because we were talking to his agent today, and she recalled an incident last year when she asked him whether he was going to get involved in entertaining the troops. She said it was a perfectly innocent question, but it seemed to touch a raw nerve in him and produced a decidedly strong response. She thought it must've been a deeply personal matter and she suggested we ask you about it. It seemed to be connected in some way to him having entertained the troops during the last war.'

'Yes,' said Doreen after a few moments of thoughtful silence. 'Now you mention it, there is one thing that comes to mind that you might call an incident – I wasn't there at the time, but I heard about it. As you said, Roy was in the army, but he was discharged. That was in 1917. Before he enlisted, he'd been on the stage, of course, so when he found himself a civilian again, he did do a bit of entertaining for the troops. Not all the time, mind – he had to start earning a living again. He mainly went to entertain the wounded troops – he hadn't been sent to the front himself, you see, so he'd escaped all that danger. I think he wanted to show his gratitude in some way. But then again, perhaps it was just guilt, because they'd been wounded and he hadn't – I don't know.'

'Where did this incident take place?'

'About half a mile from here. If you go up to Long Acre and turn right, you come to Endell Street – that's where it was. Do you know about the military hospital that used to be there in the war?'

'Is that the one that was run entirely by women?'

'Yes – they used to say it was the only hospital that was manned by women.'

'I remember hearing about it when I was in the army – it had a good reputation, the kind of place some of the men hoped they might end up if they got wounded.'

'And a lot of them did, unfortunately. But it was a good hospital, very well run. In fact, I can tell you when it happened, too – it must have been in September 1917, because it was just after the King had brought in that new medal, the Order of the British Empire, and the two lady doctors who ran the hospital both got the CBE in the very first list. We all felt very proud of that. Louisa Garrett Anderson and Flora Murray, that was their names.'

'You said "we" – were you working there?'

'I was, yes.'

'As a doctor, or a nurse?'

'Neither. I was a masseuse – there was a huge demand for massage treatment in the military hospitals during the war, and I was already trained, so they snapped me up. I was also an electrical therapist.'

'What's that?'

'It's another form of treatment – it involved putting,

say, the patient's arm or leg in a bath of hot water and passing an electrical current through it.'

Jago raised his eyebrows: it sounded alarming.

'I don't mean we hooked them up to the mains, of course,' she said, reading his expression. 'We used batteries. It was very effective for some conditions. I trained to do it because one of the doctors at the hospital said there'd be a glut of massage specialists after the war, but if you could offer electrical treatment as well, you'd be much more likely to get a job, and you'd be paid more too – and she was right.'

'So your husband went to entertain the patients there – the wounded servicemen?'

'Yes. He used to come over to the hospital whenever he could and put on a bit of a show for the men. It was only a few minutes' walk away when he was at home, so it was handy, and I think he liked it because the patients were all "other ranks" – no officers. In fact, the only officers in there were the doctors, and I always thought that was a funny set-up. They were all attached to the Royal Army Medical Corps, you see, because it was a military hospital, so they were classed as army lieutenants, but they couldn't actually have the rank because they weren't men – it would have needed an Act of Parliament to give women commissions, and I don't think that was ever going to happen. They got paid as lieutenants too – twenty-four shillings a week, one of them told me, but that was quite a step down for her because she was already doing very well for herself in private practice before the war, and so were some of the others. I suppose the RAMC thought

236

they were doing the women a big favour allowing them to practise, but I think the boot was on the other foot – some of those women did a better job than the men, and had to swallow a pay cut to do it. Roy was quite taken with the place, and he used to go up there whenever he could.'

'I imagine the men liked that.'

'Oh, yes, they were very appreciative – I mean, most of the time they had to put up with an endless round of hopeless amateurs, but Roy was a real professional, and a bit saucy too. They loved him. He didn't just tell a few gags and go home, either – he'd go round the wards and have a bit of a chat with them, to keep their spirits up. Some of them were horribly wounded. I don't know how they coped, to be honest, after what they'd been through – nerves in shreds, some of them.'

'It must've meant a lot to them. But the incident itself – what happened?'

'I'll tell you what I know, for what it's worth. Roy never told me what happened himself – he just said that was the last time he was going there, and it was clear he didn't want to discuss it. I could see something had upset him, so I mentioned it to one of the nurses who'd been on duty. She said Roy had been visiting one of the wards and chatting to the patients, but then there'd been a very unpleasant scene – one of the men who was able to sit up in bed suddenly started shouting foul abuse at him. Being a nurse, of course, she took that in her stride – the hospital staff got used to hearing every swear word under the sun in those days. It wasn't the men's fault – they were often in unbearable pain, or not in their right mind. This patient was one of the luckier ones, not too badly off at all, but he came out with some really choice language. The air was blue, she said.'

'And Roy took exception to this?'

'Well, he wasn't a shrinking violet – he must've grown up with all sorts when he was working on the market, and even in the music halls the heckling could sometimes get a bit fruity. I think it must've been the fact that it was all aimed at him personally. The nurse said the man shouted at him and called him everything you could think of – a swine, a cheat, a thief, you name it – and questioned his parentage in the most graphic terms, as you might say. They had to give him something to shut him up. Roy apparently said he hadn't done anything to provoke the outburst, but I suppose he thought why should I give my time up for these men if all I get is an earful of abuse, and he stopped doing the visits. My nurse friend said they reckoned the patient must've been delirious – it was the sort of thing that happened with some of the men who ended up in the hospital in those days. That's about all I can tell you. Roy never mentioned it again, so I suppose he just put it behind him.'

'The nurse who told you this – do you know where we might find her?'

'I'm sorry, no. She married one of her patients – another soldier. He was a New Zealander. I don't recall his name, but I think after the war he took her back there with him. She wasn't a close friend of mine, and we didn't keep in touch.'

'I see. And the fact that the patient called your husband

all those names – do you have any idea why he should do it?'

'No. Apart from the obvious – that that's what he must have thought Roy was – the whole thing's a mystery to me.'

CHAPTER THIRTY-ONE

The substantial front door of Sussex Mansions closed softly behind them, leaving Doreen Radley cocooned in her comfortable refuge, alone with perhaps some less comfortable memories, and Jago and Cradock excluded outside on the cold and windy street.

'No chance of a trip to New Zealand to see if we can track down that nurse, I suppose, sir?'

Jago chose to believe this question was ironic and played along with a serious-sounding question of his own. 'A nurse with a new married name that we don't know? Who was an acquaintance but not a close friend of our murder victim's wife, who thinks she went out there maybe twenty years ago? I can't see Detective Superintendent Hardacre being very keen to sign that off on our expenses. Besides, do you really fancy spending a month on an unarmed ship sailing halfway round the world and dodging mines, U-boats and the rest of the German navy to get there? I don't think so, Peter.'

'Now you put it like that, sir, perhaps not. Maybe we should do the same as Mrs Radley – stay where we are and accept that it's an insoluble mystery.'

'Stay where we are, certainly, and treat it as a mystery – but it's not necessarily insoluble. What Doreen Radley told us is only hearsay, so it's either true or she's just made it up. If it's true, it tells us that someone publicly accused Roy Radley of being a swine, a cheat, a thief, and perhaps other things, and if it's not true, it suggests that maybe that's what Mrs Radley wants us to think he was. It's not evidence, but either way it's interesting that those words tally quite closely with what Radley said to Charlie Stone when he was dying, and his wife certainly wasn't there to hear that.'

'That's right, yes – I hadn't thought of that. So it's a mystery we need to solve, isn't it?'

'It's what we're paid to do, Peter – or at least try to the best of our ability. In fact, it's one of two mysteries I'd like to solve.'

'Yes, sir? What's the other one?'

'Our mystery man in the theatre – the one with the number. We need to get onto that. I'd still like to find out if anyone else has seen him.'

'What about that ENSA bloke? He's in and out of the Prince Albert, isn't he? Would it be worth checking whether he's ever run into him?'

'I think it would, yes – let's take a stroll down to the Theatre Royal.'

* * *

As Reg White had predicted, their ring at the stage door of the Theatre Royal gained them entrance to its bomb-damaged splendour and up to the more prosaic environment of the ENSA office, where he seemed, as he had also predicted, to be battling against a sea of paper.

'Take a pew,' he said, gesturing vaguely in the direction of the chairs. 'I'm sorry about the mess. Every day I get memos and instructions, orders and invoices – you name it – and there always seems to be more coming in than goes out. I'm literally drowning in it. I reckon the bigwigs must have too much time on their hands, so they fill it by sending memos to people like me. You won't believe the latest idea. Someone's said that when we send people out to do a concert at a munitions factory or some such place, we should start calling it an "ENSAtainment". It's awful, isn't it? I don't know what they're thinking.'

Jago removed a box file from one of the chairs and sat down. 'You have my sympathy, Mr White. I have more than enough paperwork to deal with in my job too. Now, I'm sorry to disturb you again, but I'm wondering whether you might be able to help us.'

'Really? Well, I'll do my best. What's it about?'

'Just a minor point. Since we last spoke to you, we've had a report of an unidentified man seen in the Prince Albert Theatre recently – someone who it seems had no business to be there. I'd like to know whether you've seen him yourself.'

'Hmm . . . what did he look like?'

'We don't have much of a description to go on, I'm afraid. He's been described as youngish and scruffy, and wearing dirty clothes, like a tramp. Does that ring any bells?'

White thought for a moment. 'Yes, it does, actually. Funnily enough, I have seen someone who looked like that. It was a few days ago – I assumed he was a workman. He seemed nervous – you know, wound up tight like a spring – and I got the impression he didn't want to speak to anyone. When I bumped into him, he just stood there staring at me for a moment and then bolted. Between you and me, it made me wonder whether he might be a bit funny in the head, but he disappeared, and I never thought of it again.'

'Do you know his name?'

'No – we weren't exactly introduced.'

'Can you add anything to the description I gave?'

'I don't think so. His clothes were just like I'd expect a workman to be wearing, but I can't remember anything distinctive about them, and he was youngish, as you said – in his twenties, I'd say. I did ask Tipton, the caretaker, if he knew about it – I said I'd seen a suspicious-looking character hanging around in the theatre and thought I ought to report it, just in case.'

'And what did Mr Tipton say?'

'He said he knew there was a young man in the theatre, but he didn't know anything about him – didn't know his name or anything. I asked him why he'd let a stranger like that in, and he said it was because Sir Marmaduke Harvey had told him to – and since Sir Marmaduke owns the theatre, that was his prerogative, and it was none of his business – and none of mine either. I couldn't agree more, I said – I was only reporting it out of concern for Sir Marmaduke's blasted theatre. Thought I was doing him a favour. Anyway, whoever it was, he doesn't seem to be there now. As far as I can tell, he's gone.'

'I don't suppose you'd have any idea where?'

'Sorry, not the faintest. Tipton might know, otherwise you'll have to ask the great Sir Marmaduke himself. By the way, do you know how Tipton's doing? I heard he was in hospital.'

'Yes, he is – he was injured when the bomb hit the Prince Albert, but I believe he's making a good recovery and should be out soon.'

'I'm glad to hear that.'

'Thank you, Mr White. Well, that's all – we'll be off now, then.'

'You're welcome. But before you go, there's something else I've remembered since I last saw you. Not to do with that strange man, but it was another funny thing, to do with my key to the theatre – the Prince Albert, that is.'

'Yes?'

'The thing is, it went missing.'

'What do you mean? You lost it, or did someone take it?'

'I mean I think something odd happened between when I arrived there in the morning and when I left several hours later. I don't think I lost it, because it was still in my coat pocket when I left – but it was in the wrong pocket. I always keep it in my right-hand pocket, and I'm sure that's where it would have been when I hung my coat up in the corridor, but when I came back later it was in the left-hand pocket.'

'You think someone may have taken it and put it back later?'

'I'm not sure what I think. It's possible my coat got knocked off its hook for some reason and the key fell out, then someone came along later and popped it back on the hook and slipped the key back into the wrong pocket. But now that there's been a murder in the theatre . . . well, I just wonder whether someone might have taken it deliberately and put it back later.'

'Why do you think they would do that?'

'I don't know, but they could have taken it down the road to get a copy cut, couldn't they? Then they'd be able to get in and out as they pleased.'

'I see. And on what day did this incident occur?'

'It was Wednesday of last week.'

'Right. Well, thank you for telling us that. And if you think of anything else—'

'Oh, yes, don't you worry – I'll be sure to let you know.'

CHAPTER THIRTY-TWO

'That day White said his key went missing,' Cradock began as they came out of the theatre.

'Last Wednesday, you mean?' said Jago.

'Yes, sir. That was the same day Joan Radley said she'd been to the theatre to see her brother – Roy, I mean. I was just thinking – she could've taken it out of White's coat pocket, couldn't she?'

'It's possible, yes. And what else are you thinking?'

'Well, if she did, she could've taken it to some key cutter and had a copy made.'

'I see – yes, you're right. It could just be a coincidence, of course – there are only seven days in a week, after all.'

'I suppose so.' Cradock shrugged. 'It was just a thought.'

'A good thought, though, Peter,' Jago replied. 'A good thought.'

'Shall I check all the key cutters in the area, then, to see if anyone's asked them to make a copy?'

'No, not yet. If someone did take that key so they could get into the theatre and murder Roy Radley, they could've gone halfway across London to a key cutter and been back in good time to put the original back in White's coat pocket – and given a false name to boot. At this stage I don't want to send you off on a wild goose chase – I'd like to try and find out more about that mystery man in the theatre first.'

'Righto, sir. That Reg White didn't have much to add about him, did he, although I suppose it's interesting to know it was Sir Marmaduke who let him stay there. That suggests Sir Marmaduke must know who the man is, doesn't it?'

'Quite possibly. It's also odd that White says Tipton told him the man was there with Sir Marmaduke's permission, but when we asked Tipton in the hospital if there was anyone else sleeping in the theatre, he said no. I think that's something we'll have to take up with Sir Marmaduke when we get the chance.'

They began to walk along Drury Lane. Jago was lost in thought about the case, but ducked instinctively as a pigeon swooped low above their heads and he felt the flapped air from its wings brushing his face. The birds were no respecters of a police officer's authority, he reflected, and if they thought he was a danger to their young or their nest, they'd see him off like any other marauding threat. They seemed to be gradually taking over the city, and the attempts in recent years to reduce their numbers had largely failed, not least because of the many visitors' habit of feeding them. But perhaps the impact of war on the number of visitors and the price of bird feed, not to mention the government's recent Prevention of Waste of Food Order, was starting to bring the number of pigeons down. Added to which, he thought, the bombs must surely be killing birds as well as people.

He was beginning to wonder what the pigeons made of the war when he spotted a familiar figure farther down Drury Lane. It was Sal, the flower seller. She crossed the road to meet them.

'Hello, Inspector,' she said. 'Nice to see you – how are you doing?'

'We're fine,' he replied. 'And how are you?'

'Still walking and breathing, so mustn't grumble. But I'm getting worried. Have you heard what's going round at the moment?'

'I'm not sure what you may be thinking of in particular, but I have heard there are rumours of buried treasure at the Prince Albert Theatre – people saying Roy Radley hid a big stash of money there. I've also heard the theatre's got a ghost, but as a policeman I have to say I don't think there's enough evidence in either case to bring charges.'

'You can laugh, Inspector, but rumours can cause a lot of damage and distress. I've just discovered there's one going round about me – that I know where that treasure is. People are saying I know everyone and everything round here, that I'm always hanging round outside the Prince Albert. That's true, of course, up to a point – I've lived here all my life and I work here. But they're saying they reckon either I've got my hands on that cash already or I'm biding my time, then I'll be going in there and bringing it back out in the night or something. They're saying then I'll disappear with it and never be seen again – either that or someone else'll get there first and beat me to it, and then I'll kill myself, and there'll be a second ghost in the theatre.'

'I don't think most people round here will believe that for a minute.'

'I'm not so sure. I think some people are born mischief-makers – they come up with these daft ideas and start putting them about, then it's their idea of fun to see how many people they can get to believe them. But it's not fun for the likes of me – suppose someone believes the rumours and thinks I can lead them to all that cash? What price my life?'

'These things usually peter out of their own accord, so it's probably nothing to worry about. But if you hear any hint of trouble brewing, just let us know and we'll take appropriate action.'

'Thanks, Inspector, that's very kind of you. I wish I could say you've taken a weight off my mind, but I don't feel I'm out of the woods yet. Still, chin up, eh? Now, I've got a little something for you in exchange.'

'Oh yes?'

'It's just something I thought I ought to mention – about that man I saw going into the theatre on Monday evening. The one with the umbrella.'

'Yes?'

'Well, it's just that I've seen him again – it was down there, on the corner of Dryden Street.'

'When was that?'

'It was yesterday, not long after you'd gone – about five in the afternoon.'

'So can you confirm now who he is?'

'No, but when I saw him yesterday, he was talking to that special of yours – the one who's really a hairdresser. What's his name?'

'Stone.'

'Yes, that's the one. I thought I'd better let you know, because if you ask him, he might be able to tell you who that bloke is.'

'Thank you, I'll do that.'

'Righto,' she said. 'Bye, then.'

She turned to go, but Jago stopped her. 'Just a moment, please. While you're here there's something I'd like to ask you.'

'Oh, yes. What's that then, dearie?'

'It's about something you said yesterday – you said you know what it feels like when life kicks you in the teeth, and you spoke about Roy Radley as being the kind of person who ruins other people's lives, although you seemed to suggest that wasn't something he'd done to you. I'm beginning to wonder whether there's more to that than you've let on.'

'What do you mean?'

'Someone told us you'd had a bad experience when you were young.'

'Well, we all have them, don't we?'

'But this was apparently one that marked you for life.'

'That sounds a bit dramatic – I can't imagine what they were thinking of.'

'I think they were recalling something that Roy Radley had done to you.'

'I don't know what you mean.'

'Well, let me see if I can help you to remember. His brother George has told us that when you were young, Roy Radley jilted you.'

Sal's face crumpled. She wiped a tear from her eye with her gloved hand and looked annoyed with herself for doing so. 'Kind of him to mention it,' she said. 'All right, it's true. So what?'

'Could you tell me a little more about it?'

'If you insist. It was just one of those things that happen – like you said, when life kicks you in the teeth.'

'And on this occasion, it was Roy Radley who kicked you in the teeth?'

'Yes – I think it's what some people call being unlucky in love. Very unlucky in my case. It was all very romantic to start with, but I was young and naive, so I suppose it was the romance that turned my head. I thought it was all going to be plain sailing – you fall in love, you go to the altar together, then you live happily ever after. We did the first two bits, but then when the vicar said "Wilt thou have this woman to be thy lawful wedded wife?" Roy didn't say a dicky bird. There was just this horrible silence in the church, everyone waiting for him to say yes. So the vicar asked him again, "Wilt thou have this woman to be thy lawful wedded wife?" Then Roy just said "No." That was all – just that one word, and that was the end of it. He walked out, and I just wanted to die. It was the most humiliating thing that's ever happened to me. So yes, if you must know, did he ruin my life? Yes, he did.' She gritted her teeth, her jaw firm. 'He made me cry then, but I will not cry for him now – never.'

'Did he ever explain why he'd done that?'

'Yes. I don't think he wanted to – he didn't have the nerve to face me. But I ran him to ground later and cornered him. I said he needn't think I'd ever have him back, but I demanded to know his reason.'

'What did he say?'

'He said his family had told him I wasn't good enough for him, that's what. I was too common. They said he had to choose between them and me – and the spineless rat chose them. It made me feel like a bit of dirt he'd brushed off his boot.'

'And when you say the family told him this, do you mean his parents?'

'Yes. This was thirty years ago, so Joan was only five and I don't think she knew anything about it. Even George would only have been fifteen, although if he'd been older I think he might've taken his mum and dad's side. But old man Radley and his wife, they were as hard as nails, merciless. I vowed I'd never speak to them again, and even if I had to spend the rest of my life in the gutter, I'd never be mean like they were – and I'd never ask them for a penny.'

'Joan spoke warmly of you when we talked to her.'

'Yes, well Joan didn't take after her parents – she's always been kind to me, and I like her.'

'And George?'

'He's always kept his distance, so I've kept mine. I don't know what he thinks of me, and I don't care. But his parents – I hated them and I'm glad they're dead.'

'And Roy too?'

'Yes – I hated him, and I had good reason to.'

'And you're glad he's dead?'

'Glad? I think I'm indifferent. He broke my heart thirty years ago and walked out of my life, and I've coped – now I just don't care. I'm not shedding any tears over him, if that's what you mean, and I don't expect I shall.' She paused and looked at Jago intently, as if trying to read his face. 'But look here, Inspector, if you think I hated Roy enough to kill him, you're barking up the wrong tree. I never laid a finger on him. It felt like he'd killed me all those years ago, killed me with his cruelty, but I wasn't going to let that drag me down to his level – I decided I was never going to be heartless like that, not as long as I lived, and I've stuck to that. If you want to find out who murdered Roy Radley, you'll have to dig in someone else's backyard, not in mine.'

CHAPTER THIRTY-THREE

'I know what you said about rumours, sir,' said Cradock, raising his voice over the distressed puttering of an ancient passing motorbike as they waited to cross Drury Lane, 'but do you think there could still be truth in them? About the money, I mean.'

Jago waited until the venerable machine had gone on its way, taking its noise with it. 'Well, that's the whole problem with rumours, isn't it? You can't tell. Unless you can find evidence that it's true or false, it's just something that someone says and then someone else repeats it. That's why the Defence Regulations come down on you like a ton of bricks if you spread false information. In a case like this, what I'm more concerned about is who might've had an interest in starting a rumour like that. I've been thinking about Daisy Greenway's dad.'

Cradock struggled briefly to make sense of this, then

gave up. 'You mean the old lamplighter, sir? But he's dead – she said so herself. Or was that a rumour too?'

'No, I'm not suggesting he started a rumour from beyond the grave. It's to do with lamplighters.'

'Oh, I see,' said Cradock, although he didn't.

'I was listening to a talk on the BBC a while ago, and it said something about an interview on the German radio with one of their bomber pilots. He was flying one of the planes that come over first. You know how it goes – they drop incendiaries to start a lot of fires in the dark, then the ones with the big bombs come along and use the flames as a target. The thing I've remembered is that he said in the German air force they have a nickname for people like him, the pilots dropping the incendiaries – they call them the lamplighters.'

'Right,' said Cradock tentatively, still trying to grasp the relevance of this.

'So all I'm thinking,' Jago continued, 'is that we've heard a lot of bad things said about Roy Radley by various people. Now they may or may not be telling us the truth, but the question is, could one of them be a lamplighter? In other words, someone who didn't actually kill him but just started a little fire by maligning him so as to provoke someone else to do him harm. Someone who they knew had a grudge against him, perhaps, but one way or another would do the dirty work for them.'

'Ah, now I see what you mean. They do say there's no smoke without fire.'

Now it was Jago's turn to be puzzled, but his seniority in rank and experience excused him from unduly wasting time trying to make sense of Cradock's remark. 'I'm not sure that's entirely relevant, Peter, but the point is, let's just bear in mind that our murderer may've been induced or provoked to commit the crime by someone else who was either unwilling or unable to inflict violence on him themselves.'

'Right. Will do, sir.'

'Good. Now then, leaving that aside, I've also been thinking about that thing Billy Barratt said about the train service being so handy for getting to London – it's been bothering me, and I reckon we should go and have another chat with him. As you said, it sounds like he could easily have got up to Covent Garden and been back home in time for breakfast, albeit a slightly later one than the likes of you and me usually get. So although he lives out in the wilds in Twickenham, there's no reason why he couldn't have nipped up to London to kill someone. The question is, was he up there on Tuesday morning?'

'That's right,' Cradock replied. 'And I got the impression he was interested in knowing what time we thought Radley had been killed.'

'I know – that's why I didn't tell him.'

'But it's a bit incriminating for him, isn't it? I mean telling us about how easy it is to get up to London and all that, and asking when he was killed. So why would he do that unless he's innocent?'

'Who can say? I just keep having to remind myself that I'm talking to people who've spent a lifetime acting in one way or another on a stage, and some of them, Billy Barratt included, have good reason to feel resentment –

or worse – over the way Radley treated them. It makes me think we should dig a bit deeper, so we're going to take another trip down to Brinsworth House to beard him in his den.'

Barratt seemed surprised when they arrived. 'Oh,' he said, 'I didn't expect to see you again so soon. But as you can see, Inspector, I'm still here, soldiering on.' He took them up to his room. 'Now, can I get you a cup of tea?'

'No, thank you,' said Jago. 'We're a bit pushed for time.'

'How I wish I could say the same. There was a time when I would have, but those days are over – life moves at a rather slower pace here.'

'I suppose you miss the bright lights, eh?'

'I think that's probably it. My fellow residents and I have spent years literally in the limelight – although nowadays it's all electric light in the theatres, of course – so we're bound to be a bit nostalgic about the past. But how can I help you?'

'It's quite easy, Mr Barratt. When was the last time you were up in the West End?'

'Well, I, er . . .'

'You don't remember?'

Barratt was silent and avoided Jago's eyes.

'Were you by any chance in London at the beginning of this week?'

Barratt looked up, working his mouth as though preparing for a significant pronouncement, but when he spoke, his voice was flat. 'Yes, I was.'

'And what was the purpose of your visit?'

'It was a private matter.'

'Were you visiting a friend, perhaps?'

'Yes.'

'And this friend – was it Roy Radley?'

Barratt hesitated, as if trying to find a way out of answering the question. 'Well,' he said eventually, 'actually it was, yes. I did go to see Roy.'

'Why was that?'

'Because he wrote to me. I had a letter from him, asking me to come and see him – he said he needed to talk to me but didn't have the wherewithal to travel down here, and, in any case, he couldn't trust his health to make the trip. He said I could find him at the Prince Albert Theatre in Drury Lane – I was to ring the bell at the stage door four times.'

'Did he say what he needed to talk to you about?'

'Not specifically, but he said he wanted to put things right with me.'

'What did you take that to mean?'

'Well, he said it was about the old days, when we worked together, so I guessed maybe his conscience was troubling him and he wanted us to be friends again.'

'So you'd stopped being friends?'

'I think so, yes, though I never said so to his face, or to anyone else for that matter. There's this thing in our profession, you see – you'll find if you talk to a performer, especially if it's what you might call a middle-ranker like me, we tend to reel off the names of all the people we've worked with and we say how wonderful they were, even if they weren't. I don't think it's because we're necessarily full of love and admiration – I suspect it may be that if we say they were hugely talented and delightful, it kind of implies we are too, because they worked with us. I read a book of memoirs not long ago by a variety artist who shall remain nameless, and it was full of that from beginning to end.'

'So what ended your friendship? Was it when he sacked you?'

'I suppose so, yes. I think Roy maybe realised he hadn't treated me well and wanted to build some bridges. Perhaps falling on hard times had made him reassess his life. It's one thing when you're strong and healthy and successful – you can treat people like dirt if you're so inclined, because you think you're invincible. When you're on top of the world, you look down on everyone, don't you? But it's another thing when you're ill and getting older, when your career's failing and everything's going downhill. That's when you realise you're weak and vulnerable, and you start looking round for friends who can help you and support you.'

'And you think he was a bit lacking in that department?'

'I think that when Roy did that, he probably found his friends were few and far between – if he had any at all. He was separated from his wife, and estranged from his family as far as I could tell, and I knew he wasn't popular in the business. The crowds used to love him, but it was his act and his gags they loved really, not the real Roy Radley. I think Adelaide, his agent, did her best for him and tried to stick by him, but it was her job to get work for him, and he was making himself unhirable on account of his drinking. It got to the point where he still thought of himself as her valued client, because of the money he'd brought in for her in the past, but to her he was probably just a millstone round her neck. I imagine she'd have been only too pleased to get shot of him.'

'Did he explain all this in his letter?'

'No. The letter was short, but there was a kind of desperation in it. It was only later, when . . .'

'When you went to see him?'

'Yes.'

'I see. Yesterday you told us you hadn't spoken to each other for two years.'

'I'm sorry, yes – what I meant was we hadn't spoken to each other for two years since he sacked me.'

Jago looked at him sceptically. 'That's a fine distinction, Mr Barratt, but it seems to me to be a distinction between truth and untruth.'

'I can only apologise, Inspector. I just felt it would be a bit embarrassing to admit I'd been to see him not long before he was killed – it's the sort of thing that can easily be misconstrued.'

'Indeed it can. So when did you go to see him?'

'As soon as I got the letter. The date on the postmark was the middle of last week, you see, but it didn't arrive here until second post on Monday – you know how it is these days, with all the delays. I was concerned about what Roy might think if he hadn't received any reply from me – and given the state he seemed to be in, what he might do. So I caught the train that afternoon, thinking I'd see him and be back here before bedtime, but the train was delayed. By the time I got there it was evening, and Roy and I got into a very long conversation.'

'Was he sober?'

'Not entirely, but I think he knew what he was saying, and he was making sense to me.'

'What did he talk about?'

'He said he wanted to apologise for treating me badly and then for abandoning me. He also said he was sorry for not paying me as much as I was worth, not recognising how important I was to his act, and so on. I was watching the time, but he said he wanted to get these things off his chest – the air raids had made him realise you can't put things off till tomorrow any more. You might be killed at any moment. So we talked on, and then the sirens went off, so it was too late for me to try and get home. He said I could share his room with him in the theatre, so I did, but it was pretty awful. My days of being able to sleep on a floor are long gone, and I hardly slept a wink. I just wanted to get back here to my own bed as soon as possible, so I got up at about six o'clock and walked down to Waterloo, and took the first train I could.'

'The seven forty-three?'

'Yes – how did you know?'

'I know all sorts of things, Mr Barratt. So what time did you arrive back here?'

'That would've been about half past eight, I think. I let myself in as though I'd just been out for a walk, then had my breakfast as usual.'

'You were trying to conceal the fact that you'd spent the night in London, then. Why was that?'

'It was a personal matter and no one else's business. Besides, I just didn't want the story getting around that I'd been off gallivanting up to London and spent the night there without telling anyone. Some people are very inquisitive, and if a story like that got around it might . . . well, you know – give the wrong impression.'

'You also declined to mention this visit to us. Was that because you didn't want us to get the wrong impression too?'

'No, that wasn't the reason. The truth is I was scared. Adelaide Mansfield had told me Roy had been stabbed and was dead, and I thought if I told you I'd been in London with him overnight you might think I'd killed him. No one else knew I'd been, so I reckoned it would be safer not to say anything. I can see now that that was a foolish decision, but it's what I did, and I'm very sorry. All I can say is the last time I saw Roy he was still very much alive, sleeping like a baby.'

'Can anyone confirm when you left the Prince Albert?'

'I don't think so. There was no one else in the theatre, so the only person who might be able to confirm anything would be the man on the ticket barrier at Waterloo. He might remember checking my ticket, but it seems pretty unlikely – as I said to you yesterday, to most people I'm just part of the scenery, not a very memorable person.'

'You say there was no one else in the theatre, but how can you know that was the case?'

'I'm sorry – what I should have said is that I didn't see anyone else. But it's a big building, so there could've been someone I didn't see.'

'Have you still got the letter?'

'Yes, it's over here.' He crossed the room to a small bureau, opened the lid and pulled an envelope from one of the pigeonholes. 'Here it is.'

Jago took the letter from the envelope and read it quickly. It seemed to bear out Barratt's account of the events. He put the letter back in and studied the postmark. This too was consistent with what Barratt had said.

'Right, Mr Barratt, I may need to speak to you again, so I want you to stay here where I can find you. No more jaunts up to London or anywhere else without my say-so. Understood?'

'Understood.'

'And I'll need to keep this,' he said, holding up the envelope.

'That's all right,' Barratt replied. 'I don't need mementos of Roy. He was a pretty unforgettable man, one way or another.'

CHAPTER THIRTY-FOUR

Cradock was unusually quiet on the drive back from Brinsworth House: he seemed lost in thought. 'What are you thinking about?' said Jago. 'Billy Barratt's revised version of what took place between him and Radley?'

'No, sir – I was thinking about Sympathetic Sal, actually.'

'And what in particular?'

'Oh, I just think I've changed my mind about her, that's all. She's had a lot to put up with, hasn't she?'

'You mean you've changed your professional diagnosis from "off her rocker" to "plucky survivor"?'

Cradock sounded embarrassed. 'Well, yes, I suppose so. You wouldn't want any poor woman to go through all that. I mean, it's funny when it's a song about being left waiting at the altar, but when it's real life, well . . . He must've let her think right up to the last minute he was going to go through with it.'

'Yes, and if Sal had been a wealthy woman, she'd have sued him for breach of promise, but that's not the way it works if you're poor.'

'It makes him a liar, though, doesn't it? He told her he was going to marry her, but he had no intention of doing so.'

'We don't know what his intentions were. If you're wanting to tick off lying as well as stealing on the list, I'd say it's not quite as clear cut as pinching money from your sister.'

'Sal must've felt he'd lied to her, though.'

'Quite probably, yes. But if we're talking about Radley's apparent confession, the important thing, perhaps, is whether he felt he'd lied, and that we don't know.'

'I suppose so, yes – and we don't know whether he killed anyone either. If what Doreen Radley said about that bloke in the hospital shouting at him's true, he didn't call him a killer – but then again, if the bloke was a soldier, maybe he wouldn't bother mentioning it. I mean, if that was in 1917 and it was a hospital for wounded soldiers, just about every man in that ward had probably killed someone, hadn't he?'

'All except Radley, of course – his brother and Stan Tipton both said he'd been a PT instructor in the Gymnastic Staff and hadn't seen any fighting.'

'So if Radley did kill anyone, maybe it was after the war.'

'Maybe – if he did. We still don't have any evidence of that, and if there is someone who knows he's a killer, they haven't told us. So as far as Roy Radley's confession's concerned, I think all we can say at the moment is that we've got a tick against stealing, a question mark against lying, and a blank against killing.'

'Sal said she felt like he'd killed her, didn't she? Isn't that significant?'

'It could be, but don't forget – Sal's still alive.'

Cradock looked puzzled. 'Er . . . yes, of course.'

'And she's also told us who was speaking to the man she saw going into the theatre on Monday evening. The one with the umbrella. So let's stop off on our way and see Mr Stone.'

The sign above the shop in Maiden Lane said Maison Charles, as Charlie Stone had told them. The front window, unlike so many in London, was still intact – at least, Jago thought as they approached it, until such time as a bomb found its random target in this particular street. The premises lacked the traditional barber's red-and-white striped pole that Jago was accustomed to seeing when he went to get a haircut, but then Maison Charles was clearly no mere barber shop: the words 'Permanent Waving and Hair Tinting Specialists' emblazoned across the window promised a rather more sophisticated service. He reminded himself not to refer to it as a shop if Stone was in: it was a salon.

The proprietor was nowhere to be seen when they went in, but a young woman with perfectly coiffured hair came to attend to them immediately. 'Good afternoon, gentlemen,' she said quietly, as if not wanting to disturb the calm of the establishment, where three female customers were having their hair cut and styled by murmuring hairdressers.

Jago forestalled any inquiries about how they'd like their hair done by explaining that he and Cradock were colleagues of Mr Stone who wished to speak to him, if he was in, on police business.

'Ah, yes, of course,' she said. 'I'll go and fetch him for you.'

She disappeared through a door at the back of the room and returned moments later with Stone.

'Hello,' he said. 'Julia tells me you'd like a word. If it's police business we'd better go upstairs to the flat – I'm assuming you might not want everyone here listening in to our conversation. Would you like a cup of tea or coffee? Julia can make you one if you'd like.'

'Yes, thank you – that would be nice. Tea for me, please.'

'Same for me too, please,' added Cradock.

Stone had a quiet word with Julia and then beckoned them towards the door. 'Come with me.'

He'd told them that he lived above this salon when they'd first met him, but when they followed him up the stairs to which the door led, what they found was not what Jago had expected. He'd visited many people who lived above shops in his time, and Stone's description of it as an 'upstairs flat' had sparked a mental image of cramped, dingy and even miserable surroundings. But the neat hallway and the living room beyond it were furnished and decorated with a taste and quality that suggested considerable expense. A sign, perhaps, Jago mused, of a man who'd worked hard for his success and wanted to enjoy its rewards.

'Take a seat,' said Stone, gesturing with his arm towards a plumply upholstered settee facing the hearth. 'And welcome to Maiden Lane – or Murder Lane, as one of my regular clients used to call it.'

'Really?' said Jago, taking his seat. 'Why was that?'

'Because a man was murdered here. It was quite a sensation – an actor was stabbed to death at the Adelphi Theatre's stage door, just down the street from here. In fact, Roy Radley was something of an expert on it.'

'When did this happen?'

'Forty-three years ago. Roy used to live over the road, in Sussex Mansions – that was in the good old days, as you might say, before his troubles started. He used to take quite an interest in local history before the drink addled his brain.'

'What was the story? About the murder, I mean.'

'Well, there was an actor called William Terriss appearing at the Adelphi, and one day as he was going in via the stage door to get ready for the evening performance he was attacked and stabbed.'

'Who did it?'

'It was another actor – a man called Prince. Terriss had helped him by getting him small parts over the years, but Prince had a long-standing drink problem – he ended up deranged. By the time of the attack, he was unemployable because of the alcohol and destitute. He got it into his head that Terriss was stopping him getting work, and developed a deep hatred for him. One night he crept up behind him out there on the street and stabbed him twice in the back with a butcher's knife. The second time the knife went through his heart, and he died.'

'And the trial?'

'Prince was charged with murder and found guilty but insane – he was sent to Broadmoor Criminal Lunatic Asylum and died there three or four years ago.'

'And Terriss – did he leave any family?'

'He had a wife, although I imagine she'd be dead by now. He had a daughter too – she married Sir Seymour Hicks, the actor.'

'Ah, yes – I've heard he's running ENSA now.'

'That's right – since the war started, so I expect they all know him down at the Theatre Royal. I wouldn't be surprised if he was mates with Sir Marmaduke Harvey – you remember I told you he's the owner of the Prince Albert? They're both knights of the realm now, for their pains. They probably do each other the occasional favour.'

'I think they do – we've heard that the ENSA people have been storing some of their props at the Prince Albert since the Theatre Royal was bombed.'

'There you are, then – pals. It's a small world, the theatre.'

'It is, yes. I'm just thinking about Roy Radley – only because he was stabbed to death in a theatre not far from here. I don't suppose you know of anything that could link him to Terriss or Prince or what happened between them.'

'I don't think so – he would only have been a child

back then. His dad might've known them, though – there's always been quite a connection between the theatres and the market, you know.'

'Yes, so I understand.'

'And, of course, passions often run high in the theatrical world.'

'I'm sure they do – I've heard there's lots of jealousy.'

'True enough. But all that was more than forty years ago. You don't think it could have any bearing on this case, do you?'

'I don't know. We'll have to see what else we turn up.'

There was a timid knock at the door, and Julia brought in a tray, from which each of the men took a cup of tea.

'Will that be all, Mr Stone?' she said.

'Yes, thank you, Julia,' he replied, and she left. 'So, Mr Jago,' he continued, 'what was the police matter you wanted to discuss?'

'I'll get to that in a moment, but first I wonder if we might use your telephone?'

'Of course. If you didn't see it on your way in, it's in the hallway, to the right as you go out of the door. You can speak in private there.'

Jago thanked him and turned to Cradock. 'Peter,' he said, 'I want you to phone the War Office and ask them whether that number we were given is an army number, and if so, what's the name of the man whose number it is. Tell them it's Scotland Yard calling, and we need an answer pronto, not next week. If they can call us back before we leave here, so much the better.'

'Yes, guv'nor.' Cradock went out into the hallway to

make the call, taking his cup of tea with him.

'He shouldn't be long,' said Jago to Stone.

Stone seemed mildly amused by this comment. 'I think that rather depends on the GPO, doesn't it? If my experience is anything to go by, there's no knowing how long it'll take to get through nowadays. Only yesterday I was trying to phone my brother-in-law in Luton and had to give up. Someone told me twelve thousand Post Office engineers are in the forces now, so the army's had to send hundreds of men down here to London to help mend all the cables that the bombs have wrecked. It sounds a bit barmy, doesn't it? They should've just left some of those men where they were, then the GPO could've done all the repairs themselves. Not that I envy them – apparently, they sometimes have to wear gas masks because they're working down a hole where the bombs have broken the gas main, and if the water main's burst too they're getting soaked at the same time. Makes hairdressing sound like a holiday.'

The door opened, and Cradock returned. 'All done, sir,' he said. 'I got through to a very helpful lady who said it might be better if I hung on, in case she couldn't get a line to call us back. She looked it up in some kind of register they've got and said yes, it is an army number, and she gave me the details.'

'Very good,' said Jago. He wasn't sure he wanted to discuss confidential information in front of Stone, even if he was a sworn-in special constable. He had no reason to doubt the man's ability to keep his mouth shut, but the tendency of some hairdressers to gossip with their customers made him wary. 'You can give me those later, Peter,' he continued. 'Finish your tea.'

'So,' he said, turning back to Stone, 'how's your business? I must confess I was intrigued when you said you were a hairdresser – you're the first special I've come across who's from that line of work. What made you want to be a policeman?'

Stone laughed. 'It is a bit unusual, I suppose, but we all have our role in life, don't we? The simple answer is I just wanted to do something – my wife worries about me being out at night in the raids, but there's a war on, and I wanted to do my bit. I spent the last war in the army – cutting men's hair, funnily enough – but I'm too old for the forces now. Back then, of course, it was all just short back and sides for the men, but nowadays I do ladies' hair as well, and it's much more creative. Did you meet Roy Radley's sister Joan, by the way?'

'Yes, we did, thanks.'

'She's one of my customers – I've been cutting her hair for years. Very nice lady. I have a lot of clients from the theatres too – you'd be surprised whose hair I've cut in my time. I like to think of myself as a hairdresser to the stars, and of course it's always good for business if people know Laurence Olivier or Flora Robson might pop in for a trim while they're having theirs done. I've never had George Formby or Max Miller yet, but you never know.'

'And the special constabulary in particular? Why did you choose that?'

'Well, I was thinking of doing either that or the ARP wardens, because you can do both where you live and

272

carry on with your job, but I reckoned being a policeman might be more interesting. I wasn't sure at first what they'd make of me being a hairdresser – some of my regular police colleagues still don't seem convinced it's a very suitable background for a policeman, but I think they've already discovered I can break up a fight as well as they can. What inspired me in the end, though, was Jack Hulbert – I saw it in the paper when he volunteered to be a special, and I thought if an actor can do it, why not a hairdresser?'

'And the war – has that been good for the hairdressing business, or bad?'

'A bit of both, I'd say, especially on the ladies' side. Before war broke out, we used to do a lot of perms, like the Eugene wave, and they were good for business because they're quite complicated, but the customers had to sit around for ages. Any woman can tell you what a palaver it is – I don't suppose you've ever seen it done, but we have to wind their hair up in dozens of little electric heaters all wired up to a kind of chandelier above their head, and they have to sit there until it's dry and the perm's set. Most of our lady customers decided they didn't fancy being trussed up in all that when the air-raid sirens went off, so they changed their style to something simpler. Bad news for hairdressers who'd invested in the equipment and done the training, but that's a risk you have to take with the usual changes in fashion, never mind all-out wars.'

'And the good news?'

'Well, a lot of the ladies who used to have longer styles

273

are doing things like ARP work now and having to wear tin helmets and gas masks, so they want shorter hair and simpler styles. That means they get it cut more often, so that's good for business, but of course we're losing out on the perms. Men's styles are obviously simpler and shorter, so that side of the business is usually pretty steady, but so many men have been called up now, it's taken a bit of a slide – not enough heads to trim, you see. It's the same with the theatrical gents – they have to keep themselves looking well turned out if they want to get the work, but now that there's hardly any work to get, they can't afford it. So now I think about it, I should've said the war's all pretty bad for business. But at least I haven't been bombed out yet, and everyone has to get their hair cut sometime.'

'Oh,' said Jago, 'by the way. Speaking of the theatre, were you by any chance in Drury Lane at about five o'clock yesterday afternoon?'

'Yes, I was on patrol there. Why?'

'We're just trying to identify someone, and we have a witness who says they saw you talking to him on the corner of Dryden Street at that time. A man with an umbrella. Can you remember who that was?'

'Yes, of course. It was Sir Marmaduke Harvey. He often stops for a chat when I'm down that way.'

'Right, well thank you, that's very helpful.'

'Glad to be of—'

Before he could finish his reply, Stone was interrupted by a violent and persistent ringing of his doorbell. He exchanged looks with Jago and Cradock. 'That sounds urgent – I'd better see who it is.' He hurried down the stairs, with Jago and Cradock following. The ringing now gave way to a rapid banging at the door. Stone opened it, and Joan Radley almost fell into his arms. 'Come quickly,' she gasped. 'It's Sal – she's been attacked. She's at my flat.'

CHAPTER THIRTY-FIVE

'Let's go,' said Jago, darting out into the street. Stone slammed the door behind them and the four of them set off at full tilt for Broad Court. They were there within minutes. Inside Joan's flat they found Sal sitting on the edge of a chair, looking dishevelled and distressed, with eyes puffed, as if she'd been crying. She put down the handkerchief she was holding to her face, revealing a red wheal on her cheek and a cut to her forehead.

'Look at her,' said Joan. 'Why Sal? She's kind to everyone, and everyone loves her.'

Jago knelt down on the floor beside Sal. 'Who did this to you?' he said gently.

Sal wiped her eyes with the handkerchief and winced as it touched her cheek. 'A copper,' she replied.

'What? A police officer? Did you get his collar number?'

'No, it's not like that – I'm sorry, Inspector, I'm not

thinking straight at the moment. He was in plain clothes, like you, so he didn't have a collar number, and I couldn't tell whether he was a copper or not. But he said he was.'

'Did he show you his warrant card?'

'He did, yes. He flashed it at me a bit quick, so I grabbed his hand and had a good look, but . . . well, you know what I said about reading and writing . . .'

Jago sighed. 'And not having any glasses? Even a sixpenny pair from Woolworth's would be better than nothing.'

She nodded. 'Yes, sorry, Inspector – I will try and get some. But the fact is, I could tell it was a warrant card, but it could've been a fake, for all I knew.'

'Where did this happen?'

'There's a little alleyway near the Prince Albert where I sometimes go for a quick sit down when I'm out selling my flowers, just to take the weight off my feet and have a bit of a rest. There's never anyone down there, because it only leads to a place that got shut down when the war started, so it's quiet and private. I reckon he must've followed me down there, otherwise how would he know to find me? Anyway, suddenly there was a tap on my shoulder, and when I turned round he was standing there, blocking my way out with a nasty look on his face.'

'What time did it happen?'

'About half an hour ago. I came straight round to Joan afterwards – she lives very close, see, and I knew she'd help me.'

'Can you describe him?'

'Yes. He was shortish, about five foot four or five tall,

and thin, and I'd guess about thirty or forty. He was wearing a trench coat, light grey, and it was too long for him, so the belt looked funny – you know, too low. Yes, and he had glasses too – black frames. He had a hat like yours, and it was pulled down at the front, so I couldn't see much of his face. The only other thing was he spoke Scottish – I mean he had a Scottish accent.'

'What did he say?'

'He said he knew I was Sal, and he was making inquiries about Roy getting murdered. I had no reason to question that, and I wasn't surprised he knew who I was, because everyone round here knows that. I just thought he must be a new copper from Bow Street that I hadn't come across before. Anyway, he started asking me questions. He said something like we have reason to believe Mr Radley was in possession of a considerable sum of money at the time of his death and we're trying to trace it. Yes, he spoke like a copper too. I said that was just a rumour, but he got a bit cross and said no, you're lying. I said I didn't know anything about any money and told him to lay off, and then out of the blue he just slapped me round the face. It was a big slap, and it really hurt, and I fell back against the wall and cut my head. Then he grabbed hold of me by the shoulders and started shaking me, saying tell me where the money is. I was scared, so I went for his eyes. I've been selling on the streets for long enough to know how to look after myself. He wriggled away, but not before I'd made him howl. Then I heard some people coming down the Lane, talking loud and laughing, so I gave him a good kick on the shin. He swore at me and hit me in the face again, then hobbled off as fast as he could.'

She stopped and took a deep breath to steady herself. 'I don't know who those people were, but they saved my life. I don't want to think what might've happened to me if they hadn't.' She shuddered. 'But there's one thing I can tell you. He wasn't Scottish – he was putting that accent on, and I know he was because when he started having a go at me it slipped. And there's another thing too – I think I know who he is.'

'Really?' said Jago. 'Who is he?'

'He's an ARP warden. It was that trench coat, see. It was light grey, for one thing, and that's unusual – they're nearly always navy blue or fawn, aren't they? But on top of that, when he made off, I could see a greasy sort of stain, like oil or something, on the back. That's what clinched it for me – I'd seen that coat before, and I'd seen him before too, walking up Drury Lane wearing it. He didn't have glasses then, but he was on the short side and his coat was too long for him. I've never spoken to him, but he was the man who attacked me.'

'Do you know his name?'

'I do. It's Baxter – Joe Baxter. I reckon he's no more a copper than I am, warrant card or no warrant card.'

'Right,' said Jago. 'You stay here with Joan, Sal – I'm sure she'll look after you. We're going to see whether Mr Baxter's at home. Stone, you come with us – we may need some help.'

'Yes, sir,' said Stone as they headed for the door. 'But before we go, could I just tell you something? I think it's important.'

'OK, but make it quick.'

'Yes, sir. It's just that I've been off duty since Tuesday, and my next shift's tonight, so before you came round I was checking my uniform was all clean and tidy. I, er . . . well, it's a bit embarrassing to say this, but I couldn't find my warrant card. I know I had it when I was last on duty, so I think I may have lost it in all the confusion when the Prince Albert was bombed. Now that I've heard what happened to Sal, I'm wondering whether Baxter – if she's right and it was him – well, I'm wondering whether he might've found it. I mean, if he's an ARP man, he might've had reason to visit the site.'

'Right, thanks for telling me. We'll talk about that later, though – first I want to get hold of Baxter.'

CHAPTER THIRTY-SIX

Jago and Cradock set off immediately for Daisy Greenway's flat in Long Acre, taking Stone with them. It was only a few hundred yards away, and Jago hoped they'd be in time to find Joe Baxter there, probably nursing his wounds. If he'd decided to go to ground somewhere else it would be more problematic, but in that case they'd have to depend on his sister's willingness to point them in the right direction.

When they arrived at the flat it was Daisy who came to the door. She looked surprised to see Stone with them, but made no comment on his presence.

'Good afternoon, Mrs Greenway,' said Jago, getting his breath back. 'I'm sorry to disturb you, but I just wondered – is your brother in?'

She eyed him cautiously. 'Is something the matter?'

'No, it's all right – I've just been in a bit of a hurry. Is he in?'

'Yes, he is.'

'Good. We'd like to speak to him, please. May we come in?'

'Of course. You won't be long, though, will you? I've got to give him his tea before he goes on duty.'

'Don't worry, we won't be long.'

She opened the door wider to let them in. 'He's just through there, in the living room.'

As they stepped into the hallway, Jago glanced at the row of hooks on the wall: there were two coats hanging on them. The first was dark green, in a woman's style. The second was a man's coat – a light grey trench coat. He waited until Daisy turned away to open the living room door, then caught Cradock's eye and pulled the coat out: it had a greasy stain on the back. They followed Daisy and found Baxter sitting in an armchair.

'The inspector's here, Joe,' she said. 'He wants a word.'

Baxter looked startled and jumped to his feet, wincing as he did. He said nothing, but his face was tense. He stared at Jago as if trying to read his next move. 'OK,' he said eventually, his voice expressionless. 'What do you want?'

'I'd like to know what time you got home, Mr Baxter – you've been out, haven't you?'

Daisy looked puzzled. 'How do you know—' she began, but Baxter cut her off. 'Leave this to me, Daisy,' he said curtly. 'Yes, Inspector, I've been out for a walk. Nothing unusual about that, is there?'

'That depends. What time did you get home?'

'I don't know – just a few minutes ago.'

'This walk of yours – did that include Drury Lane?'

'Yes, as a matter of fact it did.'

'And you're about to go on ARP duty – so will that be in Drury Lane as usual?'

'Yes. So what?'

'It's a little odd to go there for a walk, come back for your tea and then go straight back, isn't it?'

'I don't think so.'

'Would you like to tell us why you went there?'

'No particular reason – it was just for a walk, like I said.'

'Did you attack a woman there?'

Daisy put a hand to her mouth and stared at him in shock. 'Joe?'

Baxter glared at her. 'Shut up, Daisy. I said leave this to me.' He looked back at Jago, his eyes narrowed in hostility. 'Look, Inspector, I don't know what kind of mug you take me for, but if you're trying to pin something on me, you've got the wrong man – and if some woman says I attacked her, she's lying. So just leave me alone, will you? I've got an important job to do, and you're wasting my time.'

'All right, Mr Baxter,' said Jago. 'You've had your say, and I'm afraid I don't believe you. You might as well come clean. I'll tell you what I think happened. You went to Drury Lane, but it wasn't just for a walk – you accosted a woman called Sal in an alleyway near the Prince Albert Theatre.'

'No, I didn't.'

'You told her you were a policeman and you demanded she tell you the whereabouts of a large sum of money. When she refused, you assaulted her, and when she resisted your attack, you fled.'

'No, that's not true – none of it's true.'

Jago ignored him. 'I'm arresting you on suspicion of assault occasioning actual bodily harm, stealing a police officer's warrant card, and falsely representing yourself as a Metropolitan Police constable for an unlawful purpose. You are not obliged to say anything, but anything you say may be given in evidence.'

Daisy stared at her brother in disbelief. 'Joe, what's he saying? What's this all about? You wouldn't do anything like that, would you? Speak to me, Joe.'

She was close to tears, but Baxter ignored her. He said nothing. His lips tightened and his fists clenched as a rage seemed to boil up within him. His eyes darted to the door, then to Jago, then back to the door. He sprang forward with a yell and flung himself towards it, arms flailing.

He slipped past Jago, but before he could reach the door and escape, Special Constable Stone, the Bermondsey boy turned hairdresser, calmly took half a step forward with his left foot, raised his fists into a boxer's position, and delivered a neat right hook to the oncoming Baxter's chin. The suspect was out cold before he hit the floor.

'Well,' said Jago, eyeing the supine figure of Baxter on the carpet, 'we'll have to add a charge of resisting arrest too, when chummy comes round. And thank you very much, Mr Stone. I think perhaps we can overlook the small matter of you mislaying your warrant card. Well done.'

CHAPTER THIRTY-SEVEN

At the time Jago and Cradock were delivering Joe Baxter to Bow Street police station for charging, most people who had more normal jobs were thinking of packing up for the day and going home. Not that it was safe to regard any job as normal these days. Expectations of getting to and from work on time had been one of the first casualties of the Blitz. For Jago, however, ever since the day he'd transferred out of police uniform into the role of a plain-clothes detective, the concept of normal working hours had played no practical part in his life. If you were a detective, you had to work whatever hours it took, whether by day or by night, to get the job done, and the extra few shillings a week of the detective allowance were scant compensation. Being a bachelor helped, of course: it was undoubtedly harder if you had a family, and he wondered whether Cradock would be able to put up with it if he ever settled down. He hadn't told his assistant yet that he intended to visit another person connected to the case before the day was out, but he had something in his pocket that he hoped would sweeten the pill. That, however, could wait, to be deployed if the young detective constable showed signs of flagging later.

For the moment, Cradock still seemed as bright as a button. 'That was good, sir, wasn't it?' he said.

Jago tried to work out what he might be referring to, but gave up. 'Give me a clue, Peter.'

'Charlie Stone knocking out Baxter like that – it was like something in a movie.'

Jago had to admit he'd enjoyed the scene himself, as it had the ring of justice being meted out in a manner befitting the crime: if Baxter had inflicted physical violence on Sal, he'd received an appropriate taste of his own medicine. He decided to keep this thought to himself, however. 'You mean the kind of thing The Saint might do,' he said, 'if he was combining his film career with signing up as a special constable?'

'That's it, sir – biffing the villains left, right and centre. Showing them what's what.'

'Well, if that's what you aspire to, perhaps you should take some boxing lessons.'

'I think I might, sir.'

Jago sighed inwardly and smiled to himself. Cradock's boyish enthusiasm always seemed to provoke in him a sense of premature ageing.

'But that other thing,' Cradock continued, 'that story he told us about the actor who got killed by the other actor.

Do you think he was telling us that just as a bit of local history, or was he trying to drop a hint?'

'What kind of hint?'

'I don't know – maybe that that's what happened to Roy Radley.'

'You mean he knows something we don't?'

'I'm not sure, sir – maybe he does know something but doesn't want to tell us, or maybe he's got some reason to try and push us in that direction with a few hints, so we'll think it ourselves. After all, it's a bit close to what's happened here, isn't it? Two actors, and one of them ends up a destitute alcoholic who can't get any work and stabs the other one? Radley wasn't an actor, but he was on the stage, and he certainly ended up as a destitute out-of-work drunk, didn't he?'

'I see your point, Peter, but in our case it's actually the opposite, isn't it? The destitute drunk with no work was the victim, not the killer, so what kind of hint would that be, if Stone was trying to drop one?'

Cradock creased his brow as he wrestled with the question. 'Er, I don't know, sir.'

'Well, next time we see him we'll ask him. And if we find out in the meantime that Radley was killed by a rich and successful actor in some sort of mirror image of the Terriss murder, I'll buy you a drink for spotting the hint.'

Cradock's face brightened up. 'Oh, thanks, guv'nor.'

'Think nothing of it, Peter,' Jago replied, confident that the chances of him having to shell out for a beer for Cradock were vanishingly small. 'Now, with all that excitement over Baxter, I haven't had a chance to ask you what the lady at the War Office said when you phoned her, apart from the fact that that number was an army number. So what else did she say? Did she give you a name?'

'Yes, sir. She said the man with that number's called William Robinson, and he's a private in the Royal Army Pay Corps. She also said he's listed as missing in action.'

'Really? That's interesting – I wonder whether that's really missing in action, or just missing in the Prince Albert Theatre. I think we'd better find Sir Marmaduke Harvey and see if he can tell us about this other mysterious guest of his.'

Jago checked his watch: Sir Marmaduke was not the person he was already planning to visit. So now they had two calls to make before finishing work for the day, but such, he thought, was life. If they proved to be fruitful meetings, it would be worth it.

'The car's been sitting here all day doing nothing while we've been wearing out our shoe leather,' he said, 'so I'll let you give your legs a rest. We'll drive over to Sir Marmaduke's office, and if his working hours are as long as he said they were, we might find him still there with his nose to the grindstone.'

Exactly how close or prolonged the contact between Harvey's nose and the grindstone had been was impossible to tell, of course, but when they arrived at Concordia House he was undoubtedly there in his office and gave every appearance of working.

'I'm sorry to disturb you, Sir Marmaduke,' said Jago, 'but I wonder if you could spare us a few minutes.'

'Of course,' said Harvey. 'I've nearly finished for today – I was just tidying up. You have my full attention.'

'Thank you. I just wanted to ask you something else concerning the Prince Albert Theatre.'

'Fire away.'

'Well, the thing is, we know that Roy Radley had been living in your theatre for a while before his death, but it's now been suggested to us that there was another man taking refuge there. Is that true?'

Harvey looked uncertain. 'Who told you that?'

'I'm not at liberty to tell you, I'm afraid, but I would like to know whether it's true.'

'Well . . . Oh, all right – yes, it is.' He seemed reluctant to say anything more.

'But you didn't think to mention this earlier?'

'No. I didn't think it was relevant. He's a harmless fellow, but he's been through a very difficult time, and I feel a certain responsibility to help him out.'

'What's his name?'

'I'd rather not say, if you don't mind.'

'I'm afraid I do mind, Sir Marmaduke. This is a murder investigation, and obstructing the course of public justice is a serious offence, so I'd be obliged if you could tell me.'

'But I gave him my word that I'd keep his identity confidential.'

Jago said nothing, but his placid stare into Harvey's eyes indicated that this response cut no ice with him.

'Very well,' Harvey continued, 'his name's Robinson – Bill Robinson.'

'Thank you. Your caretaker told us that apart from Mr

Radley there was no one else sleeping in the theatre.'

'Yes, well, I told him not to let anyone know. A cynic might say Stan Tipton knows which side his bread's buttered on and can't afford to cross me, but I'd say he's just a very loyal man. I trust him, and I think he trusts me.'

'And this responsibility of yours to help Mr Robinson that you mention – what's that about?'

'It's a long story, but I'll try to keep it short. It goes back to something that happened in the last war. I served as an infantry officer, and towards the end I had the misfortune to be taken prisoner. I was on patrol with my sergeant, and we were both captured – not a pleasant experience, but at least it meant we both survived, so I suppose I should be thankful. After the war we went our separate ways, but we kept in touch, and I was able to help him occasionally when times were hard for him and his family – a bit of money for clothes for the children, that sort of thing. He had two daughters and one son, and he's always been very proud of them all. That son's grown up now – and he's the man who's been living in the theatre.'

'As another favour on your part to his father?'

'Yes – I can't have him sleeping on the street. I'd do anything to protect him – his father was very loyal to me, and ever since those days in France I've tried to be loyal to him in return.'

'And this son of his – he was called up to be a soldier in this new war?'

'Yes – but how did you know that?'

'We've just been doing some checking, but that's not important. Tell me more about his military career.'

'OK. I believe he was enlisted soon after war broke out. He was a private in the Pay Corps, but he was sent out to France with the British Expeditionary Force and was still there when it was driven back to the sea by the Germans.'

'So he was at Dunkirk?'

'No – he didn't get out until later. He said there were still thousands of British troops left in France when the Dunkirk evacuation finished, and support units like the Pay Corps were mostly stationed miles away from the fighting. Bill said he wasn't even trained for real combat – he was a pay clerk. His unit was ordered to make its way to St Nazaire, on the west coast. They managed to avoid capture, but the ship that took them off was the *Lancastria*.'

'Ah, yes,' said Jago. His voice was sombre. 'The Cunard liner. I read about that in the paper – July, wasn't it? Terrible business.'

'It actually happened in the middle of June, but the newspapers weren't allowed to report it until nearly the end of July. The government must have thought it would be too big a blow to public morale if it got out so soon after the Dunkirk business. She was sunk by German dive bombers before she'd even got out of the estuary – three thousand troops and RAF men killed, and civilians too, men, women and children. Bill survived somehow and was picked up by a minesweeper that brought him back to Plymouth, but he still can't speak about everything he saw. I tried to get him to talk, but he said he couldn't, said I wouldn't believe him. But I saw things in France in the last war that I've never told anyone, for the same reason.'

Jago said nothing, but nodded. So had he.

'In the end I got a few details out of him, but I think that's because he knows I'm a friend and I've been in a war myself. He trusts me.'

'What happened to him?'

'He said he was down below when the bombs hit. There was blood everywhere, bodies and bits of bodies. People were going mad. Hundreds of men were killed in the hold, and hundreds more were trying to get up the stairs to the deck. He was one of the last to get to the top before the whole staircase collapsed and the men fell down into the flames. He's a swimmer, so he stripped off his clothes and jumped in – the only thing he kept on was his army identity discs, but he lost them when he was in the water. There was fuel oil everywhere, and some of it was burning – men were screaming, choking and dying. When they picked him up, he was naked and covered in black oil from head to toe. That's about all he said. The experience has clearly had a dreadful effect on him, and he's not the young man I used to know.'

'Poor fellow. I'd like to speak to him – he may've seen or heard something in the theatre that could be relevant to our inquiries. Where is he?'

'He's not in London, I'm afraid. You see, he was in the Prince Albert when that bomb hit it on Tuesday morning. It was too much for him – I think it brought back all the terrible memories he had from the *Lancastria*. He was a quivering wreck when I saw him, so I had to act quickly. I contacted a private nursing home that I have some connections with, that provides psychiatric treatment, and they agreed to admit him immediately. He's there now.'

'I'd like to go and speak to him. Where is this nursing home?'

'It's out in the country, near Chalfont St Giles. Look, it might be easier if I take you there myself and introduce you to him, reassure him, you know. When would you like to go?'

'As soon as possible, if you don't mind.'

'In that case, I'll call them.'

He picked up the phone on his desk, dialled the operator and asked to be put through to the nursing home. After a short wait he was connected. 'Hello?' he said. 'Sir Marmaduke Harvey speaking. You have a friend of mine as a patient – his name's William Robinson. I wondered if I might pop over with a couple of gentlemen who'd like a brief word with him, if he's up to it.' He waited while the person at the other end went to find out and returned. 'Tomorrow morning, ten o'clock?' He put his hand over the receiver and looked questioningly at Jago, who nodded his head. 'Very well, ten o'clock. We'll see you then.'

'Right,' he said, putting the receiver down, 'that's all arranged. It should take us an hour and a half or so in the car, traffic and the Third Reich permitting, so if you can be here by half past eight tomorrow morning, I'll take you out there.'

CHAPTER THIRTY-EIGHT

'Is that everything done for today, then, guv'nor?' Cradock enquired as he settled into the Riley's passenger seat. 'It's another early start tomorrow, and even Sir Marmaduke was about to knock off when we got there, wasn't he?'

Jago still had his final visit of the day to complete, but didn't want to puncture his colleague's hopes of a rest too brutally. It had been a long day, and while he didn't consider eight-thirty a particularly early start, he assumed Cradock was allowing for the time he'd need to down a healthy breakfast before reporting for duty. The thought of Cradock eating reminded him of what he had in his pocket.

'There's one last call I'd like to pay before we finish, Peter,' he said. 'I've been thinking about that fellow Scott that we met at the BBC yesterday, and what he said about Roy Radley.'

'Yes – a bit tetchy, wasn't he? And I've been thinking about bread pudding.'

'I'm sure you often think about bread pudding, Peter, but do you mean in general, or in particular?'

'I mean when we had lunch with him and Patricia Radley at Broadcasting House yesterday – we had bread pudding, didn't we? No custard, mind, but it was still good. But when we got to the end of it, and she was telling us about that trouble she was having with her Uncle Roy and the BBC, I thought he got really angry. He said he was making her life a misery, and he stabbed that bread pudding with his spoon like it was Radley himself.'

'Yes, he did.'

'And that made me think about what that rector said – you know, "look for where the anger is". There was certainly some anger there, and no mistake.'

'Yes, I grant you that, although stabbing a bread pudding with a spoon isn't necessarily quite the same as dispatching a man with a screwdriver. But let's keep it in mind when we're talking to Mr Scott. He said he used to work in the Variety Department, didn't he? I'd like to know whether he ever had any dealings with Radley himself.'

'Does that mean we're going back to the BBC now, sir?' said Cradock, in a tone that suggested he wasn't thrilled at the prospect.

Jago checked his watch. 'I think I'll call them when we get back to Bow Street. He might've finished work by now, but from what Patricia Radley said about the staff there working all hours and sleeping on mattresses in the Concert Hall, he might be there all night. By the way, before we go,

I was wondering – have you heard from Rita lately?'

'No, I haven't.'

Jago reached into his pocket and pulled out an envelope. 'Well, I got a letter from her this morning. Judging by the postmark it's taken quite a while to reach me, but she's inviting us to Christmas dinner at her place – on Christmas Day.'

Cradock's eyes lit up. 'You mean proper Christmas dinner, sir?'

'Well, as proper as anyone can manage when the country's short of turkeys, I suppose.'

'With Christmas pudding?'

'She didn't mention it specifically, but I can't imagine Rita thinking it was a real Christmas dinner without one, even if she has to improvise some of the ingredients.'

'Oo, I hope she makes one. I like Christmas pudding – it's the best thing about Christmas dinner for me.'

'I'm sure if she cares about you, she'll do her best – after all, you know what they say—'

'Yes, sir – the proof's in the pudding.'

'No, Peter, they don't say that. They say "the proof of the pudding is in the eating," meaning you only find out whether it's a good pudding when you eat it. What I was actually going to say is the way to a man's heart is through his stomach, which is quite a different thing. If Rita wants to see her Emily married off to you, she'll make sure she feeds you well.'

Cradock's face registered what looked like a momentary shock followed by an evasive embarrassment. 'Sir, I don't think—'

'It's all right, Peter,' Jago replied. 'I'm only joshing. But if you're a real detective you'll know a pudding isn't the first place to look for proof – unless it's a poisoned one, of course.'

Cradock looked confused. 'Er, yes, sir. Is it just you and me she's invited?'

'No – Rita says it's to say thank you for that nice American Thanksgiving meal we had a few weeks ago.'

'So she's inviting your . . . er, Miss Appleton too?'

'Yes. She said her cafe's closed on Christmas Day, and she can fit five people nicely round her best table.'

'Five, sir? But you, me, Rita and Miss Appleton make four.'

'Impressive mental arithmetic, Peter, but there's one more guest.'

Cradock's expression was apprehensive. 'Er . . . Sir?'

'That's right, Peter – Emily will be there too.'

Cradock said nothing. He'd got used to the American journalist grilling him relentlessly about the progress of his tentative relationship with Rita's daughter Emily, and if truth were told he'd secretly appreciated it, despite the occasional torment of his boss being potentially within hearing distance. But the thought of being at the same table as Emily with the two of them brought unsettling images to his mind – if not downright terror.

'Oh, that'll be nice, sir,' he replied, unconvincingly.

'It will, won't it?' said Jago, with the merest hint of glee in his voice. 'But now let's get down to Bow Street and make that phone call.'

* * *

At the police station Jago called Broadcasting House and was informed that Mr Scott had left the building and gone home. On learning that her caller was a detective inspector, the helpful person who gave him this information also supplied Scott's home address: 14 Middleton Buildings, a little lane between Langham Street and Riding House Street, very close to Broadcasting House. Armed with this information, they set off in the car, and ten minutes later they were standing outside a Georgian-style terraced house with a stucco finish to the ground floor, knocking at his door. It looked considerably more salubrious than Patricia Radley's accommodation, and Jago was still wondering whether Scott simply had a much better paid job than her or perhaps enjoyed the benefit of a private income when the door opened.

'Ah, Inspector,' said Scott, who had evidently been home at least long enough to take his tie off. 'How nice to see you. Is this business or pleasure?'

'Business, I'm afraid, Mr Scott, but I hope it won't take long.'

'Actually, I was just about to go out, but only as far as the Yorkshire Grey – that's the pub up there on the corner with Langham Street. I usually pop in there for a drink after work. You'd be very welcome to join me.'

'Yes, that would be fine – I don't want to disrupt your evening any more than necessary.'

'Good – let's go now then.'

They walked to the corner and into the saloon bar at the pub. It was quiet, with just a handful of customers. The barman stood with a bored expression on his face, idly polishing glasses with a cloth, but greeted Scott with a nod as they entered.

'What can I get you?' said Scott.

'Best if we get our own, sir, thanks all the same,' said Jago.

'Of course, yes, it doesn't look good for policemen to be seen accepting drinks from a suspect, does it?'

'You're not a suspect, sir.'

Scott laughed. 'Only joking, Inspector, but I'm glad you've clarified that.'

They got their drinks and sat at the table that was farthest away from the other customers.

'Nice little pub,' said Jago. 'And a nice quiet street to live in, by the look of it.'

'Yes, I was lucky to find it. I like the classical Georgian style of the houses, although I believe they were actually built rather later in the last century'.

'It must be very handy for work, too, being so close to Broadcasting House.'

'Definitely – that's why I chose it. I sometimes bring our guests down here after they've done a talk for us.'

'Ah, yes, you mentioned that you work in the Talks Department. What exactly is your job?'

'Oh, nothing special – I'm an administrator. There's a lot of administration in the BBC.'

'It must be an interesting department to work in, though.'

'I suppose so – it's mostly routine things, but one does get to meet interesting people. The old hands used to say it was the most exciting department of the BBC to work in, because you get a constant stream of prominent figures in to broadcast, and you meet so many famous and fascinating people. You know J.B. Priestley?'

'Not personally, but I know of him, of course.'

'Well, he liked to come down here to the pub for a drink after his talk – it's so close, you see. I used to walk back with him sometimes, and we'd have a chat over a pint here. Mainly me listening while he sat there and talked about everything under the sun, puffing away on one of those pipes of his, but it was very interesting.'

'I used to enjoy his Sunday evening *Postscripts* – but they've stopped now, I think, haven't they?'

'Yes, they were a huge success while they lasted. We reckoned that with them and his short-wave broadcasts three times a week to America he had the biggest regular listening audience in the world. But the last one was towards the end of October. He said he'd decided to stop, but rumour has it that he was pushed.'

'Really?'

'Yes. He as much as said so in one of the Sunday papers a week later – he said he was trying to make his contribution to fighting the war, but all he met with every day was obstruction, as if there was a conspiracy against him.'

'In the BBC, do you mean?'

'No – he seemed to be blaming the people high up in government. His only complaint about the BBC was that we were too gentlemanly and not assertive enough. A lot of listeners wrote to us too, suspecting that he'd been sacked, and there were plenty of people in the BBC who thought the same. I think the problem was that he said we don't just need to win the war, we've got to build a new social order when it's over. Some people said he sounded like a communist, and the BBC's airwaves weren't the place for that sort of thing. Too subversive, perhaps – but I thought they captured what a lot of people in this country are thinking, and there's no point in certain other people burying their heads in the sand. I shan't say any more than that, though – I don't want to get the same treatment as Mr Priestley. So no telling tales on me, if you don't mind, Inspector.'

'Don't worry, Mr Scott, I'm not here to interrogate you on your views on behalf of the BBC. What I am interested in is the fact that you mentioned you'd previously worked in the Variety Department. That's right, isn't it?'

'Yes, I was there until about a year ago. We had the same sort of trouble with the powers that be there too. At the beginning of the war, we weren't allowed to book any new acts unless they'd been vetted by the Ministry of Information – the government was so jittery about anything unsuitable getting on the air they didn't want to take the risk. As soon as war looked imminent the whole department was evacuated to Bristol, which was probably just as well as things turned out.'

'What do you mean?'

'Well, a few years ago the department managed to get the use of St George's Hall. That's an old theatre in Langham Place, just round the corner from Broadcasting House, and it was ideal for live broadcasts of variety shows. By the time the war started most of us worked there, including yours truly. Some people didn't like the idea of being moved out of London, but we didn't have a choice, so down to Bristol we went. Then in September of this year St George's Hall was hit by an incendiary bomb during a night raid and gutted, so I for one was glad we'd gone. That's when the famous BBC Theatre Organ that you hear so much on the radio was destroyed. Anyway, that's how I ended up in Bristol, but then later I was posted back here to work in Talks. It seems they needed someone, and Variety obviously didn't need me.' He gave a dismissive sniff, as if to suggest the Variety Department must have been fools to let him go.

'So you're not involved with Variety any more?'

'Not really. They do rope me in occasionally to deal with minor administrative matters that are more easily handled in London, but the bulk of my time is with Talks.'

'There's something I'd like to ask you about the Variety Department. When you were still working in it, did you happen to meet Miss Radley's uncle?'

Scott's face took on a guarded expression. 'Yes, I did actually – just once. But listen, Patricia said he'd been murdered. You're not trying to get me to say something to incriminate her, are you? Because if you are . . .'

'No, certainly not. I'm just trying to find out more about Mr Radley. What did you make of him?'

'Well, as Patricia said, he was trying to get work with the BBC. I don't think I made much of him at all. He turned up at the front door one day last year claiming he

302

had an appointment with the Director of Variety, but the commissionaire checked and found out of course that he hadn't. I was sent down to fob him off and get rid of him. He struck me as a rather objectionable sort of fellow, not the sort we'd be keen to hire at the BBC. Besides, Patricia had told me about his drinking – he was an alcoholic. You should have heard his language when I told him he couldn't see the director – it would make a sailor blush. I'm not surprised he was getting nowhere with his attempts to get on the air with us.'

'Miss Radley didn't seem too perturbed by her uncle's efforts to get on the radio, but it must've been embarrassing for her, don't you think?'

'I think it was, yes, but she's a kind-hearted girl. I think maybe she was just very forgiving towards him.'

'So she wouldn't have wanted to see him come to any harm?'

Scott looked startled. 'Surely you don't think—' He put his glass down abruptly and shook his head. 'No, Inspector, I don't think she would.'

'Can you think of anyone else who might have?'

'No, I can't.' He was beginning to sound exasperated. 'I mean, I barely knew the man, and I don't recall meeting anyone in his circle of acquaintance either. As far as I'm concerned, he was just a comedian who didn't have what it takes to be on the BBC and was bad for Patricia.'

'When we spoke to you before, you sounded angry about that. Were you?'

'No,' he said, pushing his chair back, the irritated tone

in his voice belying this denial. 'I don't get angry, not with people like that – they're not worth it. I just don't like to see a girl like Patricia suffering because of someone else's delusions of grandeur. It's not fair, and it's not what she deserves.'

CHAPTER THIRTY-NINE

At half past eight the next morning the blackout had ended and the sun was rising as Jago and Cradock walked up Shaftesbury Lane. It wasn't far from Bow Street police station, and since they were getting a lift to the nursing home from Sir Marmaduke, Jago had left the Riley there. When they reached Concordia House, they found him waiting for them inside the main entrance. After the briefest exchange of greetings, he led them to a car that was significantly larger and more impressive-looking than Jago's own faithful Lynx and was parked right outside the door. They had passed it on their way in, and after an admiring glance Cradock had predicted, on the basis of hope rather than evidence, that this must be the theatre owner's vehicle. When he saw Harvey insert a key into the driver's door lock, he directed a gleeful self-congratulating smile in Jago's direction.

Sir Marmaduke's car was a two-tone Bentley saloon with a strikingly long bonnet that suggested a big engine. Jago slid into the front passenger seat and was not surprised to find it was considerably more comfortable than what his trusty Riley Lynx had to offer. 'Very nice,' he said as Harvey got into the driver's seat beside him. 'And no slouch on the open road, I should imagine. Mr Bentley certainly knows how to build racers.'

'Yes. I don't think he built this one, though – they're all made by Rolls-Royce now.'

Not being accustomed to riding in, let alone owning, either Bentley or Rolls-Royce cars, Jago felt ill-equipped to discuss their relative merits, but he could confidently assume that Sir Marmaduke would have spent a lot of money on his choice. 'Good engine?' he said, reckoning he was on safe ground with this question.

'Four point two five litres,' said Harvey. 'It does the job. You should find it a comfortable ride – it's fitted with special rubber bushes, so you don't get so much engine noise or vibration.'

Jago found no reason to dispute his claim of comfort as the car purred almost silently west out of London in the direction of Buckinghamshire, nor was he surprised to find that it had none of his Riley's draughts. It wasn't long before he felt drowsiness beginning to steal up on him, and he fought to keep his eyes open. Whether it was a luxurious Bentley or a humble Riley, he had an aversion to falling asleep in the front seat of any car because he could only too easily picture himself being pitched head first through the windscreen in the event of an emergency stop, and he wanted to be awake enough to spot danger ahead and brace himself. The curse of too vivid an imagination, he thought – that and the memory of some grisly car accidents he'd had to attend in his early days as a police constable. A glance over his shoulder, however, confirmed that Cradock was dozing peacefully in the back.

They motored steadily up the A40 through Middlesex and into Buckinghamshire until Harvey announced that they were approaching Chalfont St Giles. He swung the car off onto a side road and took another couple of turnings. He seemed to know his way without the benefit of road signs, but Jago assumed that the 'connections' he'd mentioned, whether charitable or medical or some other link, had brought him here on previous occasions, of which delivering Robinson into the nursing home's care was only the most recent.

He turned once more and the road began to narrow, with only the width for one vehicle as it snaked through farmland and woodland. They encountered no other traffic, and eventually Harvey steered the car through double gates into a long drive that led up to the home. It was a grand and rambling place that might well have been an old manor house, and their approach route suggested it offered the seclusion that patients like Robinson probably needed.

Harvey parked at the front of the house, and they got out. Now Jago could see a sign identifying the place as St John's nursing home. Once inside, they were met by a slight, middle-aged woman in a white coat, who peered at them over a pair of pince-nez glasses. Harvey introduced

Jago and Cradock to her, and she gave them a half-smile of welcome.

'I'm Dr Peters. I'm the senior psychiatrist here, and I would ask you not to tax Mr Robinson with too many questions. He arrived here in a state of considerable distress and he's still at an early stage of treatment. We've given him something to sedate him, to help calm him, so he may not be quite as alert as you might wish, but I understand that it's important for you to talk to him, so a little sedative may help him to answer your questions. Please don't raise your voices, though, or do anything to alarm him – his nerves are very strained.'

'We won't be here long,' Jago reassured her. 'It's just a matter of a few simple questions, then we'll be gone.'

'Very good,' said the doctor. 'Follow me.'

She led them down a corridor and into a room, where they found just one bed, on which lay a young man with a sallow complexion and straggly fair hair, with a sheet and blankets pulled up to his chin. He was awake.

'Hello, Bill,' said Harvey. 'I've brought these two gentlemen here because they think you might be able to help them. They're detectives. And don't worry – I'll be here to make sure everything's OK.'

Robinson gave a slow nod, but said nothing.

Jago moved a chair to the bedside and sat on it. 'Hello, Mr Robinson. I'm Detective Inspector Jago and I'd like to ask you something about the Prince Albert Theatre in Drury Lane.'

The patient nodded his assent.

'Thank you. I understand that you've been sleeping there

308

recently, with Sir Marmaduke's permission. Is that correct?'

'Yes.'

'Did you know that another man was sleeping in the theatre temporarily?'

'Yes, I did – he told me he had permission too.'

He turned his head towards Harvey with a nervous look in his eyes.

'Yes, that's right, Bill,' said Harvey reassuringly.

'Do you know his name?' Jago resumed.

'Yes. It was Radley – Roy Radley. He used to be famous. He was no trouble to me – he believed what I said.'

'So he knew why you were there?'

'Yes.'

'Who else knew?'

'No one, just Radley – apart from Sir Marmaduke, of course.'

'And were you in the theatre during the night before that bomb landed?'

'Yes, I was. That's why I'm in here – I went to pieces.'

'I understand. But can you tell me – did you see or hear anything unusual that night or in the early morning before the bomb hit?'

'Only one thing as far as I can remember. It's usually completely quiet in the theatre at night – the only noise is outside – but sometime early in the morning I heard a man shouting. He sounded angry.'

'What was he shouting?'

'It was something like "You dirty cheat . . . You've destroyed my life." It took me by surprise – I didn't know what was going on.'

'Did you recognise the voice?'

'No – it was just a voice.'

'Did you notice what time it was?'

'Yes. I haven't got a watch any more – it's at the bottom of the sea – but Sir Marmaduke gave me a little alarm clock, so I checked that. It said ten past eight.'

'And did you see anything?'

'No. Like I said, whoever it was shouting, he sounded angry, violent. I wasn't going anywhere near him. I'm not . . . I'm not as brave as I used to think I was.'

'That's all right. And the shouting stopped?'

'Yes.'

'What did you do then?'

'Nothing. I tried to get back to sleep. I think I dozed off for a bit eventually, but then—' A look of fear flashed into his eyes, and his hands began to shake. 'The bomb—'

'I think we'll stop there, Inspector,' said the doctor. 'He must rest. I'm going to give him something stronger, and you'll have to go.'

'Of course,' said Jago. 'We'll go. I'd like a brief word with you outside before we do, though. Is that OK?'

'Yes. Wait in the corridor and I'll join you as soon as I can.'

Jago, Cradock and Harvey waited outside as instructed, and a few minutes later she joined them.

'So, what is it you want to have a word about?' she asked.

'Just one thing – it's to do with Mr Robinson. I expect you've been observing him, yes?'

'Of course.'

310

'Someone who saw him in the theatre we were talking about said they'd heard him reciting a long number over and over again.' He checked his notebook. 'It was eight three double-one, five double-eight. I wondered whether you might've heard him saying the same number, or something similar.'

'When he was first admitted, yes. I suspect that this behaviour was connected with his terrifying experience – it's what we sometimes call a fugue state.'

'What does that mean?'

'It's a state in which a person can become unaware of their own personality and do things they can't recollect later – a bit like sleep-walking. We also call it "dissociation of personality". It's a way that the mind tries to deal with traumatic memories. I've seen a case where a man experienced it after being blown up in the last war, and years later if he thought he heard a bomb exploding he'd lapse back into the same state.'

'So, if something happened to put him into that state, he could've done something he wouldn't normally do, and not remember it?'

'Yes.'

'And that business of the number, saying it again and again?'

'Yes, I asked him why he was doing it, and he said he thought he was going out of his mind, no longer sure who he was. The number was his army number, which he'd had to memorise when he was enlisted, and he said it was like a link with who he really was. I think perhaps he was clinging to that number and repeating it to himself as a way of holding on to his own self.'

'I see.'

'There are more people than you might imagine in fragile mental states like this, Inspector – many of them have been locked up in institutions since the Great War. We tend to think of men who lost limbs or their sight or hearing in that terrible conflict, because we see them out and about in the street, but the men whose minds were wounded are still suffering too. I fear this new war will produce thousands more.'

'So would those mental wounds include something like hearing voices?'

'Some people believe that delusions and hallucinations may be connected with past trauma, and those hallucinations can include auditory ones – hearing voices, as you say.'

'So the voice Mr Robinson says he heard in the theatre – could that have been only in his own head?'

'In principle, yes, but I don't know how one could prove it one way or the other unless there was someone else present to hear it at the time. Was there?'

'There was, Doctor, but unfortunately he's dead.'

'Ah, that makes it difficult, then. I'm sorry I can't be of more help.'

'Not at all, Doctor – you've been very helpful. I'll let you get back to your work, but I'll need to speak to Mr Robinson again – when can I come back?'

'I don't want him to be disturbed for the next two or three days. We're starting him on a course of deep hypnosis, and it's essential that he has both physical and mental rest if we're to treat his mind successfully. I think you're more

312

likely to get useful information from him once we've done that, so I suggest you telephone me in three days' time.'

'Very well. I must be frank, Doctor – is it possible that in that fugue state you described a man might kill someone?'

'It's possible that anyone in any state might kill someone, Inspector. It's a hypothetical question.'

'Yes, but I'm conducting a murder investigation. How secure is this place?'

'This may be called a nursing home, but we specialise in mental cases, some of them very severe. I can assure you our patients cannot just come and go as they please. They're under constant supervision by day, and at night we lock them in. For their own safety, you understand – Mr Robinson won't be going anywhere until we're ready to discharge him.'

'Thank you – and if he comes out with anything you think might be relevant to my investigation, please call me at Scotland Yard.'

'I shall, Inspector.'

'Good. I hope you manage to get him well again.'

'We'll do our very best, I assure you.'

'We'll be on our way, then – goodbye.'

'Goodbye, gentlemen.'

CHAPTER FORTY

The three men got into the Bentley and set off immediately on their return journey to London. Cradock sat quietly in the back: he knew better than to air his thoughts on what bearing Robinson's words might have on the case in the presence of Harvey. Jago, meanwhile, stared out of the window, mulling over what he'd seen and heard in the nursing home, but waited until Harvey had navigated the car through the twisting lanes back to the main road before he spoke. 'I have a question for you, Sir Marmaduke,' he said, 'concerning that young man we've just been talking to.'

'Really?' said Harvey. 'What else could you possibly want to know?'

'Isn't it obvious, Sir Marmaduke?'

'No, it isn't. What do you mean?'

'I'm talking about what that doctor said – she said he'd

told her the number he was reciting was his army number. Now, speaking as one old soldier to another, I don't think you should be surprised to discover that that's what I suspected it was. Consequently, I took the precaution of getting my young colleague here to check it with the War Office. They obligingly confirmed that that number was indeed allocated to a Private William Robinson in the Royal Army Pay Corps, so that's all consistent with what he said and what you said. So far so good. But the interesting thing is this: the War Office also mentioned that he was listed as missing in action. Forgive me for stating the obvious, but he can't be missing in action and a patient in that nursing home at the same time, can he?'

'I don't know. Perhaps the army doesn't know he made it back yet – it must have been chaos out there.'

'But you told me he'd been picked up by the navy and brought back to Plymouth. He would've had every opportunity to identify himself.'

'He was ill, he'd almost died. He wouldn't necessarily have thought of it.'

'And how long ago was that? Six months? No, Sir Marmaduke, there's been plenty of time for him to think of it. Unless, that is, he – or you – declined to let the army know he'd survived the sinking.'

Jago waited for an answer, but none came. 'Come along, Sir Marmaduke – he's a deserter, isn't he, and you've been colluding with him.'

Harvey gripped the steering wheel in frustration. 'All right, you win. Maybe he didn't notify the army straight away, and maybe I didn't either. But look, I had to help

315

him. He's not a criminal – he's just a pay clerk who got caught up in a war that's not of his own making. He went through a horrific experience that drove men out of their minds. Who can blame him for trying to escape? He knew he couldn't go back and face anything like that again – he's mentally incapable.'

'But he had the presence of mind to coin a new identity for himself in the middle of it, didn't he? Did he really lose his identity discs when he jumped into the sea, or did he just drop them over the side?'

'I don't know.'

'What really happened when the survivors were landed at Plymouth? And tell me the truth now, please.'

'All right, but I only know what he told me, and that wasn't much – he was in a terrible state. I told you before that he said there were civilians on that ship too – men, women and children among the dead. I think when he arrived naked as the day he was born and with no evidence of his identity, he said he was a civilian and gave a false name and address. I doubt whether there was an accurate passenger list anywhere – it was an emergency evacuation in the middle of a war, and that ship was just taking off as many people as it could pack in. In any case, even if anyone tried to check the name and address, by the time they found out they were false he'd have been long gone. The people at Plymouth gave him some clothes, and then he cleared off as quickly as he could and disappeared.'

'And he got in touch with you?'

'Immediately. He needed somewhere to shelter, and I was the only one he could turn to. He knew he couldn't go home, because that was the address the army had for him, and they'd be informing his parents he was missing in action. I got word to his father that he was safe, of course, and I assured him I'd find somewhere for his son to lie low until he was back on his feet.' He glanced briefly at Jago as he drove. 'It's what friends do, isn't it?'

'Yes, Sir Marmaduke. I don't doubt that you've been a good friend to him and his father, but that doesn't alter the fact that the man's a deserter. You must persuade him to give himself up to the military authorities, otherwise he'll be in more trouble than he is already.'

'And if I don't?'

'If you don't, you'll risk being found guilty of knowingly assisting a deserter to conceal himself.'

'And what's the penalty for that?'

'You could be facing up to six months' imprisonment.'

Harvey offered no reply, but drove on in silence, then pulled into a lay-by and stopped the car. He switched off the engine and turned to Jago. 'There's something I must tell you,' he said. 'When I was that young officer in France, a soldier in our battalion threw down his rifle in the middle of a battle and ran away. He was a good soldier, but in the end it was too much for him, and his mind cracked. I was ordered to command a firing party, and we shot him. I've never forgotten it and I've never forgiven myself – it was the worst thing I've done in my life. He'd broken the law, but in my eyes he was innocent. That day is branded into my memory – how can I even think about handing over my friend's son to be shot?'

'They won't shoot him, Sir Marmaduke – it's not like it

was back in our day, thank goodness. The army stopped shooting deserters ten years ago and they haven't brought the death penalty back in, even though we're at war again. Maybe we've all learnt something since the last war.'

'But you're going to arrest him, aren't you, and hand him over to the army?'

Jago made no response: his mind was on something more important. 'Sir Marmaduke, there's something else I want to ask you, and I must caution you that you are not obliged to say anything, but anything you say may be given in evidence.'

'What? Are you serious?'

'Deadly serious, Sir Marmaduke. Mr Robinson said the only people who knew about his true identity were you and Roy Radley. Now Radley's been murdered. You said you'd do anything to protect your old friend's son – would that include killing the only other person who knew who and where he was? Had Radley tried to blackmail you?'

'Don't be absurd – of course not. I'm not a murderer.'

'I have a witness who saw you entering the Prince Albert Theatre at about five o'clock on Monday, the evening before he was murdered.'

'So? That was just to pick up some papers I'd left there. I was only in the theatre for about ten minutes.'

'Can you prove that? No one saw you leave.'

'Perhaps they didn't – I left by the stage door, and that opens onto a dark little lane at the back of the theatre.'

'Can you account for your movements after that?'

'Yes, I can. I'm a member of the Society of West End Theatre Managers and I was attending a dinner that evening at the Garrick Club. We were in the basement, so we stayed on until late that night. There were twenty other guests who know me, and the dinner was hosted by the Earl of Pevensey – I trust you'd accept the word of a peer of the realm. Then I went home to my wife for the night. Check with any of them.'

'We will, Sir Marmaduke. But in the meantime, I suggest we get going again – perhaps you could drop us off at Bow Street police station.'

'You mean you're going to arrest me?'

'No, I'm not. First, I'll be verifying your account of your movements on Monday evening. Then we'll see.'

Harvey said nothing but started up the car engine again and drove grimly on towards London.

CHAPTER FORTY-ONE

There was a question that Cradock had been itching to ask Jago all the way back from their visit to the nursing home, but he'd had to bite his tongue until Harvey had dropped them off in Bow Street and gone on his way.

'Sir?' he said, his face creased in a frown of puzzlement.

'Yes?' Jago replied.

'Sorry to ask this, sir, but I don't quite understand – shouldn't we have arrested that bloke for deserting? Bill Robinson, I mean. Even Sir Marmaduke seemed to be expecting you would, but you didn't say anything.'

'Strictly speaking, yes, we should have, but the man's locked up in a nursing home with some kind of mental problem, so he's not going anywhere, and I think for the time being that's probably a better place for him to be than Bow Street nick.'

'And what about Sir Marmaduke? He's been sheltering

a deserter – that's an offence as well, isn't it? Shouldn't we have arrested him too?'

'Yes, we probably should have – and perhaps we will. But I was more interested in whether he could explain what he was doing in the theatre that night and whether he had a hand in Radley's murder himself.'

'Do you think he was at that dinner with the Earl of wherever it was?'

'Pevensey – not someone I've had the pleasure of meeting, but then I wouldn't, would I? We don't move in quite the same circles. But whether I think Harvey was having dinner with him is neither here nor there – we need corroboration. I want you to make a few discreet inquiries. If you can verify that he was, he may be in the clear, and if you can't – well, that might be a different story.'

'Lucky for them it was us they were dealing with, eh, sir, not Mr Hardacre – I reckon he would've nicked the pair of them on the spot.'

'What makes you say that?'

'I was thinking of what he said about that bloke who burnt his own warehouse down – what is Field Punishment Number 1, exactly?'

'It was a very unpleasant way of dealing with soldiers who didn't do as they were told in the war. They'd be tied to a post or a gun wheel for two hours a day, for anything up to twenty-eight days. It didn't get abolished until a few years after the war. People in high places said the way the men's arms were stretched out and their legs tied together made it look too much like a crucifixion, and the Army Council put a stop to it.'

'Sounds horrible. Mr Hardacre doesn't like villains, does he?'

'Neither do I, Peter, and I don't suppose you do either. It's just a matter of how we exercise our judgement about the best way to get the job done. But in the end the law's the law, and it's not our job to change it. In this case it's Sir Marmaduke's duty to report Robinson as a deserter, and if he doesn't, I'll have to. When you're a policeman you have to do your duty, whatever you might feel about it.'

'Without fear or favour, you mean?'

'Exactly – that's what we swore to do, and that's what we must. But even if Robinson's sent back to the army, they won't have any use for him in the state he's in – if anything, he's a victim, not a criminal. I suppose I feel sorry for both of them – a man who's been through a living hell that's broken his nerves, and another man who's just tried to be a friend to him.'

'And if it turns out one of them's a murderer?'

'Then I'll have no pity at all.'

Cradock fell silent: he was wondering how old he'd have to get before he could be as decisive in his judgements as Jago, and indeed whether his muddled thinking would ever reach that degree of clarity. He sighed to himself: he supposed he'd just have to hope for the best.

'There's another thing too, sir,' he said.

'Yes?'

'When you asked Sir Marmaduke whether Radley had tried to blackmail him, did you mean maybe Radley was threatening to report him for sheltering a deserter?'

'It was certainly a possibility to consider, although as

far as evidence goes, there's no more reason to suspect Sir Marmaduke than there is to suspect Robinson. The only difference would be that if Radley was trying to get money, Sir Marmaduke would appear to have deep pockets, whereas Robinson had not long since been fished out of the English Channel with no pockets at all.'

'So what you said to the psychiatrist about that fugue thing, sir – do you think Robinson could've killed Roy Radley? I mean, I can see that if Radley really was trying to blackmail Sir Marmaduke, what with his nibs being so keen to protect Robinson he might well have decided to do away with Radley. That's a proper motive, but what motive would Robinson have?'

'I don't know, Peter. The only connection we know of between him and Radley is that they were both sheltering in that theatre, but unless there was some trouble between them that we don't know about there's no obvious reason why he should end up killing Radley.'

'Unless that bomb hitting the theatre triggered that fugue state thing, like the doctor said.'

'Yes, but the bomb didn't land until after the murder, did it?'

'Oh, yes. Sorry, sir. So what do we do next?'

'We talk to Robinson again as soon as we can, but in the meantime, while we're here I want to pop round to Mart Street and see Adelaide Mansfield again. I was thinking about how Gerald Scott was when we saw him yesterday evening. He was very defensive when I raised the question of whether Patricia Radley might've wished her uncle harm, wasn't he? I think I touched a nerve there.

And he got a bit angry too, just like before. I'm wondering why. There's also something about Miss Mansfield herself that puzzles me – she was happy enough to tell us about when Roy Radley wanted to try his hand at Shakespeare, but she hasn't said anything about all that business with the BBC.'

'That's right. I hadn't noticed that – but you'd think if he was trying to get bookings on the wireless, she and Radley would've discussed it, wouldn't you? I thought that's what agents were for.'

'Well, I'm no more an expert on agents than you are, but it does seem a bit strange that she hasn't mentioned it. I think it's time we had another chat with her – I'd like to see whether she can tell us anything more about Radley's run-in with the BBC, and particularly how that might've affected his relationship with his niece.'

They crossed Bow Street and took the short walk round to the back of the Royal Opera House and to Adelaide Mansfield's Mart Street office.

'I'm sorry to disturb you again,' said Jago once she had welcomed them in and offered them a seat, 'but there's one or two things I'd like to ask you.'

'Of course, yes – fire away.'

'Thank you. First of all, could you tell me how things work with regard to variety acts and the BBC – for example, how stage performers manage to make the transition to the wireless. I imagine that as an agent you know all about that.'

'As much as anyone in this line of work, I should

think. It's something that's kept us all very busy for nearly twenty years now. When the wireless came along it opened up a new world of entertainment, but the whole business has always been a bit fraught. A lot of performers weren't keen on broadcasting at first, especially comedians, because if they did their act on the radio, thousands of people all over the country would hear it – and nowadays it would be millions. That might make them famous, but on the other hand, in the days when they just toured round the theatres and music halls from week to week that material would have lasted them a year. The theatre owners didn't like it either, for the simple reason that if people could sit at home and hear their favourite comedians, they'd lose their customers. Some of them even put clauses in the artists' contracts to ban them from appearing on the BBC. It seems to have settled down a bit now, though, and some of the best performers are a success in both worlds – on the stage and on the air. And these days a radio success can even bring business to the theatres – *Band Waggon* transferred from the BBC to the stage at the Palladium last year and it was packing the audiences in. So I'd say it's taken a while for the old world of entertainment to accept the new world of broadcasting, but now they get along OK together.'

'People have been telling us that Roy Radley had hopes of getting signed up to appear on the BBC. Is that correct?'

'Yes, it is. He wanted me to sell the idea to them, so I did my best, but frankly it was a lost cause – there was no realistic hope of him getting work with them. The

325

drinking didn't help, of course, but even if he'd been a teetotaller, I don't think much of his act would have been broadcastable. There are things you can get away with on a stage in a theatre, but broadcasting to the whole nation on the BBC – that's a very different matter. The BBC has standards and it can't afford to let them slip. Some would say people don't pay their wireless licence fee to have filth pumped into their living room, and who's to say they should?'

'So did you give up trying?'

'I did, and I advised Roy to do the same. Really, it was a waste of time, and I think it was only making him worse to be continually rejected like that.'

'You didn't mention any of this when we spoke to you yesterday.'

'Didn't I? Well, I suppose it didn't strike me as being relevant to Roy getting stabbed to death in a theatre. I mean, I know the BBC can be harsh with performers it doesn't approve of, but I don't think it kills them.' She clapped her hand over her mouth, and her eyes widened. 'Oh, Inspector, what must you think you of me? That sounded terrible. Please forgive me – I had no intention of saying anything so callous. I don't know what I was thinking.'

'That's all right, Miss Mansfield. Don't worry.' Jago gave her a reassuring smile but made a mental note: either she'd made a regrettable slip of the tongue, or she'd neatly avoided substantiating her excuse for not mentioning Radley's trouble with the BBC. He decided not to let her off the hook. 'So why would it not be relevant?'

'Because it's so ordinary. Trying to get bigger and better bookings is part of the bread and butter of a variety artist's life – and of their agent's. I can imagine that getting a booking for the wireless at someone else's expense might conceivably give someone a motive for murder, but failing to get one – well, sad as it may be, that's something that happens to performers all the time, and they just have to get used to it.'

'Mr Radley had a niece working for the BBC, didn't he?'

'Yes – Patricia. Roy told me about her, and I met her once. As far as I know, her career was going well until the war started and they closed down the television service. That must have been very disappointing for her, but she should have every chance of success if we manage to end this terrible war and the television starts up again.'

'Did he tell you he was hoping Patricia might be able to open doors for him at the BBC?'

'He did, and I tried to steer him away from such thoughts. I said what are they going to think of her at the BBC if you keep barging in when they don't want to see you? You may have been famous once, I said, but take a look in the mirror. Do you seriously think they're going to roll out the red carpet for you? I was very concerned about Patricia – if she wasn't careful, that girl was going to find her BBC career blighted, for good. It wasn't her fault she was related to him, but he obviously thought she was going to be some kind of open sesame for him and wouldn't take no for an answer.'

'And how did he take that?'

'Well, I was wasting my breath, wasn't I? Roy was desperate and he was deluded – not a good combination. He was utterly desperate for work, but he seemed to think he could just stroll onto the wireless and be a star again. He wouldn't be the first, mind you – our business is full of people who are well beyond their best but won't retire. They still crave the applause, or they don't want to let go of the fame, or they're just plain broke and need the money. I remember the days when Roy had a Rolls-Royce, and what is he now? A homeless drunk found dead on a bomb site.'

'How did all this affect his relationship with his niece?'

'I don't know what she felt about it, but I think he was blind to what his behaviour was doing to her. He was frustrated – I remember him saying he wasn't getting anywhere with Patricia. He thought it should be easy for her to get him in. To be honest, I think he was giving up on her. He told me just a couple of weeks ago that she knew a young man at the BBC who knew everyone in the Variety Department, and he was going to try him instead. Roy thought he could still charm people, but that shows how deluded he was.'

'Did he mention the man's name?'

'No, but from what he said I got the impression he was Patricia's young man, if you know what I mean – I think he called him her beau. So maybe Roy thought this fellow would be keen to help him, if only to get him off her back.'

'And did he make contact with this young man?'

'Yes, he told me later that he'd talked to him on the telephone – but that was all he said about it.'

'Thank you, Miss Mansfield,' said Jago, getting to his feet. 'You've been very helpful. If you think of anything else, please get in touch.'

'Oh, yes, I'll be sure to,' she replied. 'Roy may have had his problems and he may have hurt a lot of people along the way, but he didn't deserve to die.'

CHAPTER FORTY-TWO

'So,' said Jago as Cradock closed the office door behind them and they took the stairs back down to Mart Street, 'when we spoke to Gerald Scott and I asked him if he'd ever met Roy Radley, he said just once and told us about Radley turning up at the BBC one day last year. But now Miss Mansfield says Radley claimed he'd made contact in the last couple of weeks with a young man at the BBC who knew everyone in the Variety Department to try to get him to help. If what she says is correct, and Radley referred to this young man as his niece's beau, I think we'd be forgiven for assuming the young man in question is Gerald Scott. Some people might say a telephone conversation isn't the same as a meeting, but even so, if it is Scott, I'd like to know why he didn't mention it. I think we'd better pop back and ask him to think again about when he last saw Radley.'

'Right,' said Cradock, looking at his watch. 'And, er, any chance of—'

'If you're thinking of cadging another lunch at the BBC, the answer's no. We'll get something later.'

Cradock submitted to his fate. 'Very good, sir.'

'Come along, then – we'll get the car.'

They retraced their steps to Bow Street and drove in the relatively basic comforts of Jago's Riley to Broadcasting House, where a phone call by the man on the reception desk resulted in Gerald Scott emerging a few minutes later from one of the lifts.

'Hello, Mr Scott,' said Jago. 'Could we have a word?'

Scott glanced round the entrance hall. 'Er, yes. Things are a bit hectic up in the office, though, so could we possibly pop outside? It'll probably be easier to talk out there.'

'Certainly,' Jago replied. He noticed that Scott had arrived with an overcoat draped over his arm and wondered whether the young administrator had already assumed that this conversation with the police was one he'd prefer to keep private from his colleagues and employer. He looked tired.

Scott took them out of the building and down a couple of nearby streets to Cavendish Square, where they found a bench to sit on. 'I like it here,' he said. 'It's like a peaceful green oasis, away from the bustle, although you can see the bomb damage over there.' He gestured towards the southern side of the square. 'I think that's probably to do with the air raid when John Lewis copped it – the whole store was burnt out, just a shell left standing. Makes you wonder what'll be left of London when this is all over. Still, we mustn't get too gloomy – what can I do for you?'

'There's one small point I'd like to clear up with you,' said Jago.

'Oh, yes?' Scott replied. 'And what's that?'

'When we were with you yesterday evening, you said you'd only met Roy Radley once, and that was last year, when he turned up out of the blue at Broadcasting House. But since then, his agent's told us that he was in contact with you only recently, and that you had a telephone conversation. Is that true?'

'Well, yes, I suppose it is.'

'You suppose?'

'I'm sorry – I mean yes, it is true.'

'Why didn't you mention it before?'

'No reason, really – I just didn't think it was important. I get phone calls all the time.'

'Can you fill in some of the details about this particular instance for me, please?'

'Yes, it's quite simple. Radley said he needed to speak to me and asked for a meeting, in my office. I told him I would not be able to meet him in Broadcasting House, or anywhere else for that matter. You heard what Patricia said about what he was up to, didn't you? If there was even a whiff of suspicion that she was somehow involved in his ludicrous schemes to get on the radio it could ruin her career. There's a lot of gossip in this business, Inspector, and once the tongues get wagging it can be difficult to stop them.'

'So you wanted to stop Roy Radley?'

'I wanted to spell out to him in no uncertain terms the effect his machinations were having on Patricia. He was making her life a misery, blighting her future, and all because of his own stupid and greedy selfishness. Something had to be done about him.'

'I see. And what exactly were you planning to do?'

'I was going to warn him off – I don't know, maybe even pay him off, anything to make him stop these ridiculous attempts to get back into the limelight.'

'So you decided you would meet him, after all?'

'Yes, I did. But I couldn't afford to be seen with him in public, so I made a plan to meet him somewhere in private.'

He hesitated, as if uncertain what to say next.

'Go on,' said Jago.

'Well . . . Patricia had mentioned to me that he'd been kicked out of his digs but the caretaker at the Prince Albert was letting him stay there on the quiet. I was due to have a meeting with ENSA in their offices at the Theatre Royal, so I decided to call in at the Prince Albert on my way and have a word with Radley. I knew it would make my journey time from the BBC to Drury Lane longer than usual, but not so long that it would come to the attention of my superiors in Broadcasting House and provoke questions. My work often takes me out of the building during the day, and there's no one standing at my shoulder all the time checking on my movements. And, in any case, it was only going to be a brief word.'

'But you said you were going to meet him in private – it wouldn't be very private if you turned up at the theatre and asked for him.'

'Ah, yes, well, I'd thought of that. I could let myself in.'

'You mean you had a key?'

'Let's just say I'd obtained the use of one.'

'Who from?'

'The ENSA man I was going to see at the Theatre Royal. His name's White, and he's one of their managers. The thing is, you see, I've had two or three meetings with him in recent weeks. It's to do with a programme the Variety Department's planning to make about what ENSA's doing to entertain the troops, and it'll feature some of the acts that he manages. I think I mentioned to you that I still do some administrative tasks for Variety, and they wanted me to liaise with him about the booking administration, to make sure he wouldn't be sending any of the acts out on the road when they were supposed to be in the studio, performing in the programme. I happened to ask him how things were going with ENSA being based at the Theatre Royal, what with the bomb damage it's suffered, and I discovered that they store some of their props at the Prince Albert.'

'I see – and you thought he might have a key?'

'Exactly. I didn't say anything at the time, but I suggested he might like to meet up for a drink one evening at the Yorkshire Grey. He said yes, so we did, at the beginning of last week. I also discovered that evening that White had something in common with Radley – he liked his drink, and he let slip something that I thought I might be able to put to good use.'

'What did he say?'

'He was complaining about ENSA. You know, the usual

sort of thing – said he was doing it to serve the nation, but he had to work all hours and the pay was terrible. I was about to say that sounds just like my job at the BBC, when he looked round the bar and came over all conspiratorial. He said fortunately he'd found a way to make ends meet. I could see he was more than tipsy, so I bought him another drink and asked him to tell me more.'

'And that's when he came out with this something that you could put to good use, was it?'

'Yes, the poor fool. He gave me a big wink and said it was simple – it was part of his job to pay the artists he'd engaged to entertain the troops, so when ENSA sent him the money for that, he had some clever way of cooking the books and giving himself what he called a bit of commission.'

'So he was pilfering funds from ENSA?'

'Exactly. Now that, of course, may be your business, but it's none of mine. I reassured him that what he'd told me would remain our little secret, and then I mentioned by the by that I'd be grateful if he could lend me his key to the Prince Albert Theatre. I think he could understand the connection between those two things, and when I offered him a fiver for his trouble, he was more than happy to oblige.'

'So he knew you wanted to get into that theatre?'

'I suppose so, yes.'

'But wasn't that a big risk for you to take? When he found out that Roy Radley had been murdered there, he'd only have had to mention it to us and you'd have been incriminated. You must've realised that, surely?'

'Now you say it I do, but I didn't know Radley was

going to be murdered, did I? I just wanted a word with him where no one could see us, and my only concern was that White shouldn't tell anyone I'd borrowed his key.'

'So you didn't tell him you wanted the key so you could meet Radley?'

'No. I mentioned his name in passing, just to see whether White knew he was sleeping at the theatre, but he didn't say anything to suggest he did. All I found out was that White wasn't a fan of his – he said he wasn't surprised a liar like Radley had come a cropper in his career, and it served him right.'

'He doesn't seem to be the only person with a low opinion of how Mr Radley conducted himself in relation to other people. Did he say why?'

'No.'

'Is it a view you share yourself?'

'Well, I certainly don't think he behaved decently with Patricia, but I couldn't tell you any more than that. I didn't know him well enough.' He paused, his eyes narrowing. 'But look here, Inspector, are you suggesting I killed Roy Radley? Why would I want to do that? It'd be stupid. Yes, I didn't want him to ruin Patricia's future, but I'd never do anything to ruin my own.'

'People don't always act that rationally in the heat of the moment, Mr Scott.'

'Heat of the moment? I don't think I ever have heated moments. Besides, I'm not the killing type. My asthma may have kept me out of the armed forces, but even if I were in perfect health, I doubt very much that I'd be of any use as a soldier. I use my brain to get through life's little challenges, not violence. I make plans that I know I can accomplish using my wits.'

'And this carefully made plan to get into the theatre and confront Radley – is that what you accomplished on Tuesday morning?'

Scott snorted dismissively. 'I would have done, certainly, but there was just one small detail that prevented me.'

'Oh yes, and what was that?'

'The simple fact that my next visit to ENSA, and therefore also my planned call at the Prince Albert, was scheduled for Wednesday, and I understand that Radley was murdered on Tuesday. As a result, I never went near that theatre. I didn't even have the key. I was planning to collect it from White on Tuesday evening – ask him.'

'We will, Mr Scott. And in the meantime, where were you between seven and nine o'clock Tuesday morning?'

'I was in Broadcasting House, trying to get some sleep after an air raid. Ask Patricia – she'll confirm that for you. We'd both been working late the previous evening, and the sirens had gone off, so we both slept in the Concert Hall, down on the lower ground floor.' He paused, as if realising a potential flaw in his own argument. 'Of course, there was a row of blankets strung across the hall to separate the men from the women, so she was on the other side and wouldn't necessarily have seen me.'

'Yes, Miss Radley's told us about the sleeping arrangements.'

Scott looked surprised. 'Really? Well, you'll understand that, then. But in any case, I'm sure if you can track down the half-dozen or so chaps who were stumbling over my mattress to get to their own, they'll confirm I was there. Perhaps you could organise an identity parade with me and a few other men in pyjamas.'

'Thank you, Mr Scott,' said Jago tersely. 'That'll be all for now – but we'll be speaking to you again.'

CHAPTER FORTY-THREE

Jago jumped up from the bench, leaving Scott seemingly lost in his own thoughts. 'Come along, Peter,' he said, and began hurrying back in the direction of Broadcasting House.

'What's up, guv'nor?' said Cradock, close on his heels. 'You mean we're going to ask Patricia Radley to confirm that alibi of his about being in the Concert Hall with her when her uncle was stabbed? It's not very strong, is it? I mean, in the dark, with some blankets hanging up between the men and the women? Once the lights were out, he could've slipped out for hours without anyone noticing.'

'We'll need to ask her,' Jago replied, 'but not right now. There'd have been no point slipping out if he couldn't get into the theatre, so first I want to find out what Reg White has to say about their little arrangement concerning the key, and whether or not Scott had it on the day of the murder.'

'But someone else could've let Scott into the theatre, couldn't they? Even if he didn't have the key, supposing he persuaded the caretaker? Or what about Sir Marmaduke Harvey? He'd have a key, wouldn't he?'

'Yes, no doubt, but we'll start with White, because he's the one Scott's relying on to support his defence.'

They got to the car and drove to the Theatre Royal, where White took them up to his makeshift office as before. The ENSA man's face bore the same morose expression as it had at their first meeting, and as Jago took a seat next to his desk, he noticed an empty glass standing among the papers. He picked it up and sniffed it. 'A little early in the day for whisky, isn't it?'

'Well, it gets a bit nippy down here in the winter with the heating off. Would you like one?'

'No, thank you.'

'Please yourself.' He opened a drawer under the desk and pulled out a half-empty bottle of whisky. 'But I will, if you don't mind – I'm cold.' He poured a generous measure into the glass and took a gulp, leaving the bottle uncorked on the desk. 'So what can I do for you?'

'I'd like to see if you can help us on a point of accuracy.'

'I'll do my best.'

'When we spoke to you before, you confirmed that you have a key to the Prince Albert Theatre.'

'Correct.'

'You also said you thought someone might have taken that key from your coat on Wednesday of last week and replaced it later the same day.'

'Yes, that's right.'

'Did you happen to see the cleaner that day?'

'No, I don't think so – why do you ask?'

'No reason – she just works there on Wednesdays. I also asked you whether you'd lent your key to anyone recently, and you said you hadn't. Correct?'

'Yes.'

'I must caution you, Mr White, that you are not obliged to say anything, but anything you say may be given in evidence.'

'What are you getting at?'

'I believe you're acquainted with Mr Gerald Scott, who works for the BBC.'

White shrugged. 'What of it?'

'Since we last saw you, Mr Scott has told us that he persuaded you to lend him your key. Is that true?'

White breathed in sharply. He looked surprised, as though he didn't know what to say. Eventually he mumbled a reply. 'It's true.'

'I'm sorry, Mr White, I couldn't quite hear you.'

'I said it's true.'

'So you lied to us, didn't you?'

'Maybe.'

'Not maybe, Mr White – you lied to us.'

'All right, damn you, I lied. Are you happy now?'

'On what day did you give it to him?'

'Monday.'

'You're sure?'

'Yes.'

'So this was after your key had gone missing and then turned up again.'

'Yes, of course it was. Don't ask me why, though – I've no idea.'

'I don't imagine the owner of the Prince Albert would be pleased to hear you'd provided a stranger with a key to his theatre, and I don't suppose your employers would either. You'd have been sacked. Why did Mr Scott want a key?'

'I don't know – he didn't say. He just asked me if he could borrow one, and I said yes.'

'And you didn't think to mention this to us when you knew that a man had been murdered in the theatre on Tuesday morning?'

'Well, no, I didn't. I mean, that fellow Scott was a respectable man – he works for the BBC, doesn't he? Do you mean he did it? He killed that fellow? I just lent him the key as a favour – I wasn't to know he was going to murder someone.'

'I don't believe you, Mr White. I don't believe you'd risk your job just to do a favour to a stranger, especially one that involved providing him with the key to a theatre. Did he coerce you?'

'No.'

'Mr Scott says you told him you'd been fiddling your accounts here, stealing from your employer. Is that true?'

White banged the top of the desk with his fist and glared at Jago. 'So that's it, is it? Some good for nothing old tramp's been murdered, and you come down here to grill me about a bit of petty cash? You should try living on what I get for this thankless task they call a job. When we sent our first concert parties out to entertain the troops last year, do you know what our boss said? He said you're doing

342

national work as essential to the soldiers as food and drink. Well, that's what he thinks, but it's not what my pay packet says. Overworked and underpaid, that's what I am. What if I do take a few shillings from the till when it's no more than I deserve? We're in the middle of a war and you've got nothing better to do than persecute someone like me who's trying to do his bit for the country. Why don't you get out more and do something about the real thieves? People who lie through their back teeth and steal a man's whole life.'

'Are you talking about someone in particular?'

'What? Are you stupid? Of course I am – Roy Radley. Don't you know anything about him?'

'Not as much as you, I suspect. Tell me more.'

'The man was evil. People think he's a lovely old comedian who'd fallen on hard times, but I know better. I didn't need to meet him to know what he was like. He was a cheat, and he cheated his way right to the top of the bill.' White gripped the edge of the desk, but whether this was to steady his body or his nerves Jago couldn't tell. 'The fact is,' he growled, calming himself, 'he ruined my life, and I don't doubt he did the same to other people too.'

'What exactly did he do?'

'It's simple – he stole my act.'

'Are you saying you were on the stage yourself?'

White paused at the mention of the stage. 'Yes, a long time ago – when I was young and not as savvy as I am now. I started off as an actor – a serious actor, mind, in a touring company. But it didn't work out – for some reason I always ended up with the smallest part in the play and I wasn't getting anywhere. So I tried my hand at comedy and teamed up with a pal to make a double act. I wrote the material and he was the straight man, which meant I delivered the gags and got the laughs, so I liked that. I did quite well, really, but only on the northern circuit – not many northerners get bookings in the south. I was only playing the number three theatres, which were pretty run-down in those days, but the audiences liked me, and I thought I was going somewhere. But then the war came along, and in 1915 I went off to be a soldier. I lasted two years, which was pretty good going, but then I got wounded. They had to bring me back home, and I spent seven weeks in a hospital in London – in the end the army discharged me, and that was the end of the war for me.'

'Would you mind telling me which hospital that was?'

'Yes, it was Endell Street – a military hospital, but all the doctors were women. Why do you ask?'

'Because there was an incident there in 1917, when Roy Radley went in to entertain the wounded servicemen, and one of them got very angry. Was that you?'

'I don't remember.'

'You called him a cheat and a thief.'

'Who told you that?'

'Never you mind.'

White glared at him. 'So what if I did? All the gags he was using on that ward were mine – he must've seen us somewhere up north and decided he'd just take them for nothing for himself. It's plagiarism, but that's just a fancy name for it. I call a spade a spade, and I call that stealing.'

'So it's illegal?'

'It should be, but all we've got is the 1911 Copyright

Act, and that doesn't say anything about gags in a variety act, so pirates like him get away with it.'

'I can see that would've made you angry.'

'You don't know the half of it. Years later I had a trip down to London for a funeral – it might as well have been my own. I went to a show at the Holborn Empire, and there was the great Roy Radley, top of the bill – and this time he wasn't just telling a few of my jokes, he'd pinched my whole act. He'd changed it a bit, of course, to make it into his market porter character, but it was still my act. You can't imagine what that felt like for me. I was livid. It was like he'd stolen my life, and there was nothing I could do about it. I'd never have the money to take him to court, and even if I tried, they'd probably just laugh at me. Fred Karno shelled out two thousand pounds on lawyers when someone pinched his material, and the judge found against him, so what chance would I have? People like me who have their material stolen are just supposed to crawl back where they came from.'

'And that's what you did?'

'Of course I did. I knew I was never going to make the big time, not if people at the top were going to steal my act. That's the thing about variety – the public love to go and see the stars, but they don't realise what really goes on. It's dog eat dog – every performer wants to get higher up the bill, and they'll play any tricks they can to get there. Even if you're at the top it doesn't mean you're safe. Fred Karno was a star, wasn't he? Still is, in my book. But he said he used to see plagiarists in the audience getting out their notebooks and writing down every line that got a

345

laugh, then using it in their own acts – and when Fred took his own show somewhere, after the first house the theatre management would ask him to cut bits out because they'd already been done by other people. He called it wholesale piracy, and he was right. I tell you, I was sick of being a comedian, and that meant I was finished as an entertainer. I packed it in.'

'And what did you do then?'

'That's when I got the job at the Fortune in Bradford, like I said, and then the war brought me down here.'

'When you joined ENSA, you mean?'

'Yes.'

'And when did you find out Roy Radley was living in the Prince Albert?'

White's shoulders slumped and he stared at Jago like a lost man. 'I don't know – just a couple of weeks ago, probably.'

'The man you were livid with because he'd stolen your life. What did you do about that?'

'I went to see him.'

'And what did you have in mind?'

'To have it out with him. I wanted to tell him what he'd done to me, that he'd ruined my life. I wanted to punch him in the face.'

'So what happened?'

White moved a finger to his eye to wipe away the beginnings of a tear. 'I let myself into the theatre early in the morning, when it was still dark. It was all quiet inside, but then I heard someone moving about and a man's voice, singing some old coster song from years ago like a

Cockney. I followed the sound and saw him opening a door and going through, so I nipped over and followed him in. It was the gents' lavatories, and he was running some water into one of the basins. "Roy Radley?" I said, and he said, "Yes – who wants him?" Then he turned round, and I could see it was him. I told him I had a bone to pick with him, and he laughed. He said, "A lot of people say that to me. What's your particular bone?" What a cheek. I told him what he'd done, and that I knew. "You stole my act," I said, but he just stared at me and said, "Sorry, old chap, but it's every man for himself in this business, isn't it?" He looked tipsy and was swaying a bit. He made me angry. I said he'd killed my dream and my career – he'd destroyed my life.'

'And what did he say?'

'He said he'd never seen me before in his life, and then he just laughed again, as if it was all a big joke. It wasn't enough that he'd taken everything from me – now he was laughing at me. I decided to wipe that stupid grin off his face, so I punched him – yes, right in the face. It felt good, and I was about to do it again when suddenly he came at me like a fury. He was wild, and it was all I could do to dodge the blows. Then I saw something out of the corner of my eye on a bench – it looked like a screwdriver, so I grabbed it and waved it at him, told him to keep back or I'd skewer him. But he laughed at me again and lunged towards me. I jabbed at him and the screwdriver went . . . it went into his belly. I let go, and he fell back onto the floor by the basins and just lay there, groaning.'

'And you left him?'

347

White nodded meekly. 'Yes. I suppose I just panicked. I cleared off out of it.'

'And that's where he died. His last words to the police officer who found him were that he'd stolen, he'd lied, and he'd killed.'

He nodded again. 'That must've been his last shred of conscience, then. He'd stolen my act, he'd lied his way to the top, and he'd taken my life from me. He'd as good as killed me, and now I've killed him. I suppose we're quits. I'm sorry.' He paused, as if sobered by his own words, and bit his lip. 'Tell me, Inspector, do you ever feel like you've wasted your life?'

Jago was silent.

White shrugged his shoulders. 'I do. I had a talent once, or thought I did. I didn't bury it, but it wasn't big enough for the dreams I had, and then what little I had was stolen from me. What's a man to do when he chases a dream but can't catch it? When he ends up in a place like this? All I've got left now is regret, and regret's such a powerful thing, isn't it?'

Jago left the question unanswered. 'You're under arrest,' he said, 'on suspicion of murder.'

It seemed as though White had not even heard these words. He cocked his head to one side and gazed wistfully into the mirror on the wall of this theatrical dressing room turned seedy administrative office. 'I could have been a success, you know. A comedian, an actor – loved by everyone. Listen – I can hear the applause.' He sighed, and his face fell. 'But now I suppose the show must go on without me. Do you know that old poem, "Closing Night"?

It's about an artist's final performance.' He lifted his chin and slowly addressed his reflection in the mirror. '"They cheered him to the echo, they applauded long and loud. The audience gazed upon him, and he bowed."'

As Jago reached into his pocket, White turned towards him with an expression of intense but strangely dignified sadness in his face. He gave a slight bow of the head and an even slighter smile, then extended his hands forward, his wrists lightly touching in a gesture of submission. 'I see you've got the requisite prop, Inspector. And yes, you're right – I think handcuffs would be appropriate for this scene. Shall we go?'

CHAPTER FORTY-FOUR

They took White to Bow Street police station and saw him safely into custody, then went for a final look at Drury Lane. It was quiet, and the few people on the street looked intent on getting home before darkness returned and brought with it the threat of new air raids. The tangled remains of the Prince Albert Theatre's entrance had been carted away and the damage boarded up. The pavement outside it had been swept clean, but still the former place of entertainment and laughter had a sadly defeated look about it. As they crossed the street to take a closer look, they saw a familiar figure in the distance: it was Sympathetic Sal. She was engaged in what seemed like a friendly conversation with a customer. The man had his back to them, but when they drew nearer and Sal's expression showed that she'd recognised them, he turned round to face them, revealing that he was in the act of pinning a flower to her coat.

'Good afternoon,' said Jago. 'You're out of hospital then, Mr Tipton.'

'Yes,' Tipton replied. 'They said I was mending nicely and I could go home. It's good to be out.'

Jago doffed his hat to Sal. 'And good day to you. How are you today?'

'I'm fine, thanks,' she said. 'Have you got your murderer yet?'

'We've made an arrest.'

'Who's that, then?'

'A man called White, who works for ENSA. Do you know him?'

'No, never heard of him, but congratulations.'

'Thank you.'

'Actually, I'm glad to run into you, because . . . well, to tell you the truth, I've been feeling a bit bad about not telling you my name. You must've thought I was a crook or something.'

Jago shook his head. 'Innocent until proven guilty – that's the way it works. I expect you had your reasons.'

'I did, but it was just habit really. It's given me a bit of trouble over the years, you see. The thing is, the name I was born with was Sally Crippen.'

'Oh.'

She gave a bitter laugh. 'If you could see your face, you'd know what it was like for me. Everyone's always had the same reaction – surprise or shock, depending on how good they were at hiding their feelings, followed by everything from horror to disgust.'

'I'm sorry.'

'It's not your fault – it's just the way we are. But I ask you, what's a girl like me done to deserve that? It's about the worst moniker in the world to end up with. I might as well be called Hitler.'

'Yes, I can see that might've been a problem.'

'That's not the half of it. When I was a kid, it was fine, just an ordinary name back then – no one batted an eyelid. But when that bloke got arrested for murdering his old lady, well, it all changed pretty quick. Your lot put him in a cell just round the corner from here, at Bow Street nick, and then he was up before the magistrate at the police court next door. Thirty years ago that was, but I remember it like it was yesterday – there was hundreds of people outside, and they all wanted to get in and watch. The coppers had to get reinforcements in. I think the public hated him – and when he ended up at the Old Bailey and got hanged, well, that was it. I'm no relation, mind, but all the same, it was a right pain in the neck for me having to explain my name all the time. So anyway, I'm glad we bumped into you – it means I've got that off my chest, and you won't need to wonder what I was up to any more, wandering around with no name. You've been very understanding.'

'Think nothing of it. I'm glad I've bumped into you too – there's something I'd like to ask you, Mr Tipton.'

'Oh, yes?' said Tipton. 'What's that about?'

'It's to do with Roy Radley.'

'Right,' said Sal, interrupting him. 'If you're going to talk about him, I don't want to know. I'm just going to have a sit down on that wall over there and rest my legs.'

She perched decorously on a low wall that looked far enough away to be out of earshot but still enabled her to keep an eye on them.

'It's just a quick question, Mr Tipton,' said Jago. 'The first time we spoke to you, when you were in the hospital, you mentioned that Reg White, the ENSA man, used to pop down to the Prince Albert Theatre to deal with props and so on.'

'That's right.'

'Did you chat with him from time to time?'

'We passed the time of day a bit sometimes, yes.'

'Can you remember if Mr Radley's name ever came up in the conversation?'

Tipton thought for a moment. 'Yes, it did once. I remember him asking me what I thought of him.'

'And what did you say?'

'Not much.' He paused, then corrected himself. 'Sorry, I don't mean I didn't say much, I mean I said I didn't think much of Roy. He said he was surprised, because he'd got the impression everyone liked Roy, so I said if he had, it was the wrong impression. He asked me why, and I told him about what Roy did to Daisy and how he treated her afterwards.'

Jago turned aside to Cradock. 'There's your lamplighter, Peter, I suspect,' he murmured.

'What's that?' said Tipton.

'Oh, nothing,' Jago replied. 'Just something Detective Constable Cradock and I were discussing earlier – a police matter.'

'Sorry. I was just going to say do you think what I said

353

to White could have anything to do with what happened to Roy?'

'Not directly, no, but as far Mr White's concerned, I suspect he was itching for a fight, and what you said may've been like a match to tinder. You weren't to know, but I think it could've been the final straw that pushed him over the edge and resulted in him attacking Mr Radley.'

'Oh, no – I feel terrible.'

'None of this is your fault, Mr Tipton. You had no way of knowing what he'd do – he's responsible for his own actions, and the court will decide what becomes of him.'

Tipton fell silent, and Sal must have noticed, because she came over to join them.

'I don't want to rush you, Inspector,' she said, 'but it looked like maybe you'd finished. It's just that we're on our way to see someone. He'll be expecting us.'

'Oh, well, I mustn't detain you. Thank you for explaining about your name, though – it must've made life very difficult for you.'

'Yes, well, like I said, that name was a pain in the neck – and in one or two other places I could mention but won't.' She laughed, and it struck Jago that it was a different laugh to the one he'd heard just moments before, when she'd been talking about the past – there was no trace of bitterness in it. She slipped her hand under Tipton's arm and pulled him a little closer with a smile. 'But we're thinking we might change it, aren't we, Stan?'

Tipton looked down at her with a smile as wide as her own. 'That's right, Inspector. You know, when I was in hospital, you and Mr Cradock visited me, didn't you? But

that was in the line of duty, wasn't it? No one else came –
except Sal. I asked her why she'd come to see me, and she
said it was just because she cared. I've known her on and
off for years – she's always been around, selling her flowers,
and I suppose everyone knows her. Trouble is, back in those
days I had my eyes fixed on someone else, but it didn't work
out. It was only when I was on that ward and Sal came to
see me that I realised what a lovely person she really is.
We've decided we're going to see the rector now and have
a little chat with him.'

'That's right,' said Sal. 'It's never too late, is it, Inspector?'
She turned away, arm in arm with Tipton, and with what
Jago was sure was an unfamiliar spring in her step. She
looked back over her shoulder as they went. 'I told you,
didn't I, Mr Jago? Nobody takes much notice of me, but
Stan did – he noticed me. I like that.'

Jago smiled and watched in silence as they strolled away
in the direction of Covent Garden and St Paul's Church.

'So you reckon Tipton was the lamplighter, do you, sir?'
said Cradock as the couple receded from view.

'Yes, I think possibly he was. Not a deliberate one –
I don't think he said those things to provoke White into
killing Radley. White must've been angry and resentful
and carried a chip on his shoulder for years, and I think
what Tipton said to him just fuelled the flames of that anger
without him knowing it. So maybe Stan Tipton wasn't
exactly a lamplighter in the way I thought – more like the
man who accidentally shows a light in the blackout and
his neighbour's house gets bombed. It's only a small thing
done in ignorance, and there's no way of knowing whether

it actually caused the outcome, but one way or another someone ends up getting hurt.'

'Or even killed.'

'Unfortunately, yes. But I don't think Tipton intended any harm – it was just one of those things.'

Cradock made no comment – he seemed to be more interested in following Tipton and Sal's progress down the street until eventually they disappeared round a corner.

'Ah,' he said, turning to Jago. 'Wasn't that lovely. It's just like in a film, isn't it? You know – kind lady gets her knight in shining armour, and lonely old bloke finally finds love.'

Jago cleared his throat emphatically. 'Right, Peter, that's enough of that. I'm very happy for them, but now I think it's time for us to go home.'

CHAPTER FORTY-FIVE

Jago spared a thought for Reginald White as he and Cradock made their way to Rita's cafe on Christmas Day. Following his arrest, White had appeared at the Bow Street magistrates' court, where he'd been committed for trial at the Old Bailey and remanded in custody. Even before his downfall, Jago reflected, the man from ENSA might not have been expecting an especially jolly Christmas, but now, behind bars, it would surely be a miserable time. No chance of White getting a slap-up dinner with all the trimmings this year, he thought. Not that the general population would necessarily fare much better, of course: the depredations of war had left many of the traditional Christmas trappings in short supply. Still, he mused, if George Radley was right about the national shortage of mistletoe and Rita hadn't been able to procure any, it might prove to be a blessing in disguise for her guests.

He tapped at the cafe's door, and Rita opened it. 'Come in out of the cold,' she said, 'and Happy Christmas!'

'Happy Christmas to you too, Rita,' he replied, discreetly glancing over her shoulder as they went in and noting with relief no evidence of mistletoe. The cafe was closed, of course, for Christmas Day, and the only other person Jago could see was Dorothy, seated at a table in the middle of the room. She nodded her head to them with a welcoming smile, and Jago felt a curious warmth: seeing her made him feel as though he were in some way coming home.

'I'll go and give Emily a shout,' said Rita. 'She's upstairs fixing her hair or something. I think she's just come over a bit shy.'

Rita went to the door at the back of the cafe and shouted an instruction up the stairs in a voice that brooked no dissent. A faint cry of 'Coming, Mum' filtered back down to them.

'There, she'll be here in a minute. Come and sit down.'

They joined Dorothy at the table. Jago sat next to her, and Cradock took a chair facing her, as if keen to keep an eye on the woman who'd previously shown a disarming habit of probing his private thoughts, especially about Emily.

'Now then,' Rita continued brightly, 'I wanted to make the room look nice and Christmassy, but you know what it's like this year – even worse than last. I usually make some nice new paper chains, but I kept last year's ones just in case, and now it looks like it's just as well I did, what with paper being so short. I couldn't get any balloons either, on account of them being made out of rubber, but I did get some left-over tinsel down from the loft and I think that's made it all look nice.'

Jago suspected she would have gone into more detail about her improvised Christmas decorations, but she was interrupted by the arrival of Emily. It was some time since he'd seen her, but he was struck by her good looks: the old-fashioned word 'comely' came to mind. He glanced at Cradock, whom he knew to be her devoted admirer, and even possibly by now her suitor, though he might deny it. The look on Cradock's face was unambiguous: the lad was obviously smitten. Jago felt a kind of paternal pleasure at the sight.

Rita introduced Emily to Dorothy. 'Pleased to meet you,' said Emily, on her best behaviour. Jago feared she might be about to curtsey, but to his relief she didn't.

'And I'm very pleased to meet you, Emily,' Dorothy replied. She paused, and Jago saw Cradock tense, as if in fear that her next words would be 'I've heard so much about you.' But Dorothy was used to being diplomatic in new company. 'I'm a stranger in your country,' she continued, 'and your mother's been a friend to me.'

Cradock breathed a sigh of relief, and Rita beamed. 'And you've been a friend to me,' she said to Dorothy, 'and that's why I wanted to get us all together for a good old English Christmas dinner. I didn't like to think of you being stuck in a hotel all on your own and so far from home on Christmas Day.'

Jago imagined that if you had to spend Christmas in a hotel, the Savoy would probably offer as good a substitute for home comforts as you could wish for, but he knew Rita was all kindness, and he was touched by the fact that she wanted to take care of Dorothy.

Emily had taken the chair next to Cradock, and now she edged it closer to him: only a couple of inches, but enough for Jago to notice her movement and to draw his own unspoken conclusions about its meaning.

Dorothy threw an inquisitive smile in the direction of Cradock. 'So, Peter,' she said, 'did you go to see that movie?'

'Er, which one was that?'

'The one I recommended last time I saw you – *Pride and Prejudice*.'

Cradock glanced uncertainly at Emily beside him. 'Yes, we did.'

'And what did you make of it?'

'I thought it was soppy, really,' he said. 'Loads of women running around in silly bonnets, and so many sisters in the family I couldn't tell which one was which. And that mother of theirs was ridiculous – she just spent all her time trying to marry them off.'

Emily's face suggested disappointment.

'And what about you, Emily?' Dorothy asked gently. 'Did you think it was soppy?'

Emily was timid in her response: she'd never met an American lady journalist before, never mind being quizzed by one on the subject of Hollywood movies. 'I'm not sure,' she said tentatively. 'I don't think I'd call it soppy – I thought it was quite nice.'

'I think the experts would agree with you, Emily – the review of *Pride and Prejudice* that I read said it was a picture of irresistible charm.'

360

Emily took this as a mark of approval and felt emboldened to continue. 'I thought it was funny, too – all those snobs putting on airs and graces, but they got their comeuppance. I liked that.'

'So was it better than that other movie Peter took you to? What was it – *The Saint Takes Over*?'

Emily rolled her eyes: words were not needed.

'What did you think of Laurence Olivier?' Dorothy continued.

'I thought he was good at acting – those eyes of his made me feel all funny inside. It was a bit silly, though, with him and Greer Garson – I mean, it was obvious that Mr Darcy and Elizabeth had fallen for each other, but they didn't seem to realise it. I was sitting there just wanting to knock their heads together and say wake up, you two, can't you see it?'

Cradock shifted uncomfortably in his seat and drew a glance of concern from Dorothy. Jago felt relieved not to be the focus of her attention and did his best to remain aloof from the discussion. If asked to comment, he would plead ignorance on the grounds of not having seen the film and hope not to be drawn further.

Rita, who'd been listening carefully, joined in. 'Well, I haven't seen it, but what I say is, if it's a nice film about people falling in love and it's set back in the past and no one's killing anyone else, then it's just the ticket for times like these. We all need a bit of escapism, don't we, and even if it's romantic tosh it helps take your mind off bombs and rationing and all that. My favourite thing's those Ivor Novello shows – I love them. I went to see *The Dancing Years* last year at the Theatre Royal, down Drury Lane, before the war started, and it was wonderful. Such beautiful songs he writes – he had "I Can Give You the Starlight" in that one. It sent shivers down my spine, and that's a fact.'

She sighed decisively, as if this was the last word that needed to be said.

Jago ventured to change the subject. 'Peter and I have been spending a bit of time in Drury Lane recently,' he said.

'Oh, yes?' said Rita. 'You've been taking him to the theatre?'

'Yes, but not to see musicals, I'm afraid. We've been investigating a death at the Prince Albert Theatre, and it meant we had to visit the Theatre Royal too, and the market in Covent Garden.'

'Well, if it's about one of your horrible murders I don't want to know. It's Christmas Day and I want you all to enjoy yourselves, so we'll have no talk of grisly goings-on in the West End round this table, if you don't mind.'

'That's fine by me, Rita. I'll be very happy just to enjoy an excellent Christmas dinner – and thank you very much for all the work you must've put in to making it for us. If there's anyone who knows how to lay on a good spread for her friends no matter what the circumstances, it's got to be you.'

'Well, dear, I won't deny I was up early this morning peeling spuds and making the stuffing – and that won't be sage and onion either, because I couldn't get the onions, but I did get some chestnuts, so you'll be having chestnut stuffing instead.'

'And very nice too, I'm sure.'

'I hope it will be. I've got some help in for today too –

you remember young Phyllis, who does a bit of waitressing and stuff for me? I'm paying her to come in for the day to help out and keep an eye on things – I can't be out here being your hostess and in the kitchen being the cook at the same time. She'll be helping me with the washing-up and everything when you've gone too. And since the government's kindly decided we can only have one day off this Christmas instead of two, like we usually do, I'll be opening tomorrow morning for business as usual, so I'll be kicking you all out before it gets too late. But not until we've heard the King's speech on the wireless, of course. I don't want to miss that – I think he's a lovely man.'

'What's on the menu, then?'

'Well, dear, I've done my best to make it a proper Christmas dinner like we used to have in the good old days when you could just go out and buy whatever you fancied. I was a bit worried about whether I'd be able to get a nice bird for the table – the butcher told me the government's put a ban on turkey imports this year, so they're a bit scarce. But, er, well, being as how I'm in the catering trade I've got one or two useful poultry contacts and I've managed to get one. Only a small one, mind.' She glanced at Jago. 'Here, you won't tell on me, will you? I don't think I've done anything illegal – they said this one's from Ireland.'

Jago smiled back at her. 'Don't worry, Rita – it's the season of goodwill, isn't it?'

'To some, yes. But I'm rationing my goodwill this year – I've got none for that bloke who's causing us all this trouble.'

'The gentleman with the moustache?'

'That's the one. I'm not having him round here for

Christmas if I can help it. The way he's been blowing up the gas mains recently, I've been worrying about whether the gas pressure was going to hold up long enough for my oven to cook it – those turkeys take hours, you know. All I'm hoping is he doesn't try anything on this afternoon – I don't want any air raids spoiling our fun. But we didn't have any bombs last night, did we? Perhaps he's decided to have the day off too. Anyway, I'm off to the kitchen now to make sure Phyllis hasn't burnt anything, and hopefully dinner will be served in a few minutes.'

Rita left to attend to her duties, and shortly afterwards she and Phyllis brought their Christmas dinner to the table, with heartfelt apologies from Rita that the portions were smaller than she would have provided if there hadn't been a war on. They ate, and Dorothy pronounced the cooking excellent in every respect. Rita basked in the praise, and Jago was pleased that her hospitality had received such warm appreciation.

'That was wonderful, Rita,' he said when he'd cleared his plate. 'I'm sure I speak for all of us when I say thank you for making such a lovely Christmas dinner for us. But there's just one thing that I know Peter's particularly concerned about.'

'Oh, yes? And what's that?' said Rita.

Cradock looked nervous: were the two of them conniving to trick him into making some kind of public statement about his affection for Emily to mark the occasion?

'It's simple,' said Jago. 'Will there be Christmas pudding?'

Cradock's moment of torment passed.

'Of course there'll be Christmas pudding,' said Rita.

'What sort of hostess do you take me for? Besides, my mum always used to say it's bad luck if you don't make one. It might not be quite what it used to be, but there's been lots of recipes going around for a wartime version, so I've used one of them, with no eggs or sugar and a bit of carrot chucked in to make it sweet. Oh, and no brandy butter, of course – it'll be served with custard.'

'I suspect Peter might regard custard as more of a treat than even brandy butter,' said Jago. 'Isn't that right, Peter?'

'Oh, yes, definitely,' Cradock replied, relieved that in this respect at least it wasn't difficult to please Rita.

She smiled at him affectionately. 'I've even put a good old silver threepenny bit in it. That's good luck if you find it – as long as you don't swallow it, of course. So be careful, won't you?'

She turned to Dorothy. 'Do you do that in America? I don't mean a threepenny bit, of course – you don't have them, do you? Would it be one of your dollars or whatever instead?'

'Actually, Rita, I don't think we do.'

'Ah, well – we do. I was going to put one of those new twelve-sided ones in, but then Phyllis told me you shouldn't, because they're made out of some metal that's not safe – at least that's what the Royal Mint said, apparently.'

'My mum always used to do that,' said Cradock. 'Put a silver threepenny bit in, I mean. She used to say it meant good luck too, and you'd always have money if you found it, but I think she used to wangle it so that I got it. She used to put some other lucky charm things in too, but I was always more interested in the pudding itself.'

'Quite right too,' said Rita, 'considering all the work the mums have to put into making it. I thought I'd add a few other charms too this year. There's a little ring – that one means you'll get married – and a button that means you'll always be a bachelor, and a thimble that means you'll be an old maid. But it's only silly nonsense, isn't it?'

Jago was relieved that she seemed not to take the idea too seriously. He didn't know which would have been worse in this company, to find a button or a ring.

'There was another charm people used to put in for good luck, wasn't there?' Rita continued. 'A little swastika. Can you imagine that?'

'Ah, yes,' said Dorothy. 'Times have changed. When I was a girl my hometown baseball team was the Boston Braves – they used to have red swastikas on their caps for good luck, although I have to say they haven't had much luck in recent years. And now that Hitler's put it on his flag and painted it on his dive-bombers, I suspect no one will ever associate it with good luck again.'

'Well,' said Rita, 'I can promise you there won't be any little swastikas in my pudding. I'll go and fetch it from the kitchen now, and I hope you'll all enjoy it and you'll get whatever good luck you're hoping for. You can all make your own secret wishes.'

The knowing way she looked round the table before she left gave the impression that she was reading their minds, but Jago was confident, or at least hopeful, that this was not a skill she possessed.

She returned with a Christmas pudding and a jug of custard on a tray, and set it down on the table, then took a knife to the pudding and began to put portions into bowls for her guests. 'Remember you might have something in your piece, so chew carefully – we don't want any broken teeth on Christmas Day, do we?'

The first of them to find something was Dorothy, who proudly held up a silver threepence.

'Well done,' said Rita. 'That means you'll always have money – and Americans are all rich, so that's just right.'

Cradock looked disappointed that someone else had found the one hidden item that was actually worth finding, even if it was only threepence, but he soon produced a charm of his own. He was about to hold it up for all to see, but then realised it was a ring, and put it down quickly. As he did so, the image of Mrs Bennet from the film flashed into his mind, the mother bent on marrying off her daughters – but her face was Rita's. She'd wangled it, he thought, just like his own mum used to, although even she'd never played a trick like that on him. He blushed to the roots of his hair and hoped that no one had seen.

One person at least had seen, however: it was Jago, who smiled benevolently at Cradock's discomfiture. Poor Peter, he thought. He dug his spoon into the Christmas pudding in his bowl and felt it jar against something solid. A mild sense of apprehension crept into his mind as he prised the pudding apart, and then grew as a small object was revealed. It was the button, in Rita's scheme of things the harbinger of lifelong bachelorhood. He didn't know what to say: whether he welcomed it or bemoaned it, there were people at the table – not least Rita herself – who might take it amiss. He gave a forced laugh. 'Ah, yes – thank you, Rita.

I'll keep that for next time my shirt needs one. As you said, silly nonsense.'

He studied the button intently to avoid catching the eye of anyone else at the table, until Emily squealed with distress on finding a thimble in her pudding, and her mother abruptly switched the conversation to the recent rise in the cost of living.

Jago looked at his watch: soon it would be time to listen to the King's Christmas Day address to the nation on the wireless. After that, if Rita kept her word, she'd be kicking them out. It would be the end of a very enjoyable occasion, but it also offered the possibility that he'd get a bit of time alone with Dorothy. And that, he thought, would be the brandy butter on his Christmas pudding.

CHAPTER FORTY-SIX

As it happened, when the King finished his broadcast address to the Empire and the world, not to mention the assembled party of friends at the cafe in West Ham Lane, Rita had corralled her guests into a protracted game of charades. Only when this had run its course did she allow them to go their separate ways. They said their goodbyes, and Jago offered to see Dorothy back to her hotel.

By the time they got to the Savoy it was early evening and the streets were quiet, but the raucous singing they heard as they passed a pub suggested that people were still managing to celebrate Christmas in their traditional fashion.

'Shall we go for a drink?' said Dorothy. 'I would invite you in to the American Bar in the hotel, but it'll be full of my American press colleagues, and that would be just too much like a busman's holiday for me. Are all the pubs open today?'

'Most of them, I should think,' Jago replied. 'The only difference this year is that my boss, the Metropolitan Police Commissioner, said he's not allowing them any special extensions to their licensed hours for Christmas. I think that's the first time it's ever happened, but they can still stay open till their normal closing time. I can't guarantee we'll find a quiet one, though.'

'How about that little bar you took me to once? The Blue Moon. Back in October, wasn't it?'

'I think you're right, yes. It's only five minutes' walk from here – let's see if it's open.'

It was only when they arrived in Floral Street that Dorothy remembered. She stopped in her tracks. 'I'm so sorry – I didn't think. This is Covent Garden, isn't it? There's me talking about not wanting a busman's holiday, and I've brought you back to the very place where you've just been investigating a murder. Shall we find somewhere else?'

'No, don't worry about it on my account,' said Jago. 'It doesn't bother me. We've got a man in custody on a charge of murder, and right now, as far as I'm concerned that's all that matters.'

'So how did your case go? I can understand Rita not wanting to hear about it at her special lunch, but I'd like to know.'

'Thank you. It was about revenge, I suppose. A professional comedian who thought another performer had stolen his act and become a great success while his own career failed. It all started years ago, but it seems to have left a bitterness in his heart that never went away. Now he's in a cell, and the other man's dead.'

'That's so sad. People talk about a root of bitterness, don't they? I guess it can take hold and fill your whole life.'

'That's what seems to have happened to this man, certainly. But the fact remains he took a life, and one way or another he'll have to answer for that. I'm just glad it won't be me who has to decide how.'

'I don't envy you your job – but I'm glad it's someone like you doing it.'

He smiled. 'It's not all bad, and someone's got to clean up the mess, haven't they? Now come on, let's go and try that bar.'

They walked on to the Blue Moon and found it open. It looked about half full and sounded a lot quieter than the pub they'd passed earlier, so they took a table.

'Can I get you a drink?' said Jago. 'Last time we came here you had a lemonade, I believe.'

'You remember?'

'Yes.'

'I'm impressed. In that case I will.'

'And would you like something to eat?'

'Just a little, perhaps, but not right now – let's see how we feel later.'

'OK,' said Jago. He went to the bar and returned with her drink, and a pint of mild and bitter for himself. 'Cheers,' he said, raising his glass as he took his seat, 'and Merry Christmas.'

Dorothy raised her own in reply. 'Merry Christmas.'

'How did you like Rita's little party?'

'It was lovely – she's so kind. She was very keen not to

miss the King's speech on the radio, wasn't she?'

'Oh, yes, Rita's a big fan of the King.'

'And you?'

'I think he's a good man who never expected to be king and would've been happy living quietly with his family in the shadow of his big brother. But then when his brother decided he didn't want to be king after all, suddenly he had to take it on. I don't suppose it's what he wanted, but he's done his duty.' Jago sipped a little beer and felt refreshed. 'But I want to hear about you – what have you been up to this week?'

'Oh, writing, of course. And I'd like to point out that while your British newspapers had the day off today and won't be published tomorrow either, the *Boston Post* comes out on Christmas Day just the same as every other day of the year, so I was working yesterday, and this morning too.'

'Very commendable. And what did you write?'

'Mainly about something Rita herself mentioned, funnily enough – the fact that we didn't have any bombs last night. It was quite a change, wasn't it? She thought maybe Hitler had decided to take the day off, but I'm not sure he does that. What I was writing about is a more intriguing question – whether there's actually some kind of Christmas truce going on without anyone saying it.'

'You think that's possible?'

'Well, let's just say I was reviewing the evidence.'

'Which is?'

'Just little things. For example, last month an MP asked your Mr Churchill in the House of Commons whether he'd try to get the Vatican or some neutral state to fix it so there

372

could be a truce from noon yesterday to noon tomorrow, but Churchill said no. He was adamant – said any such idea would be rejected by your government. But then over in the States we picked up a report that Berlin had told the German embassy in Washington they were going to suspend their air raids for today and tomorrow as long as the RAF did too. It was only an unofficial report, though – Germany hasn't put out anything official on the subject.'

'That sounds a bit mysterious – I've certainly heard nothing about it. But on the other hand, Rita's right – there were no bombs last night, were there? And no sirens so far today. So maybe it's true.'

'Maybe, yes. So my paper wanted me to write something from this end confirming or denying it. Your government officials wouldn't give me any official confirmation this morning that they'd received any proposal of a truce, but unofficially I spoke to one or two people who know about these things, and I got the impression the RAF wasn't planning to mount any big raids on Germany today. So make of that what you will.'

'Very interesting. I suppose it's comforting to know the government's at work on Christmas Day, but we'll have to wait and see whether things stay quiet tonight too.'

'Yes, of course. But in the meantime, I wrote a piece this morning saying we'd heard no bombs or gunfire over London last night, and that it looked like the story was true. I did remind our readers, though, that Manchester was still reeling after that terrible raid they had on Sunday night.'

'And we don't know what they might do as soon as this truce ends, if there is one. It's all a bit grim, isn't it? Did all your colleagues have to work this morning?'

'I think so, but it's an interesting story, and you know how it is – when duty calls.'

'Ah, yes, duty.'

Jago fell silent, and Dorothy noticed. 'Are you OK, John? You look like your mind's somewhere else – is something bothering you?'

'No, not really. It's just . . .'

'So something is bothering you.'

Jago laughed. 'OK, you're right. It was just you mentioning duty – it's reminded me of something a man said to me the other day.'

'Something to do with duty?'

'Yes. He said sometimes it's your duty not to do your duty. I think he meant there can be things in life that are more important than your job. It just made me think I don't want my life to be all duty and nothing else.'

'So what are you going to do about it?'

'That's the problem – I don't know. Do you have any advice?'

Dorothy looked at him thoughtfully. 'If you really want some advice from me, I think I'd say this – it's not just about doing your duty, it's about doing what's right.'

Her counsel was simple, but when he thought about how to apply it, he couldn't find a simple answer. It was something he needed to think about, but not out loud. 'Thank you,' he said.

'You're welcome,' said Dorothy. She seemed to sense his discomfort and released him from her gaze, looking round the room instead. 'You know, it's actually really nice that we haven't heard any sirens yet, isn't it? But you kind of get used to them, and somehow it feels a bit spooky without them.'

Jago appreciated her lightening the conversation. 'Yes,' he said, 'I suppose we should just enjoy the quiet while it lasts – most of us have forgotten what a decent night's sleep is. What are people in America making of all this bombing?'

'Well, I guess for most of them it's just something happening far away across the ocean, and not everyone reads the newspapers, of course, more's the pity. But nowadays we have the radio, and I think that's making a big difference. Two of my colleagues here in London are correspondents for our big radio corporations – Ed Murrow for CBS and Fred Bate for NBC – and they broadcast fifteen minutes of news a day back to the States. Ed has a tremendous following back home because he's done live broadcasts from a rooftop in London during the air raids, so people listening all over America get a real sense of what it's like here. They say the two of them have a regular listening audience of twelve million people each – imagine that. I think those listeners appreciate the fact that the reporters are facing the same dangers as everyone else here so they can get the news out. In fact, poor Fred's in hospital right now – he got caught in an air raid a couple of weeks ago and was badly injured.'

'I'm sorry to hear that. I'm sure people here appreciate you and your colleagues too – you're putting yourselves at risk for their benefit. I admire you for sticking it out here when it's not your war.'

'Just doing our duty.'

Jago laughed. 'Not that again. I think we've had enough duty for one evening.'

'Yes – and I did have my chance to get out, didn't I, and go to China? So I've only got myself to blame.'

For the second time Jago felt uneasy: almost without him noticing, the conversation had drifted from the comfortably general to the dauntingly personal. This time, however, he decided to bite the bullet. There was something he needed to get off his chest, and talking about the perils of war for American journalists in London was another sobering reminder that it might be now or never.

'You know,' he began tentatively, 'when you had that opportunity a few weeks ago to transfer to the job in China I didn't really know what to say, but it made me think.' He stopped, unsure what to say next. Dorothy didn't help; she simply looked at him patiently. 'The thing is, you see,' he continued, 'I . . . well, I think you've become a real friend to me over the last few months, and I suppose that's something I hadn't realised until suddenly it seemed you might be gone.'

'So you reckoned you'd miss me, eh?'

He smiled. 'Yes, I suppose you could say that.'

'Well, I'll tell you a secret – I figured I'd miss you too.'

'You mean that's why you didn't go?'

'Let's just say it was one of a number of reasons – but an important reason nonetheless.'

'Would it have been better for your career if you'd gone?'

'Probably – newspapers like reporters who'll go where they're told at the drop of a hat. But a career isn't everything in life. It's like you said – other things are important too.'

'Like what?'

She looked him in the eye. 'Like . . . friendship?' When no answer came, she continued, gently, 'Sometimes we have to decide how important a friendship is, don't you think?'

Jago became aware of how warm it was in the room. He ran a finger round the inside of his collar and gulped. He was beginning to feel the need for a referee to come into the ring and call the end of the round so that he could retreat into his corner for recuperation and a pep talk, but he knew it wasn't going to happen.

'Er, yes,' he said at last. 'You're right.'

'So here's the question. How important would you say our friendship is?'

He hesitated: it was so difficult to know how she might interpret whatever answer he gave. 'Well, I, er . . .'

She waited for a few seconds before speaking. 'As important as your duty?'

This was the question that had been nagging at his mind. He knew he must give a straight answer, and steeled himself. 'Yes,' he said, with as much confidence as he could muster. 'It is – and more. Duty's what I'm paid to do – friendship's what I choose. Your friendship is really important to me.'

'Why's that?'

'Because I enjoy being with you – I think you're good for me. You make me see there's more to life than just doing my job, and to me that's special.'

'You're a special man, John – you need to know that.'

'Really?'

'Yes, really – you are. And this friendship of ours is very special to me – you need to know that too.'

He tried to find some adequate reply, but didn't know what to say. An awkward silence hung between them until Dorothy came to his rescue with a smile. 'OK, then,' she said. 'Now, shall we order a little food?'

Jago sat back and felt a weight lifted from his shoulders – the ordeal of this conversation was over, and a sweetness had taken its place. Part of him wanted to go out and bestride the world with giant steps, but for now, ordering a meal would do. A meal for two.

ACKNOWLEDGEMENTS

Visiting Covent Garden today, it's difficult to imagine that this favourite destination for stylish shopping and eating was once a bustling fruit and vegetable market, its trade, produce and workers filling the neo-classical central building and overflowing into all the neighbouring streets by day and by night in what one pre-war writer described as 'an impenetrable jungle of lorries, carts, barrows and baskets'. When it was closed in 1974 and relocated to a new site on the other side of the River Thames at Nine Elms, it wasn't just the end of a market, but the passing of a way of life, a community and a culture.

Just thirty-five years earlier, Covent Garden Market had faced, along with the rest of London, the existential threat of the Second World War, and the fact that it had always worked through the night, every night, meant that the blackout and the Blitz presented its workers with an exceptional challenge. At a thanksgiving service in 1945 in St Paul's Church, which stands on the edge of the historic Covent Garden piazza, the rector said that without Covent Garden Market London could not have carried on.

St Paul's Church has a fame of its own: it's known as the Actors' Church because of its close links with the world of theatre, which were originally forged three centuries and more ago with the nearby Theatre Royal, Drury Lane and the Covent Garden Theatre, now the Royal Opera House, both located in its parish.

The old Covent Garden was indeed where two very different worlds – the theatre and the market – met, and it was this intertwining that initially caught my imagination and now lies at the heart of the story that unfolds in *The Covent Garden Murder*.

I'm grateful for the help I've had from various quarters in reconstructing the life of Covent Garden in 1940. My thanks go to Sue Webb, daughter of a Covent Garden trader, for introducing me to the world of the cotchel, to Dave Allen, formerly a Metropolitan Police constable based at Bow Street police station in the 1960s, for walking me round his old beat and telling me stories of how things used to be, and to Rev. Simon Grigg, Rector of St Paul's, Covent Garden, for his warm welcome to the church and for telling me some of its history.

Thanks are due also to Rudy Mitchell for his advice on Christmas puddings and American English, Annette Butterworth, another market trader's daughter, for enlightening me on the history of the City of London School for Girls so that I could have one of my characters educated there, and the Ven. Nick Mercer, Archdeacon Emeritus of London, for our fascinating discussion on the history of the seal of the confessional as practised in the Church of England.

Lastly, I'd like to thank two 'expert witnesses': Dr David Love, for guiding me on the medical aspects of Roy Radley's unfortunate demise, and Dr Claire Archdall, consultant psychiatrist, for keeping my psychiatry on track.

In all such matters, of course, I must note that any errors in my application of their advice are my own.

Getting a whole bookful of words into the right order takes a lot of time and effort, and, as always, I am profoundly grateful to my lovely family for their support and encouragement from beginning to end.

Mike Hollow was born in West Ham and grew up in Romford, Essex. He studied Russian and French at the University of Cambridge and then worked for the BBC. In 2002 he went freelance as a copywriter, journalist and editor. Mike also works as a poet and translator.

blitzdetective.com   *@MikeHollowBlitz*